I0551649

Lie Zombie Lie

JACK WALLEN

ISBN-13: 0615677029
ISBN 13 is 9780615677026

DEDICATION

The apocalypse is just a grievous error away. Thankfully groups like the Zombie Response Team are real and ready to "Protect and Sever". I want to thank Morgan Barnhart and Joshua Garcia for allowing me to make the Zombie Response Team an integral part of the I Zombie series. I look forward to placing Bethany, Morgan, Josh, and company in deeper and darker peril just to see how they manage to fight their way out. Rock on!

And to my fans who keep begging for more –
fear not, I have much nastiness in store for the
world. So long as you keep reading, I'll keep
writing. And speaking of writing, let's get on
with this bitch. Shall we?

CHAPTER 1

"This is Bethany Nitshimi. I'm alive. I'm still kicking ass and broadcasting fast. After facing down the biggest horde of zombies imaginable, I managed to escape the Zero Day Collective yet again. I will not, I repeat, I will not be taken down by this apocalypse brought to us by corporate greed. I will fight, I will kill, and I will do everything I can to help mankind back to its feet. Until then, my vengeance will be merciless.

My current zombie count is one hundred and twenty two. I started that count the day I wound up on my own. That same house that saw the death of my friends Sam Leamy, Courtney Sellers, Dr. Joy Daniel Michaels, and Dirt Bag became my secret hideaway. There I grew to understand exactly what it takes to survive – how to make cold my heart and silent my fear. I can kill now without thought, without remorse, and I will not stop until that body count includes every member of the Zero Day Collective. It's been almost a year since the Zero Day Collective served up a grand buffet of gray matter to Homo Erectus 2.0. They thought it was in their right to cleanse the planet of all those they deemed unworthy. Thing is, they didn't count on the resilience of the human spirit.

Zero Day Collective, I hope you are listening

to me. I have a message to deliver to you from all mankind. Listen carefully, as I am only going to say this one time. The human race is coming for you. We will tear you apart and make you pay for what you've done. Mankind will rise again.

This is Bethany Nitshimi, for Zombie Radio. I will post the time and address of the next broadcast in the usual location. Be safe."

It begins anew...

November 16, 2016
Unknown Location, Pennsylvania USA

The first snow was both a harbinger of hardship to come, as well as a blanket of pure hope covering the landscape. That blanket covered the bits and pieces of fallen friends; and the fragments and shards of the zombie horde laid waste by the detonated hell-fire grenades strapped to Dr. Michaels. Her suicide saved my life. Had she not made that sacrifice, the Moaners and Screamers would have breached the walls of the house and ripped me and my baby to bits. Thankfully, that snow hid the carnage from sight.

When the first snow of the last year hit, it was accompanied by the gray ash of death brought on by Dr. Lindsay Godwin's Quantum Fusion Generator. Even with the comfort of innocent snow falling, being alone with a child in tow was an exercise in constant fear; especially when the undead were everywhere. They always return. The supply of the walking dead was never ending. At least now they only arrive in drips and drabs, instead of waves and platoons. But the constant presence of the zombies brings an undertow of dread. They should have started dying off. Instead, it seemed the walking dead were multiplying like undead rabbits. While time should have been the enemy to the monsters, it turned out to be completely irrelevant. The apocalypse laughed at Father Time, mocked him, flipped him off.

The apocalypse was facing a foe like no other – A pissed off mother with a secret weapon for a baby. That's me, Bethany Nitshimi. I had every intention of bitch-slapping this apocalypse right back down the throat of the Zero Day Collective. With my baby Jacob along for the ride, the child whose very blood contains the cure for the Mengele Virus, I was ready and armed with everything I needed to give the human race a second chance.

But before my vengeance could be exacted upon the Zero Day Collective, I had to survive. So far so good; but the sound of a small gathering of Moaners, coming from just outside our little refuge, warned me that I'd have yet another chance to prove my mettle against the zombie horde.

"Shhhh. It's okay Jacob. What has momma told you about crying when there are zombies near?" I rocked baby Jacob smoothly and quickly. The Moaners must have picked up the cries of my child and wouldn't rest until they had the fresh meat in their mouths.

Over my dead body.

I probably shouldn't have said that.

The sounds of the gang of monsters drifted

into the open house. The front door had been ripped off its hinges, the glass of the windows shattered. Me and baby Jacob were tucked inside an upstairs bedroom, as far away from the front door as possible.

Jacob cried out again. I popped a pacifier in his mouth to silence the sound.

"It's not going to end like this, Jake."

I could have dragged Jacob back up into the attic, but that was nothing more than a dead end waiting to trap us like wild animals. No way. My modus operandi was to beat these bitches back into the ground from which they came.

A crash from below shattered the gentle moment between me and my little guy. I sucked in a deep breath and held life within my lungs for the briefest of moments. I locked my eyes onto Jacob as he smiled up from my arms and sucked the rubber nub in his mouth as if it contained the very essence of life.

The moan below was joined by another, and another, and another. The sum total of death below grew to five. I could live with those odds – I'd lived through much worse.

"Jacob," my voice was a lullaby-whisper. If his cries were to go off again, that would be it, I would lose the element of surprise. "I'm going to leave you here for a moment. Mommy has to go kick some zombie ass. I'll be back for you, okay. Just promise me you won't cry."

A closet became my baby's temporary nativity; with Jacob swaddled in the worn blanket I pilfered from the house (the same blanket I used to cover an out-cold Sam

Leamy). The blanket was a painful reminder, but one I needed. No way I was going to forget those fallen friends – the last, closest thing to family I had. The Zero Day Collective took that away from me, but those men and women would be the last the apocalypse would ever steal.

With Jacob safely tucked away from the maw of Hell, it was *go* time. My blood ran red hot, my eyes and ears alive with sensation.

From below, the zombies punctuated their moans with crashes and random shattering sounds. They knew life was somewhere inside the four walls of the house. A full, gray-matter meal, with a side dish of brain veal, was ripe for the taking. My brain. My baby's brain.

My little black bag of tricks contained some very special toys I was anxious to try out. I cobbled together some interesting weapons from the attic that was my refuge, during the final stand of Sam Leamy, Courtney Sellers, Dr. Joy Daniel Michaels, and the rest of my fallen compatriots. But now, it was just me.

I unzipped the bag and pulled out my new favorite weapon. I had no idea what the original use of the tool was. Effectively, what I held in my hands, was a collapsible pike with a very sharp end. When collapsed, the pike was a mere two feet in length. When stretched out and locked, the beast gave me a full four feet of reach. Four feet between my jabbing hands and the gnashing stench of rot and decay.

I telescoped the pike to its fullest and locked each piece in place. When I stood back up, I could feel a smile cross my face. The whole of my new world defied logic. I was a hacker – and one of the best. Up until a year ago, the closest thing to combat I'd seen came in the form of many and varied video games. The new world order dictated even the most hard core of pacifist pick up arms. Those that couldn't defend themselves were nothing more than meat for the beasts.

Since the virus date-raped the planet, I had become skilled with a gun, a knife, a sword, fire, and now my favorite piece of phallic hardware. Four feet of hard steel.

Who said size didn't matter?

Before I made my way to battle, I gloved my hands and donned a pair of shop glasses (in order to protect myself from back splash.)

Always practice safe zombie slaying.

I walked in silence. My favorite purple Doc Martens danced over the hardwood floor, as if they didn't even touch ground. The moans from below grew louder and louder – and then fell silent. A calm before an undead storm was always the most disturbing moment. The zombies knew I was near; they could smell me. Hell, I could smell me. A hot shower would be better than sex at the moment. It's not outside the realm of the possible that they could hear my heart beating. Evolution had wreaked some crazy havoc on the Moaners, Screamers, and berzerkers on the planet. There was no reason why their sense of hearing couldn't have also fallen victim to change.

The apocalypse didn't play fair.

Once again, I held my breath. Once again, I had to fight for my life.

My instinct demanded I wait it out, wait until the Moaners finally caught wind of me and come to fight on the stairwell. Should that happen, I could at least take them on one at a time. But the fuckers could be painfully slow at catching a ride on the clue train. Instead of waiting for the fight to come to me, this bitch took it to them.

The second my feet hit the first floor, I saw them. Five of the ugliest Moaners to meet my sight in a while. They were all average size; three male and two female. All were covered in dried blood and other human remains. One of the females had a rope of intestine wrapped around her neck, like a string of macabre pearls. One of the male zombies was missing its lower jaw, allowing a length of dried up, brown tongue to dangle and flap as it moved. They were slow and, in typical Moaner fashion, dumb as fuck.

"Hey," I tossed caution in every direction to expedite the freak show Battle Royale. "Over here, you half-wit pieces of shit. You want brains? I've got a family-sized portion just waiting for your ugly asses."

The Warrior Nitshimi struck a pose, my shiny metal pike of death ready to lay waste to the band of flesh eaters.

"God, I need a soundtrack."

The first of the Moaners came up the stairs and lunged at me. I jabbed my weapon out and missed the sweet spot. Instead of impaling the monster's head, the pole easily slipped through the rotting meat of the thing's chest. It took a couple of strong yanks to dislodge the weapon.

Thankfully, the business end of the pike was now coated in thick, slick zombie gore, so when the beast made a grab for my weapon, it merely slipped from his grip.

My second strike hit home – the pencil-point end of the pike running through the right eye of the male zombie, into the gray matter, and out the backside of the skull. The Moaner instantly dropped to its knees and then down for its last and final count. I placed a foot on the thing's shoulder and removed my pike. Not a dollop of zombie spattered my Doc Martens. The thing flopped down the stairs, nothing more than a sack of worthless corpse.

"Which of you walking bags of ugly is next?"

This time, it was 'Jaws' that attacked. The lolling tongue made me laugh. I wanted to grab the tongue and yank down hard to see if the zombie's eyes would roll back like some strange circus toy. Instead of grabbing the meaty dangly bit, I ran my zombie-killing phallus through the soft palette of the beast. The innuendo of the action was not lost.

With a slam of the flat end of the pike to the stair below, the Moaner deep throated the pole. When the zombie's head hit the hardwood, I yanked up to free the staff, just in time to defend myself from Pearls.

I hated gore. I really hated it. It wasn't just the sight or the smell, but the sound. The slopping, wet squish of raw human meat was nothing but a gateway to dry heaves – or worse. The sight of this she-bitch, with her string of human sausage around her neck, made me want to go beast-mode and poke out my minds eye. That might well be the only way sleep would ever visit me again. Otherwise, I was certain to have nightmares of an undead Grand Slam Breakfast.

I hated sausage.

Pearls, and the remaining zombies, decided to not play fair and attack me all at once. Pearls grabbed my pike and yanked me down the stairs. Thankfully, all the years of ballet training allowed me to remain on my feet.

That's right, I said it, ballet.

The zombies surrounded me, tipping the odds in their favor. But I had my pole and hours upon hours worth of Jackie Chan footage looping in my head.

Be Jackie Chan. Be the crap out of Jackie Chan.

Fortunately, the pike was as light weight as it was deadly. It spun in my hands like a majorette's baton from Hell, buzzing low enough to impress a Jedi Knight or a didgeridoo master. I was fairly certain zombies didn't give a shit about Star Wars, or about music – especially indigenous Australian music.

Even more reason they should die.

The bravest of the three zombies lunged at me. I didn't have time to skewer his skull, so I side stepped his attack. I could smell the rot permeating his own flesh as he tripped by. When Klutzy tumbled to the ground, I turned my attention back to the more competent foes. I knew the grounded meat sack would be back for another round, but he wasn't nearly the threat the upright dinner guests were.

The other female zombie took a shot. I jabbed the pike out and the point made hot monkey love to her shoulder. The death metal pole exploded out the back of the beast. When she jerked her shoulder, she forced me around. The bitch was a hell of a lot stronger than she looked.

"You wanna dance girl? I don't play on your team, but I'll try anything once."

Sometimes it just felt good to mock those of a lesser IQ.

I forced the blunt end of the pole to the ground, put my foot down to keep it from moving, and yanked up hard past the fulcrum of the pike. The tearing sound of the zombie's shoulder was vile, but not nearly as bad as the cracking of bone when I dropped the entirety of my weight on top of the weapon.

The metal pole tore through the bottom of the monster's shoulder. Chunks of meat and thick, gooey, brown blood slopped to the floor.

Another stab with the pike, this time the point demolished the undead, she bitch's skull. The body dropped without complaint. It was now just me, Pearls, and Klutzy.

Pearls was slow, thanks to her over-sized frame and high heels. In who's fucked-up, fetish-filled nightmare did zombies wear heels? The last standing undead female squared her shoulders at me and lunged. With a smooth jab of the pike, the point sliced the space of her neck in two, severing the spine and rendering the zombie officially un-undead. The bitch dropped to the floor, her string of meat-pearls snapping and spilling out around her.

Cafe Noir was officially closed.

Except for the last remaining meat sack. He sized me up, but when the sound of Jacob crying tumbled down the stairs, Klutzy decided, since fresher meat was now on the menu, to make his way upstairs. What Klutzy failed to realize was that he'd have to go through one very pissed off mother before he'd reach the second floor deli. I dashed around the zombie to place myself between him and Jacob.

The Moaner caught up and, as soon as he was within range, I ran the pike through the center of his abs and out his lower back. The pole was just wide enough to sever the spine, thus rendering his legs useless. It didn't matter how undead you were, a severed spine was a severed spine. If your legs didn't get the motor impulses sent by the brain, those boots would no longer be made for walking.

True to form, Klutzy rolled down the stairs, grasping at the banister to try to stop his descent. When the zombie hit the bottom of the stairs, his eyes staring up at me, his hands reaching out, I jammed the point of the pike deep into the bowels of his brain. The last neuron fired and put the Moaner to his final rest.

A cry from Jacob reminded me there was no time to bask in the glorious victory. I had a baby to protect – and to quiet. I carried the pike, aka my new best friend, up the stairs with me, back into the bedroom that hid my precious cargo away from sight. When I hit the top step, I collapsed the pole back into its packing position. There was no way I would take a chance on running Jacob through with the angry end of that stick.

"Hello, my little brave boy. Momma saved you from the big bad beasts. Did you hear the noise?" I had Jacob in my arms, a soothing antithesis to what went on below.

We had to leave. If five Moaners could find us, who knew what other happy tricks fate had up her skirt. A pack of Screamers or a single berzerker could come crashing through the walls of the house any minute. A few Moaners I could take down. A Screamer? Maybe. A berzerker? No. Freaking. Way.

The single most important favor I could do for me and my baby was to find a group of fellow survivors. I had a group. They kicked ass. In the end, chaos reigned supreme and all but me and Jacob met a grotesque demise. The ugly lesson? The fewer you had in your party, the quicker you went down.

Task number one – find some new buddies to system.

There was one slight problem. It was almost night. Me and night didn't get along so well since the great cleansing began. At night, everyone can hear you scream, and screams were certainly rampant. There was no way in shazam I was about to pack up the babushka and chance running into a cadre of night-owl zombies ready for a little nightmare waltz.

So, we camp ... inside. At least there were four walls and a roof. In the morning I would do another broadcast and then Jacob and I would be on our way.

To where? I have no idea yet. Hopefully, by morning, I'd know.

CHAPTER 2

November 17, 2016 4:15 AM
Unknown Location, Pennsylvania, USA

My friends all sat around me. Jacob was there, and Dr. Godwin. Susan, Michelle, Gunther, Danielle ... they all sat around me in a circle. The night air kissed the skin of my naked body. I was pregnant. Baby Jacob was neatly tucked and folded back inside my womb. From behind, I felt hot fire.

Everyone stared up at me, smiling, holding up their hands as if they were praying or testifying to some strange religious faith I knew none of them actually had. They spoke, but I couldn't understand the words. The strange tongue was part moaning, part spoken word. It was a beautiful sound, but completely foreign.

From behind the circle of friends, glowing eyes appeared in the night. At first the eyes seemed like nothing more than distant stars, but the regularity of their position, and the swaying movement gave the haunting orbs away.

A blackened smoke rose up from behind me. The smell of cooking meat assaulted my nose. The meat was me. I was tied to a pole, over a fire, with my friends circled around me. Their hands were praising some odd god as they held out plates. They waited to be served my flesh. I tried to cry out, but the sound wasn't me – it was the sound of a baby, my baby. Jacob cried out, from inside my womb, begging for release. I knew the second he came out, either the cannibals around me or the glowing eyes in the night would devour him. I had to hold my baby in as my backside flesh cooked to a crispy well done.

It was all a nightmare. The sound of crying wasn't me, it was Jacob. He was hungry. The surrounding darkness served only to confuse me further. When I jerked awake, that haunting sensation of not knowing if I dwelled in reality or some dream-state still fogged my mind. Jacob's continued crying hatefully jerked me into reality.

With my eyes half opened, I rummaged in my bag and pulled out a can of formula and a bottle. It would have been so much easier to breast feed the baby, but with the apocalypse came a glorious, constant hunger. I hadn't been able to feed myself enough to produce sufficient milk for Jacob. So every chance that presented itself, I looted a grocery, or kitchen, for as much formula as I could. I was surprised the shelves hadn't already been picked clean of the stuff. It never failed – there was a steady supply in every store I flash mobbed.

As soon as the rubber nipple popped between his toothless gums, Jacob hushed. In a half-asleep trance I fed and rocked the baby. After he sucked down the entire contents of the bottle, he was back off to his own little dream world. God I hope the visions that danced in his little head were nothing like mine.

To sleep, perchance to dream. Shakespeare had no idea!

***

November 17, 2016 9:30 AM
Unknown location, Pennsylvania USA

This is Bethany Nitshimi once again broadcasting for Zombie Radio. I survived another attack. They brought it, but not as hard as I. I learned a lesson – going at it alone isn't easy now. And so, I have to call out to anyone listening. It's time to band together, form an army, and take back the planet from those that thought it their right to go anal on the first date with mankind. I'm not going to lie to you, I'm packing a child, an infant actually. But I also carry with me what is probably the only hope the human race has of puking up this shit sandwich and making it out alive. So here's the deal – you know where my web site is; on that site you'll find a link to contact me. Tell me where you are, who you have with you, and your plan for survival. I'll read through every email and decide which best suits the needs of the many. When I find you, there will be much to do. I have a cure to create and distribute. I have a collective of ass bags I must find and destroy. And I have a very special child I must protect and raise.

If you're curious about who I am and why you should care, go to my site, download a copy of my ex lover's book, I Zombie I, and read it. Once you finish the Bible of the New World Order, you will understand the importance of my survival.

Please, contact me. Let me know you're out there. This is Bethani Nitshimi for Zombie Radio. Out.

Out is right. Unlike the previous voice of the Zombie Radio Nation, I had no music to play. My broadcasts would be nothing more than succinct call-outs in an attempt to bring some order to the whirling chaos trying desperately to look up our skirts. I wish I had something to entertain the masses, some shtick to stem the tide of hate and hell washing over the land. At the moment there were simply more important tasks than making people laugh, cry, or dance. If I have my way, the world will be saved and there'll be plenty of time for dancing ... after the fire.

I had Jacob packed up and ready to roll. The reality of the situation was that I had no fucking idea where I was going. There was no poetic wind to fill my sails. All I had was some broken inner compass carrying me on in random directions. Randomness was never a part of my makeup. Up until a year ago, my life was about order in absolutes. Binary. Ones and zeros ruled supreme. But with the apocalypse, anything was possible.

I had fashioned a make-shift baby sling to carry Jacob. His tiny weight resting on my breasts and belly was an unfamiliar comfort. My arms would be necessary and I wasn't about to put the little guy on my back – not with Moaners and Screamers on the loose. The chances of a zombie going stealth and snatching my baby away were slim to zilch; but

I wasn't about to take a single chance. Jacob was far too important. Besides, I'm a nerd. Chance and I don't play well together. Give me calculation, hard numbers, facts and I'm all sexy, sexy.

It was bitter cold outside. As soon as the too-early winter wind slashed and smacked the exposed skin of my face, I thought twice about continuing on. The house we just left seemed like a paradise compared to the Polar Icecap-like weather we were experiencing. It wasn't enough to have to deal with the end of the world, but a record-setting cold front and snowflakes the size of my fist? In what level of Hell is that fair?

Jacob was bundled up tight against the cold. My only concern for the bundle of joy, was whether or not he could actually breathe underneath his wrappings. I stopped, paranoid that his swaddling was too tight. When I felt a tiny rise and fall of his breathing belly, I knew it was safe to move on.

The snow served to silence the area. The sight was lovely. There was something about the scene that reminded me of my childhood. Maybe it was snow crunching under foot as I walked with my Grandmother, ready to drop to the ground and make snow angels. Or maybe it was recalling something Jacob had written in his journal about the snow and ash falling, and the zombie he called 'Flaky'. No matter what it was, something flipped an emotional switch in me and tears threatened to freeze on my cheeks.

The apocalypse was no time to allow my

inner traveling pants girl to slip out. No, it was time to channel my inner tomboy. Or, better yet, my inner kick-ass red neck. Zombies wouldn't dare fuck with a red neck.

A laugh spilled out, along with a puff of smoke-like air. God it was cold.

A roaring sound stopped me – stopped my feet, my breathing, and nearly my heart.

"Oh fuck," the whisper accidentally spilled out from between my chattering teeth.

My brain sent the *run* signal to my feet, but they succinctly ignored the command.

"Hide." I whispered.

The roar grew louder.

"Run." Again, I whispered.

The roar drew nearer.

"Fuck!"

The roar vibrated in my skull.

Finally, my feet received the order from my brain and took off running. I ran to the nearest shelter, which happened to be a car parked in a drive way. Fate was kind to me and the car was unlocked. I carefully, and quickly, pulled off the sling and slid into the front seat of the car. I sat Jacob down in the passenger seat and quickly searched for keys.

The roar vibrated the glass of the car's windshield. I so wanted to ask myself whatever was that monster making all the noise. Unfortunately I knew all too well the bearer of those horrific tidings.

A Screamer.

The undead food chain was simple: Moaners < Screamers < Berzerkers. For those of you less math-ly, that reads: Moaners, are less than Screamers, are less than Berzerkers. Moaners are your made-for-tv zombies: slow and shambling, without plot, plan, or point (other than to consume your gray matter). Screamers are mad bastards, faster and stronger than anything you'd have ever seen (other than maybe Chuck Norris). Berzerkers? You don't even want to go there; because the second you do, you're dead. And I'm sure by now there's some form of big nasty that has evolved beyond that of Berzerker.

At the moment, the sound crashing the party was all Screamer. One Screamer, it seemed. But even that one beast could peel the flesh off my bones and make a pinata with my bladder in less than thirty seconds.

Not that I've actually timed them.

I locked the doors to the car and hunkered down with Jacob to try and wait out the tornado made of rage and pain. It would pass. It had to pass.

Another roar threatened to shatter the windshield of the car. The thing was close – too close. One ridiculously ear-splitting scream made it all too clear the thing was just outside of the car. This was it, I was going to die. The car started rocking back and forth. Roarzilla knew I was inside, knew a delicious, tasty treat awaited his black, rotten lips.

The instant the rear window shattered, I could smell the thing's corpse-rot breath. Panic decided it wanted a play-date with my heart and mind – a maddening threesome. I grabbed for my pack. Deep inside the pocket was a weapon I didn't like to use. 'Boomsticks' and 'bangbangs' were great for taking down zombies quickly, but the noise was sure to bring about an instant, undead block party. I had no choice – I had to use it. I pulled the pistol out of the pack and unset the safety. The second the fucker peaked his ugly face in the window, his third eye was going to be permanently opened.

I cocked the hammer, extended my arms and waited. Jacob cried out. The Screamer roared and violently rocked the car. Jacob squealed in displeasure again and the beast shattered the passenger-side window. When his raging face shot into the cockpit of the car, the explosion of the gun cracked and promised some serious tinnitus. Somehow, even in the shock of the moment, my aim was dead on. The zombie dropped, its thick, brown blood slowly oozing out of the hole in its forehead.

When the high-pitched ringing finally subsided, Jacob's cry took over, reminding me I had just shot a gun within a couple of feet from my baby.

I was never going to win Mother of the Year.

As soon as I picked Jacob up and pulled him tightly to my chest, his cries began to wane. He was safe – for the moment. That moment would soon be over. The noise of the gunshot would surely draw the attention of a horde of Moaners and Screamers. We had to get the hell out of this little suburban nightmare, and fast.

With Jacob snuggled back up against my chest, my pack on my back, and my gun in my hand, I went in search of intact transportation.

We were in the middle of the stereotypical, American town. Surely someone left the keys to their car on a kitchen counter top.

And while in the kitchen ... maybe a snack or two.

***

November 17, 2016 12:15 PM
Unknown Location, Pennsylvania USA

It only took looting three houses to find both snacks and car keys. The snacks were packable – packaged junk food that would last forever. I learned early on, in Munich, that junk food was probably going to be the only sustenance to carry the survivors through the apocalypse. And as much as I'd love a good Cob Salad or brazened salmon fillet, Doritos, Fritos, and Munchos were just going to have to suffice.

A garbage bag served as a fitting carryall for the collected food. I hauled the black plastic sack out to my new best friend – an Audi A4 (nothing fancy like Tony Stark drove – just a standard issue Quattro). With the car loaded, me and my baby pulled out of the streets of *suburgatory* and into the grand unknown.

There had to be a fitting song for such an exit. Unfortunately the FM airwaves where bereft of broadcast. What I wouldn't do to have the original Zombie Radio DJ back, spinning tunes and weaving strange tales of conspiracy with a Captain James T. Kirkian sensibility. Quirk collided with cool and gave birth to that voice. Too bad the zombie a GoGo got the best of him and he went Linda Lovelace on a pistol. Even though I took up the reins of Zombie Radio, I had no quirk to offer the listeners. It was nothing but raw facts mixed in with a touch of vitriol.

The Audi did have a CD player. The collection of CDs accused the auto's owner of serious hipsterism. Nothing but singer-songwriter, folk-fusion, and retro-pop. There was no accounting for tastes – even during the end of the world.

By accident, my finger nudged the band mode button on the stereo and switched the radio to AM. The crackle of old-school broadcast was actually soothing to my ears. Sometimes falling back in time was comforting. I hit the Seek button to see if there was life out there in the airwaves. After a few stops of random noise, the radio landed on a real broadcast.

You simply can't assume this was a political ploy. What you can assume is that something has gone terribly wrong and we are on the brink of extinction. But there are rumors drifting around about a small army collecting on the outskirts of town. What they are planning, I have no idea. If I were to guess, I'd say they were nothing more than a pissed off militia hoping to take out what's left of our government. Honestly, I don't care why they are together and what they plan on doing – so long as they take out a few of those walking dead bastards along the way.

We have a caller. You're talking to Mike on

Tiny Radio AM. Let's hear it.

Hey Mike! I just wanted to say I love your show. I've been listening to you since I was a kid. Me and my dad...

Yeah thanks for the sentiment there guy, but we're dealing with the apocalypse. What we need are reports. If you have nothing to help save lives, then spare us all. Next caller.

Yo Mike! Thanks for taking the call. I just wanted to pose a simple question. It's been, what, a year since the Mengele Virus hit and we still have power. How is that possible? In the movies they never have power for more than a few days, maybe a week tops. What gives? I'll hang up and listen to your response.

That's a good question. Here's the thing – so much of America's power comes from coal – that power wouldn't survive without people working those systems. Solar, wind, and nuclear power could certainly continue on though. My guess is that either we have some real heroes; men and women in the coal industry, working in the background. Either that, or some genius out there somewhere has managed to tap our main grids into a pipeline of renewable energy. A year is a long time, when most industries have collapsed. In the end, I don't have an answer for that. But I would love to hear from anyone in the know. If you're in the coal industry, or someone who knows enough about the power grids keeping us in electricity, shed some light on the subject.

I was worried the guy had no idea what he was doing. The power of radio could well be the only means which to bring survivors together, or at least educate everyone into some form of self sufficiency. If I knew his phone number, I'd call the station and help him lead the human race out of Hurricane Zombie.

I continued driving, hoping good ol' Mike on Tiny Radio AM might get a caller with enough information to clue me into where I needed to go next. I had nothing. Actually, Mike had nothing, outside of a few irrational conspiracies. But it was nice to hear voices. The only companionship I had for the last few days was the cooing and crying of Jacob. As much as I adore and cherish my baby, he's not much for conversation.

"Fuck!"

A Moaner decided to play chicken with the Audi and caught me off guard. I slammed into the monster hard enough to snap its head off its shoulders. The body fell under the car and must have caught up on one of the axles or the exhaust. I could hear the meat dragging over the pavement, like a giant slab of raw bacon. I hit a speed bump fast and hard enough to dislodge the beast. A quick look in the rear-view mirror and I saw the thing roll to a stop on the street behind me.

The RPMs of my heart matched those of the Audi. I was surely going to stroke out any second. But before I could, the sound of a woman shrieking had my attention. I slammed on the brakes. The unfortunate squealing of rubber probably caught the attention of every zombie in the 'hood.

I rummaged in my pack, grabbed my pike

and gun, and jumped out of the car. I wouldn't budge from the vicinity – not with Jacob strapped into the passenger seat and the sound of a wailing woman echoing in my ears. My pike was extended and locked, my gun loaded and cocked.

Much ass was about to be kicked. God I loved power.

"Help!" The shrill female voice was drawing near. I took a chance and called out.

"Over here!"

Either some helpless woman or a hungry plague of zombies was about to ascend on me. Actually the latter was probably most likely, considering one generally beget the other in this golden age of the Scream Queen.

Just as I expected, a young girl came flying around a corner, followed by – fuck – a Screamer. I ran around to the passenger side of the car and flung open the back door.

"Over here! Jump in!"

As the girl picked up speed and aimed her body for the car, I ran back to the driver's side door, hoisted my pistol, and took aim for the beast. I had no idea if I could pick off a target moving as quickly as a Screamer. Now was not the time for second guessing. Now was the time for dumping truck loads of confidence powder all over my bad-ass self and pumping lead into the skull of the fast-approaching monster.

The Screamer gained ground on the girl. I sucked in a deep breath, relaxed my shoulders, and slowly squeezed the trigger. The sound detonated in my ear and the bullet left the gun with a velocity far too fast for the human eye.

To my surprise the bullet struck home. Unfortunately 'home' was very much where the heart was – not the brain. The hit didn't even so much as faze the beast, who continued to gain ground. The fucker was going to catch the girl and make a snack of her thought meat.

"Run! Run! Run!"

I couldn't help but toss out the clichéd encouragement.

The Screamer lunged and barely missed grabbing the girl by the hair. I leveled my gun for one last shot, held my breath, and pulled the trigger. This time the shot struck gold – or gray, as it were. The Screamer dropped like an over-sized, maggot-infested meatloaf. Thankfully, the girl continued running and, when she was close enough, dove straight into the back seat and jerked the door closed.

Without hesitation, I sat my ass in the driver's seat, closed the door, and sped off.

In the back seat, the girl cried to hyperventilation. I let her continue, not wanting to interrupt the catharsis prematurely.

"You okay? Did that thing bite you? Have you been bitten by any of them?" I Gatling-ed the questions too fast for the overwrought girl to comprehend.

"Fu-uck!" My new passenger screamed through the hiccups. The disjointed word made me want to laugh. "That was aw-some!"

The girl's last proclamation threw me for a loop. Awesome? Seriously? This girl just shot up near the top of my list of 'huh?' I glanced back in my rear-view and immediately considered slamming on the brakes and tossing the girl out of the car.

Emo chick. Of all the people I could have possibly saved, I had to pick up an emo chick. Her hair was nearly every shade of the rainbow – and not in the fun, clown-wig kinda way. Her bangs hung over her eyes, so she constantly had to brush them aside. She had piercings in her nose, her right eyebrow, and her lower lip. I couldn't get a complete picture of what she was wearing, but I swear I saw an orange and green mesh tutu.

Good god.

I had to make small talk before the never-ending diatribe of whining disenfranchisement spilled out of her sparkly, glossed lips. "What's your name?"

The girl's coal-rimmed eyes looked back at me through the mirror. "Echo. What's yours?"

"Bethany. Bethany Nitshimi."

"No fucking way! Seriously?"

I didn't like where this was going.

My new bestie kicked the back seat of the Audi with her pink Chuck Taylors and squealed. "Oh my god! I'm hanging with a freaking super star! You're all over Twitter and Tumblr. Everyone's talking about you being the savior, like you are the rebirth of Jesus himself. Holy shit, isn't that a bitch – all the religions being wrong. The Messiah's a chick! That rocks."

This is so not gonna work.

Totes.

Just as if things couldn't get any worse, Jacob let out a shriek of displeasure.

"Whoa. You have a baby in here? OMG,

please tell me that's Jacob?"

Jacob cried out again. I patted around the passenger seat until I found his pacifier. Before I attempted to blindly pop it in the little guy's mouth, I gave it a wipe or two on my pants until I realized there was only one way to make sure the rubber nub was clean enough for a baby. I jammed the paci in my mouth and sucked off the dirt.

There are things we do as mother's we'd never dream of otherwise.

The second the pacifier entered Jacobs's mouth, his cries went silent.

"Yes, this is Jacob. How do you know his name?"

Echo leaned in over the front passenger seat to get a look at Jacob. "Everyone knows about baby Jacob. He's like our last, best hope right? This is so Star Wars and he's our Obi Wan. Am I right?"

I couldn't do it. This little fan girl I'd picked up wasn't going to work out. There was already enough to deal with. As if a baby, zombies, the apocalypse, and the Zero Day Collective weren't enough – now I had super fan girl OMGing over every aspect of my life. I didn't need this. The world didn't need this. I pulled the car off to the side of the road and jerked it into park.

"Look Echo – I'm glad you're safe and I really appreciate the kind words, but I can't handle the love-fest you've got going on here. It's really messed up out there and I could certainly use some help making it through this nightmare. But if you're going to be my sidekick, you've gotta tone down the worship. I don't deserve it."

Echo was aghast. Her mouth dropped open to reveal a not-so-surprising tongue piercing.

"I'm sorry. I was just ... fuck, I'm really sorry. I didn't mean to make you uncomfortable. It was just, well, of all the people to save me from certain suck, it was you. You! I mean you're—" Echo's voice faded off as she realized she was about to add another layer to this already too-thick, sticky-sweet sandwich. "Sorry. Look, you're a hero. Seriously. And every young girl I know aspires to be you. I read Jacob's book and listened to Zombie Radio every waking moment. I already know what you've done and what you're planning on doing. If there is anything I can do to help you, please ... at least give me a chance."

Echo's huge, blue eyes unintentionally pouted at me. How could I resist? I could use the help. Hell, if anything, it was nice to have another human being to talk with – even if much of the talking would wind up in abbreviations and acronyms.

When I smiled at the young girl she squealed and, with the speed of Bruce Lee, had her smart phone out.

"What are you doing?"

Echo looked at me as if I'd just spewed pea soup and spoke a dead language.

"I'm posting on Twitter that I'm hanging with *the* Bethany Nitshimi!"

I matched Echo's speed, reached into the back seat, and grabbed her phone from her.

"No. You can't tell anyone. I'm still trying to

work out a plan and I can't have certain people knowing where I was and who I was with. Besides, it'd put you in danger. I've already had enough blood spilled on my watch."

Echo glared at me. I knew I might well have unleashed Teenageddon, but I had to have the element of surprise on my side.

"I'll give you your phone back, but you have to promise me you won't tweet, face, or tumble anything about who you're with or where you're going." Another check in the rear-view. Echo was a lip-biter. Great. "Deal?"

The teen reached her hand across the plane between the front and the back seat and spoke the one word I had to hear.

"Deal."

I handed Echo her mobile back. She didn't immediately proceed to go social on me. There was hope after all.

"So, what's the plan? We gonna find the ZDC and kick some corrupt corporate ass?"

There was a lot of hope.

I had to confess to my new sidekick there was no plan other than to drive and wait for one to fall into our laps. Surprisingly, she was cool with that. To her, this was probably just some road trip dream come true. In the meantime, we grilled one another about our pasts. Echo seemed to know more about me than I was comfortable with. I guess that's what happens when you make your life completely public as I had with Jacob's book and my own blog. I did, however, get to learn plenty about the young girl in my back seat.

She told me she was eighteen. I didn't buy

it, but I figured I'd leave that doubt go for now. She had been living on the streets for the last couple of years, after escaping a tragic foster situation. As much as I hated to even think her sad fate in any positive light, it was somehow reassuring to know I was traveling with a real survivor, and not some whiny-ass teen who'd come undone the second her BFF showed up with same trashy word plastered across the ass of her sweats.

Echo also confessed to already taking down a few Moaners. I was starting to like the little punk-rock waif.

***

November 17, 2016 8:50 PM
Unknown Location

We drove until I started feeling the warm, inviting fingers of sleep caress my eyelids. The car was in need of gas, so I pulled off at a truck stop to fill up. Surprisingly enough, the pumps were still working and there was still gas in the tanks. As the Audi gulped down fuel, I went into the station to explore and, hopefully, stock up on some chow. I didn't fully trust Echo enough to leave Jacob behind, so he was happily bouncing along in his sling.

Thankfully, the stop was abandoned. The last thing I needed was to come across a gang of curious survivors or, worse, a gang of curious zombies. After casing the joint, I realized this might well be the best place for Echo and I to set up camp for the night. We could hold up in the stop, get a hot shower, lay down some cheap knock-off Indian blankets, and get some sleep. I could also slap an air card into my laptop and drop another broadcast to the masses, if there are still masses out there to listen.

I hadn't checked my email in a while. Shit. A geek like me not checking email? What has the world come to?

Oh yeah ... the end.

Fuck.

Jacob cried out and nearly started break-dancing in his sling.

The world, and all its wonders, could wait until morning. I was exhausted and Jacob was getting cranky. Time for sleep.

CHAPTER 3

November 18, 2016 10:10 AM
Unknown Location

The second I woke, the über-nerd in me took over and demanded I do geeky things. The first of those things was to check email. Truthfully, I'm surprised I'd made it this long without a single check. Such is the apocalypse.

I recently set up a number of email filters to help me sift through the onslaught of mail. Since the original Zombie Radio DJ had me on his show, I started getting quite a large amount of 'fan' mail. As much as I wanted to sift through each and every one – there were far more pressing matters at hand. The most important of those matters was to figure out where in the Hell my side kick and I were to go.

The answer to that all-important question arrived in the form of a single email from an old friend – a fellow hacker.

Jamal Tisdale.

Jamal wasn't just any hacker, he was the one person I knew who could go toe to toe with me in LAN party kernel hacks. We used to host parties to see who could break into a given server's kernel the fastest. No matter the stakes, the game always wound up with two remaining contestants – me and Jamal. He was good and I fully trusted the man. His email was powerfully encrypted and simple:

Bethany (aka, my old friend ZeroOneZero),

It's been a long while. It seems the apocalypse has been kind to you, or you've been kind to it. Either way, I want to return the favor you've given us all. I've started forming a small, underground city beneath the streets of Seattle, Washington. Our goal – amass an army to help you take down the Zero Day Collective. But we need a leader. Join us Bethany. Help us help you. Use your old pal Google and locate The Underground Tour of Seattle. You'll find it. And if I know you as well as I think I do ... you'll join us.

J-Tiz.

Well, that was that. How could I turn down not only an old pal, but an invitation to help create an army whose sole purpose was to sate my personal wet dream of wiping clean a little filth and grime known as The Zero Day Collective? My reply to Jamal was succinct and included a .jpg of our route to Seattle. Thank you Google Maps.

J-Tiz,

On the way.

Z1Z

Jamal was connected in more ways than Kevin Bacon. If I knew my J-Tiz, he'd be playing God for the duration of this road trip. It was like having my own St. Christopher along the way. How he'd pull off keeping us safe, I had no idea. But Jamal could work some serious mojo.

I wasn't in the least bit surprised that Echo was thrilled at the prospect of a road trip.

"It'll be dangerous."

Echo laughed as she munched peanut butter and toast. "I eat danger."

I wanted to pat her on the head like a puppy, with a nice 'Oh I bet you do, you sassy lil' girl.' I refrained. The truth was, the girl probably believed her words. In her world she was an indestructible street ninja, who'd likely have fought off starvation, sickness, loss, and who knew what else. The never-ending onslaught of the zombie horde was nothing to an orphaned teen girl.

"So, who's this J-Tiz dude? Ex boyfriend?" Echo had that 'look' in her eyes that girls get when they're wanting some scoop. I had no scoop – at least not scoop I was willing to share at the moment. But who knew, we had a long ass drive ahead of us.

"I need your help. We have to load the car up with anything and everything that will help us make it across the country." Non-stop, the drive would take us nearly two days. Thanks to the apocalypse, non-stop no longer existed. We'd face zombies, riots, militia, and who knew what else between Pennsylvania and Washington. Having an infant and teenage girl on board, well, those complications went without saying.

Echo's eyebrows arched with excitement. "So you mean like guns, knives, grenades, gas masks?"

"I mean like food, water, baby formula,

diapers. You know, the boring stuff that'll keep us alive. Don't worry though, I'll take care of arming us."

And I did. While Echo visited as many of the neighboring houses as needed to fill up a trunk-full of provisions, I did the same looking for weapons of undead destruction. The one thing about suburbi-land – although it seemed incredibly safe – people had secrets and secrets were the one thing worth keeping safe with the help of boomsticks and bangbangs. This fact o' life was made even more real when that which is being hidden from prying eyes had a hefty price. The secrets of the wealthy were protected with expensive weaponry. So a big 'thank you' to white-collar crime!

Teenage mistress? Hello Colt 45.

Extortion? Meet my little friend semi-automatic.

Laundered money? May I introduce you to AK 47?

Along with the big guns, came a nice stockpile of swords that belonged in museums, as well as a crate of flares, an axe, a couple of claw hammers, various saws, and a few handy Tasiers (one even bedazzled with fake pink jewels).

The last thing I bothered to locate was a stack of CDs. Tiny Radio Mike would only last so many miles, and even I have my limits with talk radio. So, the handful of compact discs would have to do. What I wouldn't give for my blessed MP3 player. I'd spent untold hours perfecting my playlists. Oh well. Cest la vie, as it were. Or at least it was when we were in

France. But we won't always have Paris.Before we slammed the doors closed on the Audi and Pennsylvania, I had one last task.

This is Bethany Nitshimi – still alive and still kicking ass for Zombie Radio. Hopefully you caught the update on the site, leading you to the auditory Nirvana that is my voice in the now. As always, I must apologize for not being able to sound off a regular broadcast, but when you're on the lamb from someone like The Zero Day Collective, you have to be as cautious as possible. That is the why of the secrecy. And you'll have to pardon the cryptic as well. Even though I'm fairly certain not a single member of the ZDC is clever enough to locate this encrypted broadcast, I'm not about to give away precious information like my location.

So, for all intent and purpose – know that I am here and you are there. Where here is, I'll leave up to your imagination. But when I get to where I am going, I promise you there will be major announcements. Why? Because your DJ has happened across something big, something beautiful, and something that might well flap the wings of this chaos effect so hard, the ZDC will feel the ripple to their bowels.

I have a new sidekick by the way. Her name is Echo and she's bad ass. So everyone better think twice about getting in our way or we will take you down.

Right now would be the perfect time for a song. It's too bad I can't oblige directly. But I can make a suggestion. As soon as I end this broadcast, I want everyone to spin up

'Interstate Love Song' by Stone Temple Pilots. If that song doesn't make you want to don your beat-the-fuck-up straw cowboy hat and sweat across the country, nothing will. Keep the emails coming in. Talk to me my lovelies. I'm out.

Echo watched every second of the recording like I was making magic. I hated that the poor girl had to find out the Zombie Radio broadcasts were no longer live. It wasn't something I could risk. So I recorded them, fed them to a server, and looped just the new 'cast for the given time period posted. It was the only way I could ensure the ZDC couldn't track me. I had to lead them on, astray, and away from our goal. Honestly, I had no idea what kind of disorder I was heading into. I trusted Jamal implicitly, but I knew wrangling the post-apocalyptic cavalry was like herding cats. Whatever Jamal had in store would be better than facing down the Zero Day Collective alone.

Once I had the file uploaded and the link set, it was time to punch the gas and hit the highway. A road trip. Who'd of thought I'd be going on a road trip? It was clear that Echo was even more excited than I. She had the passenger seat all decked out with various accoutrement associated with the sport of cross-country driving. It was actually endearing.

Echo had also managed to dig up a baby seat for the car – one of the bourgeois, rear-facing models that would save Jacob should I T-bone a horde of Screamers. The girl got it. Survival. What I thought was going to be a teenage albatross around my neck, might well turn out to be a serious asset.

Our first targets on the map were Akron, Ohio and Fort Wayne, Indiana. My goal was to try to stay on a highway that would take us through as many larger cities as possible. We were going to have to keep a steady stream of supplies coming in, and I would need network connectivity to keep in touch with a select group of people. I couldn't always count on the aircards I had collected for connectivity. When I had larger files to upload (or download), I'd need the speeds of wireless or a hard-wired connection.

The Audi gracefully pulled out of the driveway. The tiniest part of me would have enjoyed the irony of backing over a Moaner. The mighty crush of its skull would have been the sweetest of music. That didn't happen. The only sound was the rich rubber of the tires gliding over the smoothest pavement I'd ever driven on.

Eat the rich baby.

CHAPTER 4

November 18, 2016 12:25 PM
Zombie Response Team, Pennsylvania Unit

The Screamer had the young girl pinned to the ground, his cold, white fingers tangled in her curly, red hair. The thing pulled the girl's head up close and personal to its mouth and let loose a raging, primal scream. The girl had already fallen just under the surface of consciousness and couldn't feel the wind and smell the rot from the mouth of the monster.

After a second hell mouth roar, the zombie cracked the skull to the ground. The wet thud made it clear this wasn't the first crushing blow. Under the skin, the bone had already caved in. Shards of bone sliced through the blood-brain barrier, rendering the girl's brain nothing more than an entrée for the undead.

The Screamer lifted the skull to its face and roared once again. This time, when the head met the sidewalk, the bone and flesh gave way. An oozing pool of blood flowed between the monster's fingers. The zombie flipped the girl over, dug its fingers into the newly fashioned hole, and pulled apart the skull.

Lifeless fingers dug into the human-head pudding and pulled out chunks of brain. The slippery, rubbery mass went from finger to mouth. As the dead man chewed the first bite of his meal, his nearly-useless eyeballs rolled up into his head – a living dead ecstasy.

"Shit, that's disgusting!"

Olivia's whisper sailed on a brisk wind all the way to the ears of the dining zombie. The Screamer dropped its meal and let loose a skin-shrinking scream.

"Oh fuck Olivia! It heard you." Jon panicked. Jon always panicked. If his partner had a bullet for every time he panicked, she'd have enough ammo to wipe out the entire zombie population.

Olivia refused to acknowledge Jon's mental anguish and instead connected the silencer to her pistol.

"Let me show you how the Zombie Response Team takes care of brain-munchers like this."

The Screamer rushed the duo; as one crouched and aimed, the other pissed his pants. Olivia sucked in a deep breath and held her torso tight.

Thirty yards.

"Olivia! Do something!"

Twenty yards.

"Come on!"

Ten yards.

"We're gonna die!"

The huff of the silenced weapon sent the bullet charging through the air and into the space just above the right eyebrow. The Screamer dropped instantly. The only sound was the moaning and whining of Jon, who had knelt to the ground with his head covered and his eyes closed tight, the smell of his urine rising to meet anyone around and above him.

Olivia knocked Jon over with a knee to the

shoulder.

"Get up chicken shit. The meat puppet is down."

Jon stood and brushed his pants off. When he realized he'd pissed himself, his face burned bright red and his jaw quivered.

"Don't worry, Missy, I won't tell anyone you wet the bed." Olivia laughed as she double-tapped the Screamer.

One of the prime directives of the Zombie Rescue Team was to ensure all undead not get up for a third shot at life, that meant double-tapping – or sending a close-range killing blow into the skull. Take no chances; leave no trace of life behind.

Olivia pulled out her mobile and dialed Morgan Barnhart's cell. Morgan was one of the founders of the Zombie Response Team. Originally from Texas, Morgan had temporarily relocated to Seattle to help Jamal with the Washington division of ZRT.

"Morgan, this is Olivia Stemler, Pennsylvania Unit. The last of the Screamers has been neutralized in the area we believe should be their last pit stop in the state. What are our orders?"

The orders were simple and clear – remain in the area until the travelers had cleared and passed the area. Once they were sure Bethany was on her way out of the state, the ZRT Pennsylvania Mobile Unit could return to their headquarters and back under the charge of the senior state officer.

"Yes ma'am." Was all Olivia said before she hung up.

When she turned back to Jon, he was gone. She found him digging through the trunk of the car for a pair of pants. It was cold and the soaked crotch of the pair he wore was growing chilly.

"Don't you have any sweats or something I could wear?"

Olivia laughed. She was lucky to have packed extra sleeping gear. Pants? Doubtful.

"I might have a skirt in there you could wear." Olivia laughed.

Jon turned and flipped the girl off.

"If it were warmer, I might take you up on that."

"I'd pay to see it."

Jon turned his full attention to his partner. "How much?"

Another round of laughter peeled from Olivia's mouth. "What does it matter? You can't spend it anyway. Didn't you get the memo, jackass? The only currency of value now is food and ammunition. Everything else is shit."

After a bit of rooting, Jon came up with a pair of old Carhart overalls.

"Wow, 'Liv, didn't know you were in the closet! Sexy."

Before Olivia could smack Jon upside the face with a razor-sharp retort, the sound of car tread had them diving for cover.

"Why are we hiding?"

Olivia hadn't filled Jon in on every finer detail of the mission.

"We have to make sure no one is tracking Bethany. So we stay in the shadows until we know for sure she's in the clear. If she is being followed, we take them out. That's all I know."

The couple tucked themselves into the car and locked the doors. Olivia had parked the black sedan, in a lot among other autos, to keep it from looking out of place.

The Audi pulled into the abandoned gas station slash food mart and came to a stop at one of the gas pumps. Bethany stepped out of the car, stretched, and began the process of filling up. Before she could get the gas flowing, she had to head inside and okay the 'sale'. As she was walking toward the building, a younger girl stepped out of the passenger seat. The girl had her head buried in a cell phone. When she came up for air, she danced around a bit and opened the back door of the car. After a moment, she pulled back with a baby in her arms.

"Holy shit." Olivia whispered.

"What? What is it?" Jon sat up to get a look. "You mean the chick?"

Olivia smacked the back of Jon's head. "You're a fucking tool bag Jon. No, not the chick, the baby, don't you know who that is?"

Jon stared ahead in silence, clearly ignorant of what he was witnessing.

"That's baby Jacob."

Silence.

"Jesus crap Jon, don't you know anything? That baby might be the new messiah, the second coming, the fucking savior of the human race!"

"As in biblical?"

Olivia stared on in silence for a moment. "Kinda. Yeah."

Bethany returned to the car and began filling up the tank. She instructed the other girl to run inside. Before the younger female took off, she handed the baby to Bethany. When the woman held the baby, her face lit up as if the apocalypse had never happened.

"I have to get this on film." Olivia pulled a digital camera out of her bag and started snapping shots. "Morgan will be thrilled to see these."

Jon stared at Olivia as if the woman was starting to sprout extra appendages. "Is there something going on I don't know about?"

Olivia continued snapping pictures. "Like what Jon?"

"I don't know. Like are we really the good guys or does the Zombie Response Team have something planned for Bethany they'd rather not share with the rest of the world?"

The photo-shoot ended abruptly with Olivia punching Jon in the shoulder.

"The ZRT saved your ass from certain death you piss face, dirt bag. What good would it do for us to spend every waking moment saving people like you from this plague of death, only to off the one woman who could single handedly save the planet?"

Jon's eyes lit up like roman candles. "I never implied you were planning to kill her. What made you think that?" The young man started stuttering in fear. "So you are planning —"

"Jon, listen to me. The Zombie Response Team is not going to harm Bethany or her baby. The only plans they have are to make sure that woman reaches Seattle safely and then let her help in rebuilding an army to take down the Zero Day Collective. You know, the bad guys."

"Shit! Duck!"

Jon grabbed Olivia and yanked her down hard, as the Audi rolled out of the gas station. As the dust settled, Jon hopped back into the driver's seat and started to fire up the engine. Olivia pulled his hand away from the ignition and grabbed her mobile. As she dialed the number for the Zombie Response Team headquarters, she removed the keys from the ignition and dropped them in her lap.

"Morgan, this is Olivia Stemler reporting in. Bethany has just left the station. They should be exiting the state within the hour. We'll hang back and wait to see if anyone was tailing them. Once we know they're in the clear, we'll pursue the car. It's a gray, Audi A4. I didn't catch the license number. Right. Thank you."

Olivia hung up and turned to Jon with a look that could easily char his soul to a bitter black. "You don't listen well, do you?"

***

The ZRT unit waited fifteen minutes before Olivia handed Jon the keys. They filled up the tank, and cleaned the remaining scraps of food from the quicky mart before taking off after Bethany. Jon was instructed to do everything he could to catch up to the Audi, but remain out of sight. Bethany couldn't know they were there.

"This would be so much easier if we had a helicopter. I'm licensed to fly, you know." Jon's bragging fell on deaf ears.

Olivia had military-grade binoculars glued to her eyes. If they lost Bethany, the mission could fail. If the mission failed – who knew what would happen to mankind.

"Watch out!"

A Screamer leaped out in front of the car, catching Jon off guard. Just before the car would have driven straight into the walking bag of death, Olivia grabbed the wheel and gave it a jerk. The car veered off to the side of the zombie with an angry screech. Jon managed to right the trajectory just before the sedan threatened to t-bone a fence. The car came to a jerking halt in the middle of the road.

Jon was just about to celebrate his driving heroics, when Olivia's gunshot yanked him back into the world of the real.

"Drive, Jon, drive!"

The roar of the monster, and another gunshot, threatened to deafen the living. Olivia's aim was off its usual mark. The Screamer jumped onto the car before the tires could announce their exit.

"Oh my God! Oh my God!"

"Jon, drive!"

The car tires barked on the pavement as the pedal hit the floor. The Screamer held on. It knew what delicious treats lay within.

"What are we going to do Olivia?"

Olivia dropped her window and undid her seat belt.

"Olivia, what are you doing?"

"Saving our asses, chicken boy. Keep the car on the road, moving forward preferably."

Without another word, Olivia stood, the upper half of her body hanging out of the window. As soon as the Screamer noticed the girl, he started pulling his way to the passenger side of the car. The beast let loose a roar to shame the screaming car engine.

A pale, white hand of death reached up from the hood of the car. Olivia knew that one hand could crush her skull. She aimed the pistol, held her breath, and squeezed the trigger.

A brown, sticky rain splattered the windshield before the Screamer was thrown to the pavement. Olivia slid back into the passenger seat just as Jon hit the windshield washers. At first, the mess smeared the glass and blocked his view. A rush of fluid cleaned the way to reveal a zombie-free highway ahead.

"Fuck!" Oliva released what tension remained.

"That was amazing. Jesus, you are fearless."

"And we are lucky bastards." Olivia pointed ahead. The line drawn between her fingertip and the horizon revealed a small, gray blur on the road ahead. Olivia pulled her binoculars to her eyes to confirm what she was already certain of. "It's them. Don't get any closer. We can't let them know they're being followed."

CHAPTER 5

November 18, 2016 9:15 PM
Near Chicago, Illinois

Eight hours. I drove eight hours straight. We stopped a couple of times for gas, food, and potty breaks. My legs threatened to revolt and leave my upper body stranded. What was truly astounding was that nothing stood in our way, no Moaners, Screamers, Zero Day Collective operatives, starving survivors, break downs, or teenage meltdowns. It was a strange miracle; something I would never have believed in, something I still question and probably will until my last, dying breath.

But I do fear that our luck would soon wear thin. I pointed the car on the straight and narrow to Seattle, thinking the quickest route between two points was the most logical. My logic failed to take into consideration the population of a city like Chicago. It's 2016, the big city headcount was reaching four million. If even just a quarter of that population has turned, that is still one million brain-munching zombies. Our odds of surviving those numbers are infinitesimal.

"Christ Bethany! Look at the road." Echo's model-thin arm was reaching forward – nearly into the beam of light cutting through the thickening fog.

Abandoned cars littered the highway. They weren't so thick as to keep us from moving forward, but the further we drove in, the thicker they became. The gray ash, from the explosion a year ago, still coated the landscape as if time decided to ignore the area. A fraction of my brain wanted to turn on the car radio and tune into some creepy music, just pretend this was nothing more than a movie.

Wouldn't that be nice? Close my eyes and make believe I was sitting on a couch, with a huge bowl of kettle corn in my lap, watching an old Romero zombie flick. Or "The Stand." Gary Sinise would run by any minute and scare the shit out of me. The popcorn bowl would fly out of my lap and who ever I was with at the moment would point and laugh.

But that's not our current truth. The hate-filled horror ahead of us was reality and now, more than any other moment in history, reality bites.

"What do we do?" Echo whispered, adding to the creepfest surrounding us.

"We keep driving. But we're going to not go through the city. I was hoping to look for a friend and find a decent hotel to stay in, but there's no fucking way I'm risking this. It was a stupid idea to begin with. Grab the map and find us the most direct route out of here."

Echo didn't argue. Why would she? I admitted to my mistake and hastily changed our course immediately. The only problem we had was the highway was growing more and more clogged with abandoned cars, trucks, and semis. It looked like our path forward wouldn't take us much further. I really had no desire to back track.

"In about a mile there'll be an exit; take that and it should get us around the city. Go either West or South – whichever way."

There was a hint of doubt in Echo's voice. Now was not the time for doubt. I had her read off the exits and nearest highways. She was right. The next exit was our target.

"Oh shit."

Echo's whisper filled the car with doom. We'd finally reached the national impound lot. Abandoned cars blocked the way. There was no going forward. I stopped the car with enough room to turn around and opened the door to step out.

"What are you doing? Are you nuts?" Echo grabbed for my arm but I slipped out of her grasp.

"I'm just going to see if we can get around the cars. I won't go far."

I didn't need to go but a few yards from the side of Audi to know there was no way we were going forward. The highway was a graveyard of vehicles. The only sound was the cold wind whipping and weaving in between the abandoned hulks. I closed my eyes and took in the absolute nothingness of the moment.

At least the silence was not interrupted by screaming, moaning, or gunshots. At this very brief second, I got to experience a peace I hadn't felt in a long time. I could keep my eyes closed and that peace would remain. I could die right now with a lie to free my conscience.

As I drifted deep within the wells and recesses of my mind, I saw Jacob – In the cell, lying on the floor in shock, standing with

Susan holding handfuls of candy, in a bathroom drooling over my panties. His warm smile comforted me.

Those memories would never leave. They were the only connection to a past I had. It seemed my life began at Jacob and would probably end at Jacob as well. It was the apocalypse; at least I had something to hold on to. The only thing most people had to grasp for was the hope to stay alive, to not become a meal for the monsters.

"What are we going to do?"

Echo's voice startled me. I was so lost in my head I didn't even hear her approach.

When I turned to look at the young girl, it was clear the threat of defeat lay just under the surface of her psyche. She needed something to hook her sanity to. I couldn't give that to her now. I could, however, give her human comfort. So I wrapped my arms around her tiny frame and squeezed as tightly as I could.

"We're going to get in that car, have a bite to eat, lock the doors, and go to sleep. When we wake in the morning we'll turn around and get ourselves back on track."

It wasn't ideal, but it was our best hope at the moment. I was exhausted. I couldn't drive another mile without the threat of nodding off at the wheel. I hated the idea of falling asleep in the middle of an open area, but we really had no choice.

"I'll pull the car up so it blends in with the rest of them. Once we seal ourselves up inside, we'll be safe."

I lied. I had no idea if a car could seal our

scent away from the zombie olfactory.

"I hate this silence. I'd love to hear the sounds of cars, or laughter, or a concert right now." Echo smiled up at me. "I guess that's what happens when you grow up on the streets. You get used to a symphony of chaos around you and silence becomes your enemy. I can deal with gunshots, riots, gang wars – but silence? Not so much."

Note to self – grill Echo with twenty or so questions.

We got back into the Audi and I pulled it within inches of another car. It blended in perfectly. With the lights and engine off, we were nothing more than another empty metal container.

"In about an hour or so it's going to be really cold in here. We have to try very hard to fight off the temperature without starting the car. The less noise, the likelier we'll survive. What's say we break open some groceries and have ourselves a picnic, post-apocalyptic style!"

Echo smiled and hauled out a sack of food. It was junk food, but would fill the tanks. And honestly, the chocolate snack cakes, pretzels, and warm soda would go a long way to curb what might well be a flood of PAMS – Post Apocalyptic Menstrual Syndrome.

Chocolate. Was anything ever so incredible?

As we were eating, Jacob woke and grew restless. Before the little guy could let loose his first wail of the evening, I took the initiative and changed his diaper. With that mess out of the way and out of the car (Sealed in an airtight, zipped up baggie, in case Moaners could smell baby scat), it was safe to give the boy a bottle of less-than-cold formula. He balked at the temperature, but when the nourishing liquid hit the back of his throat, he greedily sucked it down.

"Can you imagine how nice it would be to have such ignorance and innocence on your side? To not know what the world was suffering at the moment? Do you think Jacob has any idea what's going on around him?"

I wanted to say 'no way', but something inside me was fairly certain this baby was more aware than anyone would ever imagine. Understanding of the apocalypse coursed through Jacob's blood. When he looked up at you with those big brown eyes, it was clear his knowledge ran contrapuntal to his age. I held in my hands a prophet of an infant.

"I think he's asleep again. And I think I'm going to join him now."

I carefully cradled Jacob in the car seat and snapped him in. The soft sound of his breathing was the only noise to be heard. The back seat was going to make for an uncomfortable bed. It was, however, better than sleeping in a grave.

Echo was already spread out in the front seat, her be-socked feet pressed up against the driver's side window. I sat up and looked over the front seat at her. She smiled up at me.

"Thanks B."

The nickname struck me hard. It was the name Sally gave me back in Paris, just before she was ripped apart by Moaners.

"Most people wouldn't have bothered with

me. It took Armageddon to get someone to notice and care enough to take me in."

"You mean apocalypse."

Echo looked at me; confusion lined her big brown eyes.

"Armageddon is actually a mythical place where the messiah and Satan are supposed to fight some end of times battle."

The confusion on Echo's face changed to a warm smile that lit up the inside of the car.

"What?"

"You're so smart B. I really envy that. And I hate that I may not survive long enough to be like you."

I waited for tears to well up in Echo's eyes. None came. Instead she grinned, stuffed a chunk of chocolate in her mouth, and laid her head back down. "Night B."

"Good night Echo."

I fought off sleep as long as I could. Nerves did their best to keep me from the task of nodding off. It wasn't until I started thinking about the drive ahead of me that I grew bored and weary enough to drift off.

CHAPTER 6

November 19, 2016 1:35 AM
Outside of Chicago

My own chattering teeth woke me. When I sat up every muscle in my body complained. From my mouth, the mist of winter expelled from between my lips. We hadn't thought of blankets – that was a huge mistake (one we'd rectify during our next stop). As much as I hated to start the car, we needed some heat. Even if I could stand the cold, Jacob wasn't strong enough to withstand such chill. I had him swaddled in plenty of blankets – his perfect skin wouldn't be touched by the cold air. But breathing in the O2 of winter would certainly wreak havoc on his lungs.

"Echo." I nudged the girl. She didn't so much as show a sign of rousing.

"Echo, wake up!"

The sprawled girl moaned. She was alive and teen-enough to whine about it.

"What do you want?" One of her eyes opened and glared at me.

"I want you to sit up, start the car, and turn the heat on. We're going to freeze if we don't get some heat in here."

The girl's eyes went pie-wide. "Are you mental? If there are any Moaners or Screamers around, the sound of a car will bring 'em all raining down on us! No way. No fucking way."

I couldn't argue with her logic, but the truth of the matter was, we'd die anyway. And I could think of far sexier ways to die than freezing to death in an Audi on Interstate 80.

"It's below freezing out there. We have to get some heat in here or Jacob could get sick. We'll figure out a better way to stay warm later. But for now, start the car."

Echo complained again, but sat up and turned the ignition over. Thank God the car had an excellent muffler. The car was as silent as a combustion-driven machine could be.

"Give it a few minutes and crank up the heat. Once we get the edge off the temperature we can shut the car off and go back to sleep."

The hum of the engine was hypnotic in the dark, silent night. There was something comforting to still have machines at our disposal

"Do you know how much this sucks Bethany?"

All I could do was laugh. I'd been asking myself the same question for a year. Never once had the answer changed.

"Tremendously."

"What was it like in Munich?"

The question took me by surprise, punched me in the gut.

"I read the books B. How could I not. Jacob's book, your blog – required reading for a post-apocalyptic society." Echo sat up, cross-legged, in the front driver's seat. "So? Munich?"

Just as I was about puke forth my take on living through ground zero, a gunshot broke the silent, eerie night. The sound shut us up and stiffened our necks. The shot was close.

I eyed the ignition. Echo immediately received the hint and shut off the still-cold car. The doors were locked. The only sign of life from the car would be the fading exhaust fumes.

"Get down," my voice hardly audible. Fortunately Echo understood and scrunched as far into the shadows of the front seat as she could. I tucked myself down in the spaces between the front and rear seats. My brain wished to will my body as small as possible.

A second gunshot pierced the darkness, followed by maniacal laughter.

"Run, mother fucking coward! Run!"

The raging voice out-shined the sinister crack of the gunshot. Something wicked out there was on its way and I wanted no part of it.

The sound of running footfalls drew near. Something slammed up against the car. The sound of heavy breathing pierced the veil of safety. I wasn't sure about Echo, but the only movement from my body lie deep inside my chest, pounding mercilessly.

Another gunshot.

"Fuck!" A frightened male voice from outside the car pitched fear to the four winds. "God damn psychotic piece of ass trash!" The thick Chicago dialect couldn't be mistaken.

"There's the son of a bitch! Get him!"

The fight outside the car wasn't the run of the mill scrap. These people meant business.

"Now, you fucking piece of shit, I'm going to show you just why you shouldn't go around raping poor defenseless women; especially when one of those women happens to be my God damn wife!" A new voice joined the fray.

"What are you going to do to me?"

A laugh that would shame Tim Curry's evil clown made me want to poke out my ear drums.

"I am going to fuck you up, that's what I'm going to do. You see, there's only one thing worse than death now – infection. And since anarchy seems to be reigning supreme, I can do whatever the hell I want and no one will do fuck-all about it. So, the only answer for a piece of shit like you, is to tie you up and let the monsters have at your bony ass. Grab him boys."

Another scuffle broke out. This time, the tragic horse play was accompanied by cackling laughter best suited for an Asylum.

There was no way I was going to chance voyeurism now. The Mengele virus wrought more than just the undead on the human race. Along with the zombification of the majority of the population, came the psychopathic panic of the survivors. What Echo and I were hearing was only the tip of a very large and jagged iceberg.

"No! Don't leave me here!" The desperate, hoarse voice cried out. "They'll tear me apart!"

"That's the plan, motherfucker!"

The manic laughter was accompanied by gunshots. The gunshots were chased by cries for help. Whoever it was out there, wasn't going to survive making that much noise.

"Should we help him?"

I was surprised by Echo's question. She was a survivor, a casualty of a very broken system. The girl knew better than to let her heart bleed for the unknown, especially when said unknown was nothing more than zombie bait.

"Bethany? What do we do?"

Right before I opened my mouth to tell Echo she was foolish for thinking we should bother saving the man's ass, my conscience bitch slapped my mind. The man was still out there, screaming a siren song for every Moaner and Screamer in the area to hear. If we were going to do something, it had to be now.

I sat up and scanned the area. Sure enough the 'zombait' was tied to the rail of a truck bed about twenty yards away. He looked youngish, maybe mid-twenties.

"Stay in here Echo. Have you ever shot a gun?"

Echo's head shook back and forth, like she'd become possessed by Captain Howdy and his band of evil renown. So much for my backup. "Fine. Just stay in the car."

The young girl grabbed my arm and looked deep into my heart, concern and fear lined her face. "Don't die B."

"I don't plan on it."

I slowly swung the Audi door open and stood up from the rear seat. The gun I tried to offer Echo was in my hand, ready to rock. I wanted that gun to give me some sense of security; it didn't, quite the opposite. Using the pistol meant willingly making enough noise to draw the attention of the walking dead.

"Fuck! Lady, come and untie me. Please. Oh my God hurry."

The man's panic was understandable. In the distance the familiar cattle-like lowing sound was drifting through the cold night air. Zombies. They were coming, en mass. I had to make a decision immediately. Should I untie the man, knowing one of two things would happen; either he'd take off running, or he'd demand refuge with our little trio. I liked trios. Three was a prime number, it only had two divisors – perfect order – the *anti* to apocalypse. I needed that order. But there was a life in front of me that could be extinguished with a single bite.

The cattle were coming.

"What are you waiting for?" The man cried out.

I halved the distance between us to get a better look. The male was a bit older than I thought, his neck covered in a large bar code tattoo.

I hoisted the gun up and pointed it in the sweaty-faced kids' direction. "What's your name?"

Confusion drifted across the face of the male.

"What the hell does it matter? Untie me before those sons of a bitches get here!"

The zombies couldn't have been more than a block away. I had to make a choice, now. Either save the poor man, or cut my moral umbilical and haul ass.

Tears began pouring down the man's cheeks. I couldn't help myself. I ran to him.

"I won't hesitate to use this gun. You fuck with me, prepare to be fucked back – and I use no lube."

The rope holding the man was a maze of knots. I tried channeling my inner Boy Scout, but nothing worked. The moans drew nearer. The man struggled at the binding, which only served to draw the knots tighter.

"Will you stand still? You're making this impossible."

"Lady, if you don't hurry we're dead. Oh fuck! I see the bastards."

Don't look, don't look, don't look. The thought plowed through my mind. Finally, the only solid plan my panic-filled brain could come up with struck me hard. I aimed the gun at the rope, steadied my hands, and fired. The bullet sliced the rope enough so a swift tug would break him free.

"Come on! Run!"

I didn't bother to wait to see if the stranger followed. All I cared about was making it back to the Audi and getting my baby to safety. Echo already had the driver's side door open for me and was perched in the passenger seat. I flopped into the seat, slammed the door shut, turned the car over, and punched the gas. Just as the car spun out into a half-donut, the rear driver's-side door slammed shut.

He made it.

"Okay, first things first. Don't touch my baby. Second, don't fuck with either of us or you'll get it back tenfold. Now, what's your name and why did those men tie you up?"

"Whoa dragon lady. What's up with the

firing squad?"

He saw my eyes burning holes in him through the rear view mirror. His hands shot up in the air. "Okay, I get it. You don't know me so you don't trust me. That's the new world order. We're all guilty until proven innocent. Fine, fine. My name is Gabriel Wright. Full disclosure, I stole some of their food."

Echo squawked out her disapproval of his excuse. "No way. Those dudes were going militia on you. You did more than that."

Gabriel glared at Echo as if a Moaner had exploded out of her chest and lunged for his face. "You're kidding right? You know what it's like out there on the streets. Fear is the driving force behind every action. You can't look someone in the eye without them thinking you are after anything and everything they have. It's brutal. Yes, that's all I did. I took some food and ate it. I was starving. It's every man, woman, and child for themselves now."

A stare-off silence drifted down between Echo and Gabriel. I wasn't sure, but Echo looked like she was about to ram her fist through the man's face. I placed my hand on her knee to try to cool her off. As soon as my fingers found purchase, her shoulders relaxed, and the eyes returned to their normal size.

"Thank you, by the way, for saving me."

A single, broken sentence and my resolve melted away. How can you continue to be angry at politeness? Seriously, it's the apocalypse. When someone has the forethought to drop a *thank you* and *please*, you can't just brush it aside. After all, the human race set aside manners when the Zero Day Collective drop kicked us in the nuts.

"You two have names?"

I was afraid of this. It was one thing to let Echo into the center of my world – she's a young woman, I could take her if necessary. A man? That, I'm not so one hundred percent on at the moment. So, when Gabriel asked for names, my first thought was *How far would he dig?*.

"Name's Echo. That's all you get, for now. And don't bother asking about a last name. I don't have one."

The temperature inside the car seemed to drop a few thousand degrees as the Ice Princess unleashed her special brand of cold shoulder on the stranger.

Gabriel scoped me looking at him through the rear view. He was waiting for my go at the game.

"I'm Bethany and that's my baby in the back."

I gave our new recruit the low-down on what was going on. He seemed straight-forward with us, there was no reason I could think of to lie in return. He got everything but the core of what was going on. For him to know about the Zero Day Collective, and my plans to rip them asunder, required an earned trust. So we were now four. I wasn't perfectly settled inside with the change, but knew we stood a better chance with an extra pair of hands in our group. Besides, a male among us couldn't hurt.

Gabriel seemed amenable to joining our little crew.

We chit chatted until we were far enough away to be safe. It was now just after three AM. My eyelids were at war with gravity, and gravity was certain to win. Morning would come all too fast.

The rest of the night, I would sleep with my gun in my hand and the proverbial one eye open.

CHAPTER 7

November 20, 2016 9:05 AM
Zombie Response Team Minneapolis, MN Unit

"Minneapolis unit, checking in. This is Franklin Tash. Check, check."

The Minneapolis division of the Zombie Response Team was one of the largest in the north central United States. Because of their size, they were all business, all the time. The color of military flowed through the very veins of every member of 'ZRT MinSin'. No one knew where the nickname came from, they just knew it existed and everyone was expected to use it.

"Officer Tash, this is Morgan Barnhart. What's your SITREP?"

"All units in place and ready for action. If a Moaner or Screamer breeches our perimeter, we'll know it immediately and neutralize the threat."

"The target should be arriving in your location within the hour. Make sure the area is cleared. Morgan out."

Franklin pocketed his mobile and picked up the walkie to radio his squad leaders. "Operation clean and sweep is – "

The unit leader was cut short by a hideous chorus of screams, shortly after the squeal, the radio went silent.

"Sir, we have a sizable group of zombies heading our way. Type is Two. Your orders?"

'Type Two' referred to Screamers. Franklin

and his men had faced down only two Screamers so far – and that was a challenge. Now there was a group of them on the way.

"Fuck." Franklin's jaw nearly released itself from the top portion of the skull. Once again, he spoke into the radio. "Incoming. Type Two. Shoot on sight. Repeat, shoot on sight."

Everything went silent. The brief period before war always seemed to have that tiniest of moments where time seemed to lose its relevancy. Ten seconds could stretch out into ten hours. Breath was held, hearts refused to beat. All was placed on hold.

And then, Hell was unleashed above ground. What seemed like a small army of Screamers descended upon the unit. The second the first pair of sour-milk eyes was spotted, the tattoo of machine gun fire filled the air. It was on. War. And this time around, it was good for something – for killing zombies.

"Drekker! Behind you!" One of the soldiers cried out, but too late. The Screamer was on top of the young man before he could turn and fire. Cold, dead fingers tangled within the hair on either side of the man's head and pulled hard. Hair and flesh released themselves from their permanent residence around the skull. The soldier screamed out as the zombie slowly dug its fingers into the exposed skin of the man's head. The rotting flesh of the fingers had already peeled back to expose sharper bone. Those bony tips of the phalanges easily wormed their way into the space between flesh and bone. Once the deadly fingers were buried under layers of skin, the zombie yanked its hands out, tearing away the flesh like wet paper.

The soldier passed out from the shock of pain. The Screamer wrapped its fingers around the skull and bashed it on solid ground. It took only three cracks, before blood began to pour. After five cracks, the skull was sufficiently ruined to allow greedy fingers inside.

Franklin, and the rest of the Zombie Response Team, had been trained well. But that training only applied to Type One Zombies – the slower Moaners. The reality of the Screamer went far beyond anything the Minneapolis unit had experienced.

"Sir, what are your orders?" The second in command shook the leader out of his fear fugue.

Franklin Tash had no orders. He couldn't think. His brain misfired. The only command he could think of was 'fire'. That had done no good. His men were going to die.

"Sir! Your orders?" Again, the second demanded.

"Fire." Franklin half-whispered.

"We've been unloading on them and it's done nothing but piss them off."

The commander had another meaning of 'fire' in mind – a literal meaning. Without a word of warning, Commander Tash pulled away and headed back up the hill to his truck. In the bed of the pickup he had what he hoped he'd not need, a secret weapon.

Franklin's feet carried him faster than he ever thought possible. He knew how short time was. Bethany would arrive soon and there could be no danger in the area. Tash had one task, he wouldn't fail it.

As soon as he reached the truck, he jerked open the topper hatch and lowered the tailgate. The gleaming metal of the portable flamethrower spoke to him, begged him to put it into action. It would get its wish.

The tanks were heavy with fuel. The dual metal pods slammed against his back, assuring him they meant as much business as their wielder. With the tanks strapped down tight, Franklin grabbed the nozzle and lit the device. The 'fwump' and hiss were a subtle music of death and mayhem he needed to hear. The liquid flame that spilled from the nozzle promised redemption for those members of his team that had just perished. Franklin Tash would uphold the honor of his men.

When Tash returned to battle, the contents of his stomach were upturned and spilled to the ground at his feet. The Screamers had snuffed the life of every member of his squad. With no brain matter left to dine on, the zombies pulled limbs from torsos and sucked marrow from bones. The thick stench of blood flooded Franklin's senses. The heaves of vomit dried and stomach cramped; but the flame of redemption continued to fan from the hose.

"Hey! Over here. The last big brain matter in the area. You want it; you better come and get it."

The Screamers gladly complied with the command. All at once, the monsters descended upon the flame wielding sole survivor. The second a zombie was within reach of the fire, the rotting clothing and skin ignited. Once alight, the beasts began aimlessly wandering around, screeching like pitchforks on chalkboards. Franklin had to do a bit of sidestepping and dancing to avoid becoming nothing more than a collateral fire sale.

The smell of meat seared by liquid fire was caustic. One by one, the Screamers dropped to their knees and gave up their final ghost. The crackle and pop of burning flesh was replaced by a sickening black smoke. Franklin's flamethrower spit up its last life and went cold.

Commander Tash stood, motionless, staring out at the carnage of a battle that took less than fifteen minutes to fight. He lost every man on his team, but the goal was achieved. The path was cleared for Bethany. Even still, Franklin couldn't find the silver lining. Though he lived, his existence was at the cost of every man he commanded.

"Fuck." Was all Franklin could get out.

The flamethrower clanked to the ground, the sound echoed to the heavens. He knew he was supposed to leave no trace, but there wasn't time to clean up. No time for shovels, buckets, and body bags. Bethany would arrive any moment and every member of the Zombie Response Team was instructed to leave the site before the target appeared.

Franklin took off toward his truck. As he ran he pulled out his mobile and hit the speed dial entry for headquarters.

"This is Morgan." The sweet voice of the young ZRT leader chimed out of the speakerphone.

"Franklin Tash. The zombies have been neutralized. The area is clear for arrival. But ... I lost my men."

A brief, awkward silence sucked the air out of the conversation.

"How many men were lost, Frankin?"

Another, darker silence.

"All of them sir."

As expected, Franklin was commanded to remain in the area, out of sight, until Bethany arrived and took off safely. Should the target pass through the area, Tash was to follow, at a distance, until the route was clear.

The eyes and ears of the Zombie Response Team had his orders. He tucked himself away, inside of the main building of the Flying J Truck stop. His position offered clear site of the area and clean shot, should something befall Bethany.

The unexpected always had a way of following Franklin Tash. As he sat, waiting For Bethany's arrival, he saw movement coming from the pile of bodies that was the remains of his men. It wasn't possible. He torched every Screamer in the area.

"Oh fuck." The realization hit him in the gut, like a punch in the night from a too-large boogeyman. The men that had limbs and intact skulls were amplifying. There was something strange about the whole situation. The process of infection never happened so quickly. Infection to amplification normally took, at least, twenty-four hours.

The swelling chorus of moans proved that assumption very wrong.

Franklin scrambled for his weapon, but came up with nothing. He'd dropped his pistol in the melee and, obviously, left the extinguished flame thrower out in the parking lot. He had nothing for defense.

A gust of wind swung the door to the building open.

"Shit!" Tash scrambled to the door, slammed it shut, and twisted the dead bolt. He knew the door would hold the zombies out. The multitude of glass panes, on the other hand, was a different story. It would buy him enough time to locate some form of weapon. No matter how dire the situation was, he knew he had to do everything he could to clear the area for arrival. Keeping Bethany safe was above even his own life. And now he had, maybe, ten newly amplified zombies to take out by himself; with no weapon of significance.

Franklin dashed around the inside of the building, in search of something that could do damage enough to neutralize the walking dead. Connected to the convenient food mart was a diner. The smell of grease and trucker body odor had long since evaporated. All that was left was a slick floor and empty cupboards. Fortunately the cooks' cutlery was left behind. The knives weren't quality, but they had a point and held an edge. A cheap knife was better than nothing at all.

He grabbed the biggest blade he could find. The song the knife sang as he picked it up from the counter brought some reassurance that things could possibly work out. Franklin Tash could survive yet another battle with the undead.

The dead walked toward the building. The lumbering gate of the new-born zombies was the antithesis of how his men were in life. At least there was some strange comfort in knowing that. If Tash was about to go up against the soldiers that had served under him, he'd never survive. Type One zombies? That's a different story.

His confidence peeked just as the zombies were about to reach the building. But before the first blood was drawn, the gray Audi pulled into the parking lot.

"Bethany." Franklin whispered as much in awe as he was in fear. Quickly that adoration washed away to be replaced by a sense of panic. He'd failed his one duty and had to rectify the situation. The target had arrived and zombies were present.

The situation called for swift action. Franklin took an inventory of what weapons he knew to be in the area. Caution was tossed out the window when he realized there were automatic weapons in the trunk of his car. All he had to do was make it thirty yards across a parking lot, grab a weapon, and unload on the men that were once his colleagues.

Bethany had yet to swing a leg out of the car. For Franklin Tash, this was now a race against an apocalyptic clock.

CHAPTER 8

November 20, 2016 10:15 AM
Flying J Truck stop Minneapolis, MN

The Audi was as low on gas as my bladder was low on space. It seemed almost a tragic relativism, my bladder versus our survival. But even in the given circumstances, the Audi running on fumes at least held some truth and validity over our survival. My bladder was nothing more than a discomfort. Even still, when the Flying J appeared on the horizon, I could finally uncross my mental anguish that radiated out from just below my uterus.

Of course that relativism was shot to Hell when the small band of Moaners made themselves known in the parking lot. At that moment, my hands wanted to jerk the wheel and head back to the freeway. The only problem with that plan was that we'd not get very far. The combustion engine was still very susceptible to inadequate amounts of fuel. So somehow, I had to first hope there was fuel in the tanks and, second, figure out a way to take out a small group of the undead.

I stopped the Audi just on the periphery of the parking lot, its nose pointing directly at the shambling mini-horde. As the engine idled, the idea hit me. I had spent enough time with Sam Leamy to know the blunt force trauma of a car's grill could quickly bring a flight of angels to sing these zombies to their rest.

The gas pedal hit the floorboard. The engine roared, bringing the attention of the zombies my way. My brain scrambled for a pithy Shakespearean quote. The only thing I could come up with was "To die, to sleep; no more." *Cliché* and *touché* at the same moment.

Just as I was about to release my foot from the brake, a male came screaming out of the building. He wasn't a Screamer, of that I was certain. Who he was, and what he was doing, was clearly lost on me. I thought maybe he saw the car and was making a break for us, but he was running in the wrong direction. What the man was doing was suicidal.

"What the heck is going on with that dude, B? And why are you revving ... oh no, you're not going to do what—"

Echo was a clever girl, much more clever than her years should allow. But this was the apocalypse. People had to grow up damn fast now.

"Echo, strap yourself in. This is going to be a bumpy ride. Gabriel, grab a hold of Jacob. Don't let anything happen to him."

"Bethany, couldn't we just pull out a piece and pump their asses full of lead? Why risk our only means of getting the fuck out?" Gabriel's words momentarily stopped me from pushing the car into a maximum overdrive zombie smack down.

And then tragedy struck. The Audi choked and chugged until the engine went silent. The gas gauge clearly proclaimed the car was bereft of fuel. Now, we had no choice. It was full-on war. Before my conscious mind could grasp what was going on, my hand grabbed the gun and my legs insisted I leave the car. These were Moaners. Moaners die.

I channeled the spirit of Jacob and the balls of Sam Leamy to go full-on hero. I was a La Femme Wrecking Ball, about to go beast mode on a small gang of brainistas.

"Hey! Over here! IQ of 161 on the menu. Gray matter so sweet and delicious, it'll make you smack your momma!"

And like the film of my inner marine badass, I dropped to one knee, brought the pistol to bear on the pack of monsters, took in a deep breath, and took a shot.

The explosion was far louder than it should have been. When I saw more than one Moaner go down, I realized what had happened – someone else had taken a shot. Two of the Moaners had been dropped, the rest of the pack split in two; half coming after me, the other half after the mystery shooter.

Three Moaners. I had no idea how much ammunition was left in the weapon. Now was not the time for doubt. Now was the time for kicking ass – and willing extra bullets to magically appear in the clip of my pistol.

Another breath in. Another shot taken. Another Moaner down.

I wanted so badly to do a bit more channeling, only this time the Count, from Sesame Street.

"One dead zombie! Hahahaha!" The words actually came out of my mouth.

The explosion of the larger weapon was heard, followed by a scream. Whoever the mysterious militiaman was, he was likely either dead or infected. Either way, his life was forfeit.

Another breath, another shot, another dead bastard.

I had one zombie left and he was getting much too close for my comfort. At first, it seemed the best plan of attack was to head back to the car, climb on top, and take my last shots from up high. But drawing the undead anywhere near Jacob was an obvious mistake.

So, I took off the other way.

But the zombie bastard continued on toward the car.

"Holy fuck!"

The zombie reached the car and set his sights for the rear passenger seat – Jacob's side. When the soggy bag of meat made it to within licking distance of the window, it just stood and stared; its body slowly waving back and forth. Inside the car I could hear the sounds of panic rising and falling – mostly rising.

But the beast just stood there, like it was transfixed on some hidden dimension only meant for the rotting eyes of the undead.

"Hey!" My voice shattered the magic moment. The zombie turned to me and let out a sound I hadn't heard from the walking dead. The sound was tonal, but more than one tone – a chorus of well-trained operatic cows, or like some special effects in a really bad sci-fi movie, only this was all too real.

My hand held the pistol, steadily pointed at the bastard's forehead. But even with the bangbang ready to knock the son of a bitch permanently into a state of slumber, the thing went back to the car window. I didn't have to think too long and hard as to the why the zombie was so enamored of the contents of the Audi.

"Jacob."

When the realization hit me, the pistol unloaded three shots into the Moaners head. Just as the thing hit the ground, the anonymous gun blast went off behind me. Shortly after the overly-loud gunshot, the male that screamed out of the building earlier stumbled into the parking lot. He was hurt. My gut told me the boy had been bit. As soon as he was near enough for my eyesight to adjust, my suspicion was confirmed.

"Help!" The boy cried out, holding his arm. Blood sprayed out from between his fingers. The Moaner that bit him must have ripped through an artery.

"Stop!"

I couldn't help him. The boy was gone, already infected.

"I need help." The boy drew closer.

"I said stop. You've been bit. You're infected. There's nothing that can help you."

The boy continued forward.

"That's not true. You're Bethany right? You have a cure. You can save me. I risked..."

The boy dropped to his knees. He was bleeding out. I didn't have the heart to tell him there was no cure. I wasn't sure if he would bleed out before he amplified. If he amplified first, the blood loss wouldn't matter.

The pistol in my hand had an empty clip. If

the boy amplified, he'd be on me in an instant.

"Please. You have to help me. Just give me the cure. You can even toss it to me and I'll inject myself. I was a nursing student. I know how to—"

The boy started convulsing and screaming. He was turning. I dashed to the car, threw open the door and grabbed for my bag. I always had a spare clip.

"Fuck! Where's my clip?"

I turned back to the car and saw the clip shining in the driver's seat. It had fallen out when I grabbed the bag.

As soon as I turned back, I heard the scream of the boy. He'd turned. He was a Screamer.

Before I could slam the clip into the pistol grip, the Screamer was on me. The bastard dragged me to the ground and forced me to my back. The best I could do was reach my hands up and block the Screamer from getting close enough to bite. I could smell his already rotten breath, look into the curdled orbs of his eyes.

With all my strength, I did my best to heave the beast to the side. I kicked up, sent a knee into his groin; everything I could think of. Nothing worked. The monster insisted itself upon me. Gnashing teeth drew nearer. This was it. I was finally about to get pimp slapped by the bitter hand of irony.

The hot scream of the zombie was in my ear when the gun went off. The shot was made from the side, so all back spatter sprayed out and not down.

The Screamer rolled off, an un-lifeless

lump. When the corpse was out of my line of sight, I had a perfect vision of Gabriel, holding the smoking gun.

"Chicago style." Gabriel smiled down at me and offered a helping hand.

Finally upright, my knees decided they hadn't had enough of being down, and gave out. I couldn't believe it. I had already gone to Hell and back, swam naked in the River Styx, got raped and reamed by Satan himself. So why was I afraid? Zombies had become common place and I had seen everything the undead nation had to offer. And yet, one simple Screamer had me pissing my pants. One. Screamer.

"Bethany!" Echo was out of the car and on her knees at my side. Her concern was not only genuine, but touching.

"I'm okay. Really. Just shaken up a bit. I'll be fine."

Once more unto the standing room only breech, I took my chances and braved gravity. This time, however, my knees did not decide to give into the Earth's pull.

"Thank you Gabriel, for saving my life. I owe you one."

Gabriel started to protest the owed favor, when I stopped him silent. I knew he'd need that favor returned some day. I only hoped the return didn't have me pulling a trigger of a gun aimed square at the boy's brain.

"Let's get the fuck – "

Before I could complete my thought, two cell phones rang simultaneously – one in my pants pocket and the other somewhere on the grave-still zombie. Curiosity got the best of this kitten and I rolled the monster over with the heel of my foot. A smartphone dropped out of the boy's pocket. The name on the screen read ZRT – Seattle. I couldn't resist. I answered the phone.

"Yeah?"

"What's the status of the target?" The voice on the other end of the line spoke out.

I looked over at my phone to see Jamal's name on the screen.

I hung up the dead zombie phone and answered my own.

"J-Tiz, what do you know about ZRT?"

There was a pause. I didn't like pauses. A pause was Hollywood-speak for hidden agenda or secretive information.

"Never heard of 'em girl. Now, what's taking you so long to get here? I thought you perfected the hyper-drive already?"

It was my turn to pause. There was something to these two calls coming in simultaneously. I don't know. Maybe I've grown overly paranoid since the Mengele Virus hit. Or maybe my blood runs cold with conspiracy. Either way, on one phone line or other, something was amiss.

"Straight up, Jamal?"

I was greeted with another silence. Now I knew something was awry.

"Straight up B. Are you okay? You're starting to worry me? Girl, this shit done hit the fan and splashed all over the God damn planet. We don't need you dumping more feces on the fire." Jamal was good. He always did know just what to say to put everything into perspective. And that was the way it was with our relationship. From day one it was always a push and pull between brother and sister and lovers. We never really knew where we stood. Honestly, I was happy I'd get another chance to challenge that relationship to see where it would go.

"I'm good Jamal. We'll be there in a few days. Just – " something had me hesitating. There was something left unsaid that needed to be said. I couldn't quite put my finger on it though. "Just stay in touch with me. I need to know you're still there waiting."

And with that, I said my goodbye.

"What's going on B?" Echo was out of the car and by my side. "Who's the dead guy? What's up with the phone calls? Is it safe to stock up now?"

Teens had this uncanny ability to speak entirely in questions. It was like they were incapable of doing the slightest bit of research on their own.

The truth, however, was that I owed it to everyone on this apocalyptic three-hour tour to remain as open and honest as possible. Enough lies had been told since the Zero Day Collective hacked the planet's DNA. I wouldn't be part and parcel to spreading more untruths.

I looked to Echo and smiled. "Honestly, I don't know what's going on. But I'll find out. Trust me on that one. The dead guy? I have no idea who he was. If you really want to know, you can rifle through his pockets and see if he has anything that might give up his identity.

Just be careful you don't get any of his juice on you. I don't want to have to put a bullet between your eyes."

The look on Echo's face was priceless. Who said it was wrong to have fun in the middle of an apocalyptic crisis?

"I'm kidding. Sort of. I mean, just grab a bag and fill it with any kind of edibles you can get your paws on."

It only took a smile to get Echo moving. She was right to question. And honestly, I hope like hell she keeps the questioning up. I needed that girl to keep me honest. The second I start hiding information is the second this whole nightmare hay ride derails.

Gabriel chased off after Echo. I watched him run after her wondering if it was going to be necessary to keep my eye on him. Little was known about the man and little would be tolerated. The second his dick falls out of his pants is the second his ass hits the pavement. I'd rather take on a horde of Screamers than a second of teen drama.

I had to get the Audi to the gas pump. I reached in, put the car in neutral, released the break, unlocked the steering wheel, and started to shove. I was actually surprised the metal beast started moving forward. As soon as the car started picking up a bit too much speed, I realized I was on an incline. I hopped in and steered the slow-moving German vehicle to the gas pump.

The big fingers-crossed moment was nigh. I inserted the gas nozzle, tapped the high-octane option, and ran inside to okay the sale. We had yet to come across a station with empty tanks. How? I have no idea. The only logical conclusion I could draw was that, with nearly eighty percent of the population zombified, there were simply not enough drivers to drain the petrol coffers.

Inside the Quickee mart, I grabbed a glance to see that an underage quickie wasn't going on and tapped the blinking button for pump number five. So far so God-damn-good.

"B. Bad news. Shelves are empty. No food."

I knew it was bound to happen sooner or later. But now was such bad timing. We still had some food left in the car, but not enough to get us to Seattle.

"Wait. I found something." Echo called out, derailing my train of thought on the doom and gloom express. When I looked back her way, she was holding up a bag in each hand.

"Dog and cat food. I've eaten worse. And there's plenty."

I didn't want to know. I really didn't. I also couldn't believe my life had devolved to the point where animal kibble was what's for dinner. But, Echo was right. In a pinch, we could survive on the mangy meals.

"Hey, maybe it'll make our hair shiny and healthy." Gabriel chimed in.

"And you'll probably start licking your balls."

"How do you know I don't already?"

The two 'kids' continued on while I ran back out to fill the Audi's tank.

On my way, the dead zombie's phone rang again. I pulled the handset out of my pocket and looked at the screen. Again the caller was ZRT. I wasn't completely convinced the caller wasn't the Zero Day Collective hiding under the guise of a different acronym. I don't know if it was my overly paranoid conscious mind, or the fact that the letter 'Z' will always and forever be associated with the crew that destroyed mankind.

Sesame Street be damned.

Of course, there was no way I was going to answer the phone. No way in Hell. As far as I knew, I was off the ZDC radar, and it was going to stay that way.

CHAPTER 9

November 20, 2016 1:23 PM
Zero Day Collective Mobile Headquarters

"Sir, we have confirmation the package is en route heading west by car. We're working on pinpointing her exact location. Are we to mobilize?" The communications officer spoke over the ever-present, low-thrum of the transport vehicle. The noise wasn't loud, nor was it invasive, just always there, in the background, reminding the ZDC survivors their permanent headquarters had been lost.

"Remind me, Sergeant, what exactly are we to mobilize? We are currently rebuilding and re-harvesting an army." The commander wanted to crack the whelp across the back of the skull, but soldiers were hard to come by now. The last time the Zero Day Collective tangled with Bethany, they lost thousands of men and women and even more zombie foot soldiers. This time around they wouldn't be so careless. Their next battle would be more carefully planned; better informed decisions would be made. And with a mole practically at Bethany's side, they'd have their way the second they were flush with boots to hit the ground.

Until that moment, it was all about planning. Bethany Nitshimi wasn't your average civvy. Bethany was smart, resourceful, and she had something no one else had –

Jacob.

The commander's communicator beeped.

"Commander Faddig here."

The voice on the other end was crisp, as if they were standing to the side of the officer. "Commander, I think you're going to want to come into the lab now."

The transport had but a few 'stations' tucked within its shiny metal box – a command center, a sick bay, a kitchen, and a lab. All of this took up a single floor, with very cramped quarters.

"On my way."

The tech only ever called the commander into the lab when they had something good to share. Faddig's skin tingled. Something big was coming.

Faddig had taken control of the Zero Day Collective when it seemed the entire order was about to collapse under the bloated weight of a collection of leaders more concerned with profit than executing the righteous task of the cleansing. Faddig was the only member of the board with balls enough to remove the dead weight and push the cause forward. With strong enough ties to the remaining military contingency, Faddig managed to pull The Collective out of the growing heap of ash that threatened to drown what little hope the new human race had.

New Human Race.

The thought alone gave him chills. Wiping clean the slate, ridding the race of its chaff and debris, Faddig was to be the prophet of the next iteration of mankind.

"Sir. This way." The lab technician gestured for the commander to follow into a secured, sealed anti-chamber. Inside the chamber was a cube made of clear, three-inch thick Plexi. Inside the cube a zombie, perched on a chair, slowly rocked back and forth.

The lab tech picked up a phone receiver and held it to his ear. After pressing a button on the receiver, he spoke into the phone.

"Subject 001. Stand up."

The zombie slowly stood.

There was none of the tell tale signs of zombie-dom. This was just a skinny man slowly standing out of a chair. The zombie stood in place, nearly motionless.

"Subject 001. Turn around and face the rear wall of the room."

Again, the zombie obeyed the command.

"Brilliant." Faddig whispered, in near shock at what he beheld.

"Subject 001. Speak your name."

In a freak show, monotone voice, the undead man spoke. "My name is Subject 001."

The lab tech tossed a sideways glance toward Faddig and then back to the cube.

"Subject 001. What is your purpose?"

There was a brief hesitation, as an uncomfortable silence blanketed the room. Faddig stepped in closer to the cube and placed his hands on the Plexi. The zombie looked up and made eye contact with the new leader of the ZDC. The monster's eyes were not the cloudy white he'd grown used to, but could have passed as human, save for the jaundiced whites.

"My purpose is to eliminate Bethany Nitshimi."

The breath was punched out of Faddig's lungs. He stood, staring at the zombie, momentarily unable to breathe; his brain too overloaded with amazement to remember the lower functions.

"How did you ... Is this ... When can we..." Faddig's mind released a deluge of questions at once, all of them tripping over his tongue to be the first asked.

"All in good time sir. All in good time. The test subject is not ready to be deployed. Subject 001. Please return to your seat and wait further instruction."

The zombie slowly turned, made his way back to the chair, and sat. There was no complaint, no hesitation, just capitulation.

From chaos to order.

"Sir, follow me." The lab tech gestured for the door.

As soon as they were clear of the anti-chamber, Faddig turned to the technician.

"What is your plan for that thing? And why was I not informed of its existence?"

The tech closed his eyes and inhaled a deep breath. "This is something I've been working on since the relocation. I discovered some of Dr. Michael's notes that hinted at the possibility of returning cognitive function to the zombie brain. As soon as I read her hypothesis, I knew it was possible. As for my plans? Well, I don't really have any plans at the moment."

"But – "

"The subject was just repeating something I

gave him – just a seed of a thought. Even so, it does prove, once lower functions are returned to the brain, it is possible to implant action and even determination. The implications, as one might say, are limitless."

Faddig looked deep within the wells of the tech's eyes. "I want Subject 001 ready for deployment in twenty-four hours. And don't bother objecting – I own you, so you will do what I say. Twenty-four hours. That zombie better be ready to follow my lead."

And with that, the leader of the Zero Day Collective left the room in a show of strength and closure. There was no doubt left in the tech's mind. Faddig's will be done, else the consequences be dire.

"So much for a good night's rest." The tech turned to the cube, grabbed Subject 001's chart, and took off for his lab.

Subject 001 looked up in the darkness of the room, his lips nearly curling up into a grin.

CHAPTER 10

November 20, 2016 7:35 PM
Fargo, North Dakota

I never thought I'd see the day when Fargo was in my headlights. But there it was. In all its frozen tundra and thick northern dialect glory. All I could think about was poor William H. Macy and Frances McDormand. The thought of that brilliant film made me wonder if Hollywood was officially and permanently irrelevant. All apocalyptic films had either been proved completely right or completely wrong. The undead rendered the rom com completely laughable (and not in the good way). Reality TV was no longer, well, real.

In the end, who really cared? Television was never anything more than a means to a mind-numbing end. Now the human race had another way to rid their minds of thought, emotion, and memory. Ultimately, however, the only thing that truly mattered now was survival, and that would certainly go to the fittest.

"Where are we?" The sound of Echo's exhausted voice rose from the dead of the passenger seat.

"Fargo."

"You mean like the movie? Seriously?" Echo looked out the passenger window and nearly screamed. "Holy shit! I've never seen so much snow! It's exactly like the film."

She was right. The tundra was frozen and looked to be as bitter as American soil could get. As we drove into the town, the snow crunching under tire, a question came to mind. Could zombies survive in below zero temperatures? Or did the lack of functioning internal organs give them some super-human ability to survive extremes of temperature? I assumed, being in Fargo, we'd get the chance to find out.

But then something occurred to me. During this whole road trip, we'd only really seen any semblance of the undead in Minneapolis. How was it possible that a road trip that currently spanned nearly thirteen hundred miles and over twenty-four hours would reveal only a the smallest handful of zombies?

I didn't believe in luck.

I didn't believe in karma.

I didn't believe in destiny.

Or that guiding hand of fate.

I sounded like a Rush song.

Digress much?

"Gang, we have to stop. I have to eat, pee, and sleep. Who's with me?"

What I really wanted was a shower. Sure it was the apocalypse, but I was starting to smell like sour onions.

"Oh my God Bethany. Look!"

Echo's pointing finger jerked to my side of the car to point out what I could only describe as Mecca.

A hotel. And hotel's meant beds and possibly showers. I didn't care if there was electricity or even heat – I just wanted to clean up and lie down.

"Can we stop?"

I laughed. It was the only reaction that seemed suited to the moment.

"Are you kidding me? There's no way we're going to pass up this opportunity. But we have to be careful. Just because it seems like some secluded bastion of open-armed warmth and protection, there's nothing saying a small army of zombies aren't hold up inside. We do this, we do it safely. Are you with me?"

Echo held up her hand for me to high five. Under normal circumstances I'd pass on the frat-boy jocularity. But for some reason, at this very moment, it just seemed fitting. So, I high fived my girl.

I pulled the Audi into the U-drive at the front door of the hotel. I hated to look so obvious, but it was better than hauling supplies, and Jacob, from the parking lot. Out in the open, one random Screamer could easily take us down.

"Gabe, grab food out of the trunk. Echo, grab some clean clothes for us. I'll get Jacob and my pack. We head to the door as one. Got it? And make it quiet. Ninja quiet."

The wonder twins nodded and went to work. The silent dance we did was a thing of beauty. Even Jacob played along, still napping, as I pulled his car seat from the back of the Audi. As soon as I had my pack on my back, we were ready. We closed up the car, locked it up tight, and made our way into the hotel. Only to get smacked upside the head by the smell of rotting corpses.

Echo nearly dropped to her knees as soon as her sinuses were assaulted. "Oh my God! Make it stop!"

"My eyes are burning. What is that Bethany?"

I knew what it was. It was actually quite obvious – the floors and furniture were lined with bodies. Wall to wall death. Every square inch of the reception area and the visible halls were flooded with the rot and filth of death. The stink of methane hung in the air. A single match would blow this building to Munich, where this nightmare started.

"Can we get out of here?" Echo started to bolt.

"Echo. I know it's bad, but we really need to find beds and get some rest. We'll go upstairs and try to locate less morgue-like rooms."

Echo stopped and gave off a moan to beat the undead band.

"If we don't find anything, we'll leave. I promise."

Thankfully, Echo capitulated and we moved on, our mouths and noses covered. The stench was really as bad as it sounded. The floor was greasy with rot and ooze. Every time a foot went down, it was like stepping on ice. Only if you slipped and fell, the slop you landed in would haunt you until your dying day.

Be a tightrope walker.

Be one with balance.

"What do we do if a zombie gets up and attacks?"

For some reason, Gabe's question stopped us all in our tracks – like we were part of some strangely humorous reality TV show that followed a train wreck of a group of ghost hunters.

"We run Gabe. We run like Hell." Echo whispered her answer, giving away the fear that had to be boiling in her gut.

At the end of the corpse-carpeted hall, we were greeted with stairs and an elevator. When Echo reached for the elevator button, I grabbed her hand and slowly pulled it away.

"I don't do elevators. We'll take the stairs."

Gabriel and I shared a look. I knew what he was thinking. He'd read Jacob's book and my blog and knew what could happen within the four claustrophobic walls of an elevator.

Death could happen.

Without saying a word, Gabe grabbed the handle of the stairwell and held the door open. Before I crossed the threshold, I stopped at his side and pulled a pistol from my back pocket.

"Can I trust you with this?"

He nodded. I handed him the pistol.

"You shoot anything but zombies, you won't live to regret it."

Gabriel took my threat seriously and acknowledged with a quick nod. I grabbed the second gun from my other pocket and stepped into the stair well.

The smell almost instantly cleared up. We all stopped and enjoyed the fresh, cool air.

"We don't know what's above us. As far as we know, there could be a horde of Moaners and Screamers up there. We'll stop on each floor until we find a room worthy of our group. Everyone okay?"

Both Echo and Gabe nodded. We fell into a marching order with Gabe leading the charge and me pulling up the rear. I didn't like having Jacob so exposed in the back, but any member of the undead party would have to go through my ass to get to him. Fat chance.

We slowly, quietly marched on. I could hear Echo's heavy breathing ahead of me. I wasn't sure if she was winded or frightened. Fortunately the apocalypse did one thing for me – got me in shape. I've never felt so athletic in my life. Of course, at the moment, I'd trade my old lethargy any time for some order and security.

As soon as we hit the first floor landing, Gabe grabbed the handle of the door and gave it a turn. He was able to push the door open about six inches before it came to a sudden halt.

"Jesus Christ!" Gabe let the door slam, holding his hand to his mouth.

"What was it?"

Gabe looked at me, with a slight hint of madness in his eyes.

"Slashed up bodies. Broken bones, guts, blood ... men and women turned inside out."

I'd seen that before. Zombies could wreak havoc on the human body. Once the brain was fully consumed, some Moaners and Screamers would gladly tear open a body cavity in search of other meats to bring them peace. It never worked. Those fuckers could dig through every inch of the human body and not find a single morsel to quiet the sound driving them mad. It was brain paté or nothing.

I was at a bit of a crossroads. Part of me wanted to curl up into a ball and weep away the rest of my life, while the other part knew strength was the only way me and my baby would ever survive this monster mash. The Girl Scouts never prepared me for this. Their motto lied. But then, how in the name of differential equations could anyone be prepared for the apocalypse?

Damn it. I just wanted to curl up with some C++ and code myself to sleep. Right now, however, I'd settle for a shower. We had to forge on. Or up.

"Next floor." I nodded to Gabriel who immediately took off, onward and upward.

When we reached the third floor, the door swung open easily. I certainly didn't want to jinx us, but it was possible we'd found our refuge.

"Spread out. Try to find an unlocked room clear of the dead or the undead." I tried to make a joke, but realized now was not the time. The failed attempt at humor also only served to remind me of Jacob, the baby daddy Jacob.

I wanted to punch myself for even thinking in such terms. Trash did not become this girl.

My weary legs carried me off, away from Echo and Gabriel. It took more energy than I really had to keep from either dropping or swinging the car seat bassinet hard enough to wake Jacob. Fortunately, my little man was a sound sleeper. He could have easily ruined our chances of survival a time or two. One loud enough cry at the wrong instance and we'd be surrounded by brain-craving monsters.

Over my dead body didn't really work so well at the moment.

Just as I was about to reach out for the door handle, an ear-drum shattering screech rattled the walls and my nerves.

"Echo!"

I turned in time to see a pair of Moaners practically fall out of a room in a contorted attempt at reaching Echo.

"Run Echo!"

Gabriel appeared from out of a room and screamed. His reflexes were almost super-human. As soon as Echo zipped past him, he had his gun leveled and his sights on the forehead of the Moaners. The first shot was dead on and dropped one of the beasts in a spray of brownish blood and rotted brain. The second zombie turned its attention on Gabe and the noise maker. Echo was by my side faster than she could say *LMFAO*.

Once Echo realized exactly what was happening, she screamed at Gabe to *watch out*. The angst that billowed from her mouth was powerful. Echo's screech could shame a Screamer.

I started to raise my own gun, but before I could, Gabriel had knocked out two more shots, the first grazed a cheap wall sconce, the second pierced the frontal lobe of the zombie's brain. The undead bastard dropped like a wet bag of Spam.

We all stood, motionless. Once again my little group managed to take down a small contingency of zombies. But how many more would there be? I could whip out a TS-100 and calculate the probability that more Moaners would show their ugly, flesh-eaten faces, but there was no time for math. There was only time for survival – and that meant tucking ourselves away in a room.

Then, as if on cue, Jacob started crying. It never ceased to amaze me how quickly everything could spiral down the drain to Hell. Jacob's screaming kicked our search for undead amnesty into high gear. We stuck with the original plan and split up. One of us would find a safe haven that we could barricade ourselves within.

"Bethany!" Echo's whispered voice teased the far reaches of my hearing. Instinct had my feet following the sound before my brain registered what they were doing.

Echo stood in a doorway and waved me to hurry up. I walked as quickly as I could, but with a crying baby hanging in a car seat from my arm, sprinting was not an option. Gabe followed suit, his gun swinging in a one hundred and eighty degree arc across the hall.

As soon as Gabe slipped into the room, he pulled the door shut behind him and slid the dead bolt closed. He wasn't finished. Somewhere, within the man, a newfound survival instinct switched on. He went to the four-drawer dresser, grabbed it, and jerked the piece of furniture toward the door, It wouldn't budge.

"Fuck! It's bolted to the ground. What the Hell? Do they think someone is going to walk off with this cheap crap?"

"No Gabe, I think they're worried someone is going to try to barricade themselves inside a room with it."

My jab brought a nervous laugh from Echo. Fortunately, when Echo laughed, Gabe didn't try to pull some alpha male shtick on me. Had that happened, I'd have to make it very clear who the alpha male was, and it certainly wasn't male.

After a quick inspection of the door, it dawned on me the easiest means of keeping said door from swinging open was to pull the closet around until its edge bumped up against the door to the room. Should undead cleaning come by, manage to smash through the deadbolt, and try to enter our hide out, the door would stop as soon as the handle caught the edge of the closet door.

Instant protection without a hernia or need for tools.

With the room secured, it was time to bring us a little silence. Jacob was turning bright red. A quick check of the diaper gave a good indication the poor boy was starving. Gabe had the bags of food already on the bed. I grabbed a can of formula and prepared it for the baby. As soon as the nipple slipped between Jacob's lips, all was silent again.

We exhaled together.

"That was close." Echo was the first to voice the obvious.

"Do you think there'll be more?" Gabe asked the impossible question.

"Probably. I mean, most definitely. You saw the size of this hotel – it's huge. The likelihood that a place this big would only have three Moaners is slim to zero. In fact, it's binary. Yes, there will be more. Many more. The best we could hope for at the moment was to hold up here, get some much needed rest, and try to bust out tomorrow."

I hated to drop that bomb on Echo and Gabe, but hiding the truth would serve no purpose other than to shield them from reality. I'd rather make sure they both knew just how ugly the situation really was. The apocalypse required some serious tough love and that job fell squarely on my shoulders.

"You two shower first. Jacob isn't finished eating. Once he's done and asleep, I'll grab a nice hot shower."

Echo called *dibs* on first shower. Gabe didn't argue. The boy was starting to grow on me. He'd finally proved where his loyalties were, so time for sleeping with one eye open was gone.

Sleep, perchance to wake up and have all of this be one nasty-ass nightmare. How many times had I made that wish and how many times did it not come true? After a year I would have thought an endless supply of the undead would have beaten hope out of me. But there it was. Hope. It still springs forth. Hope. I wanted to wallow in it for a while – lap it up, drink it in, wrap its warm arms around me like a fuzzy robe after a hot shower.

The sound of water running yanked me from my odd revelry. That sound was a delicious music I never thought I'd hear again. My eyes closed and my mind swam in deep seas of memory. A shower with the adult Jacob back in Munich. A warm summer rain. A high school chess club car wash. Skinny dipping at band camp.

This one time...

And then it hit me. I hadn't cried since I lost Sam, Danielle, Courtney, and Dirt Bag in Pennsylvania. Why now? The sound of running water? Or maybe it was just having human contact and a bed to sleep in. I was certain tears of joy were an indulgence from a past we'd never see again. But there they were, running in rivulets down my cheeks.

I turned my face so Gabriel couldn't see. There was zero desire in me to explain my emotions to a young man. As if a young male could understand the roller coaster emotions of a female. The great mystery of life.

The 'E' spot.

"Do you think we'll be safe here tonight?"

Gabe's voice interrupted my moment of self-indulgence. How could I answer such a question? There was no such thing as safety now. No guarantees in this tabloid reality. The horror of horrors crept out of man's collective nightmare and cut a swath of terror into the land so deep we would never arrive back at safe. And none of this shit storm was about to slow down. My arrival in Seattle would hail the beginning of a new era. That era would be called 'vengeance'.

A dish I would most certainly serve ice cold.

"Yeah, we'll be fine in here."

I lied, or maybe exaggerated. Hell, maybe I was telling the truth, but even I didn't believe the words as they spilled out of my mouth.

But Gabe just smiled, a deep, caring look in his ice-blue eyes. I had to admit, he was handsome. Not my type – too young and unknown. His hair was close cropped, his lips and chin finely chiseled. Minus the foul mouth, barcode tattoo, and the shady background, Gabe could have walked out of a Wall Street internship or the cover of a GQ magazine. When he smiled, his teeth were toothpaste-commercial white. When he laughed (on the rare occasion that he did), the sound aired out of a fraternity house – all fist bumps and high fives to the tune of some unlikely urban hip hop. Like I said, not my type.

But the boy was here, and making it to the Pacific Northwest was far easier with him in tow.

Jacob finished his bottle. After a quick burp he was back in his tiny world of peace and sweet dreams.

"I wonder if he understands what's going on around him." Gabe nodded toward the silent baby. "I'd give anything to just not know."

He had a point. It would be a glorious thing to be ignorant of the hell that was our reality. But some day, even Jacob would grow up. His generation would either be responsible for continuing on the race of man, or making sure it ended. One way or another, that boy was going to have a massive weight on his shoulders.

The bathroom door swung open and Echo appeared with a towel wrapped around her waif-thin body. The look on her face could only be described as transcendent.

"There's hot water! I could have stayed in there forever. Don't worry, I saved plenty for you guys. Who's next?"

Gabe gestured for me to go, but I overruled him saying I wanted to make sure Jacob was fully asleep. The truth was, I wanted some alone time with Echo. Thankfully, Gabe gave in and headed for the bathroom. As soon as the door was shut and the water was running, I sidled up to Echo and whispered.

"Should we trust him?"

My question caught the young girl off guard.

"Why not?"

I was surprised by her reaction. Echo had lived on the street, so she knew the score with trust. It was a rare commodity. Or maybe I was just too paranoid. With everything I knew about the world around us, it was nearly impossible for me to trust a single soul.

"What would he stand to gain from playing two ... wait, you think he knows about you and realizes what you're worth? Seriously?"

"Why do you think that? Has he given you any reason to believe he knows about – wait, has he said something to you?"

Echo broke out in gales of laughter.

"What? What's so funny?"

Echo continued to laugh until her cheeks turned bright red.

"Us. It's the end of the world and we're acting like little school girls."

She was right – about the school girl thing. She was wrong about the end of the world.

That was always a fallacy. The world, the planet Earth, would continue on. There would be no end to the world. Man was insanely arrogant to think itself powerful enough to destroy an entire planet. Now, the end of the human race? That would be a different story to tell – one not couched in lies and dogma. But once man was dead, Earth would continue on until some other parasite crawled out of the muck and mire to begin the cycle anew.

Ultimately though, I had to tuck my paranoia away for the moment. That mistrust, however, would remain, just under the surface, until the time came when I needed to play that card and possibly save my ass.

"So," Echo started, "what was it like, being there at ground zero?"

The shock that jolted my heart had to have registered on my system. If it did, Echo gave no indication of perception.

"It was absolutely indescribable. There is no way words could paint the picture of chaos we endured. No way."

"Worse than now?"

The question should have been simple. It wasn't. Now is filled with fear, violence, and perpetual unrest and death. Munich was another story all together. Ground zero was a vacuum of loss and twisted perception. It was nearly impossible to put the release of the Mengele Virus into words.

"The beginning should have been the end. That's what we all thought – that the world had ceased to exist and we were thrust into Hell."

And that was that. The only words I could

form to describe what we went through. Of course there was an unspoken layer I just could not dive into – the loss of Jacob Plummer. Even thinking about being responsible for sending a bullet between my lover's eyes threatened to force me to any given corner of the room. My eyes could roll back into my head in search of some patron saint of sanity.

Fortunately that swan dive into madness was interrupted by Gabe stepping out of the bathroom. He was naked from the waist up. I couldn't help but notice Echo's eyes lingering on Gabe's tight torso. I should be feeling something so very wrong at the moment. To be honest, I was too tired to address the fact that Echo was very much a minor, and Gabe would quickly wind up tied to a lamp post if he tried anything.

Out of nowhere I was reminded of Susan, my little angel. The thought of the girl punched me hard in the heart. Without making eye contact with anyone, I slipped into the bathroom and wound up sitting on the toilet seat. My head found its way into my hands. Tears dropped effortlessly to the ground.

I hated these moments of weakness. The apocalypse wasn't very forgiving of the weak. Fortunately, I was able to steal away so no one had to witness me come apart. As far as Echo, Gabe, and the rest of the world knew, Bethany Nitshimi was a rock. I had to be. And now that I was a full-on mother, there was no time for displays of fragility.

There was time, however, for a shower. As

soon as I turned the water on and the steam greeted my lungs, I knew that bliss was still an achievable dream. The heat was perfect. I wanted to weep again, only this time for joy. For a short moment, the undead, the conspiracies, the Zero Day Collective all went away. I was in heaven. I was clean. The stink of death and rot spiraled down the drain with the dirty brown water.

When I stepped out of the shower, and wrapped a plush towel around my body, I felt pampered. And for a brief second, that was the only thing that mattered.

The door to the bathroom eased open. It took me by surprise to see Echo and Gabe already asleep. Echo was lying on one side of the bed and Gabe in the center of the other bed. Maybe my suspicions were unfounded and the two weren't plotting some dark hallway booty call.

I gave Jacob one last check, slipped into the bed, and turned out the lights. The darkness that blanketed the room was genuinely glorious.

CHAPTER 11

November 21, 2016 03:09 AM
Fargo, North Dakota

Darkness had become my enemy. And this time the darkness was a sentient being, hot and probing. The heat of the blackness seeped inside and around every possible inch of my body. My skin came alive with the fear of the unknown. And just as the unknown became the known – everything changed. I was soaking in a hot mud bath within a spa. The sounds of tranquility were everywhere. God-awful zen music, the kind everyone seems to think is so relaxing, droned on. Yanni on Valium. Some God of a naked man, chiseled abs and chin, knelt beside my bath and offered me a drink. Inside the shiny crystal glass was a thick, brown liquid. Floating on top of the brown water was an eyeball. The eyeball looked at me and blinked. I thrashed about in shock and realized the mud bath was actually a rank, human chum-filled tank.

A tortured chorus of baby cries filled the room, like the chime on a clock made in Hell. And then – a thunderous, vibrating 'thunk' was heard. Before the echo of the first 'thunk' faded, everyone in the spa of doom scattered.

Thunk.

Thunk.

Thunk.

The maker of noise finally appeared. It was

probably ten feet high and nothing but muscle. The entire body was covered with a skin that looked like brain. The brain-skin pulsed at random intervals. What would be the head was nothing but a jagged, rotten tooth-filled hole. At the end of the right arm was no hand, but a giant, grafted hammer made of human bone. The thing hoisted its hammer high and brought it crashing down to the floor.

I ran. My feet slipped and slid on viscera and discarded entrails. By the time I reached the door to the spa, I was covered in brown, red, and black goo. The smell was nauseating. My gore-slick fingers slipped off the door handle. My mouth opened to scream, but nothing came out.

The foul stench of the brain-man's breath overtook the air around me. With each exhalation I could feel the sticky strands of hair on my cheek dry and crust over.

Just as it seemed the monster was going to open wide and devour me whole, the Hell-baby clock chimed. The reverberating sounds of the cry sent shock waves of terror through the monster's muscles. The thing turned and ran from the room, bashing its bone-hammer at anything that dared be in its way.

I woke, the sound of Jacob, his cries piercing my eardrums. With eyes half-open, I got out of bed and rummaged through the food pack. Another can of formula, another bottle, another feeding. Jacob went silent as soon as the liquid hit the back of his throat.

God, being a mother in the apocalypse was a real pain in the ass.

It took the baby no time to suck the bottle dry. Hopefully, he'd make it through the rest of the night without another bottle or a diaper change – at least that was the plan. I needed sleep or we'd never make it to Seattle.

When my head hit the pillow, my conscience locked onto some fragment from the dream. My subconscious mind was trying to warn me of something. I fumbled in the dark for a pen and paper. I found a pen, but no paper. On my left forearm, in giant letters, I wrote:

SPA.

It had to mean something. Hopefully, a rested mind in the morning would help me decipher this clue.

CHAPTER 12

November 21, 2016 10:15 AM
Fargo, North Dakota

"Bethany. Wake up!"

The sound of the voice pulled me back from sleep. Thankfully, no other fucked up nightmare haunted the dark recesses of my mind.

When I finally sat up, and my conscience was up to speed with my cloudy eyes, another sound blew the fog of sleep away.

Moaning.

"Where is it? Where are they?"

I sat up, trying my best to remain as calm as possible. There was no reason to panic my baby and tagalongs.

"I don't know. Everywhere. What are we going to do?"

Echo was near hysteria.

My brain instantly dropped into survival mode. As if it didn't live in that state permanently.

"Quick. Hand me my laptop."

When in doubt, always fall back on what you did best. I was a hacker. Gabe handed me the backpack containing the laptop that helped me crack the Mengele Virus code. That piece of hardware would go to my grave.

As soon as the computer was booted, I plugged into a network jack and waited for the laptop to snag an IP address from the hotel's router. When the network indicator informed me all was good to go, I fired up my favorite network topology tool to get the lay of the land. It didn't take long for me to locate the server hosting the feeds from the security cameras around the inside and outside of the building. Within seconds I had control of every electric eye on the premises.

"Shit."

What I saw was not good. Every floor of the building was overrun by Moaners. There was no way we were getting out the same way we came in.

"Oh my god! Bethany, what are we going to do?"

Echo finally reached full panic. I grabbed her by arms and steadied her. I stared deep into the girl's eyes and tried to will her to calm down. It didn't work. I had to come up with a plan and do it quickly.

So I went back to the laptop. The cameras had all the information we needed. That information would be our freedom. I clicked through every internal camera. There was no way. The floors were flooded with the undead.

It wasn't until I switched to the outside camera facing our room window that I got the idea.

"We're going out the window. It's only a few flights, so we can create a rope out of the sheets, climb down, and get to the car."

Even before I could get reactions from the crew, I was yanking sheets from the bed and tying overly cautious knots at the end of each.

"You can't be serious. How are we going to

get Jacob out there?" Gabe surprised me by turning chicken.

"We'll lower you two down first. After you're on the ground, I'll lower the supplies and then Jacob. Once you have everything, I'll climb down, we'll get in the car, and drive the fuck out of here."

There was no push-back from either Echo or Gabe. It looked like we had a plan. We immediately put the plan into action and started packing everything up. It was a shock our voices didn't draw unwanted attention from the undead tourists.

"Who first?" Echo looked at me, ready to launch.

"We should send Gabriel down with a gun. He can make sure the area is cleared before we send send anyone else, Echo."

"I'm good with that." Gabe nervously nodded his head as he spoke.

It took a moment for Echo to give in, but she did. I put Echo and Gabe in charge of splicing together the rope. I had a last minute task I wanted to take care of before I packed up the laptop. Having network connectivity was a luxury I knew wasn't going to continue on forever, so I needed to take advantage of it while it lasted.

The task was looking up 'ZRT' – the number on the downed man's phone at the truck stop. A Google search brought up plenty of results, but it wasn't until I hit the fifth page that I got what I was looking for.

Zombie Response Team.

That had to be it.

JACK WALLEN

They had a website. I checked it – they were legit. According to their site, the *Zombie Response Team is a group of individuals dedicated to the eradication of the walking dead.* I had the direct hotline to this group. I wrote down a few of the more prominent names for later use: Dan Parker, Joshua Garcia, and Morgan Barnhart.

With that information in my hands, I shut down the laptop, packed it away, and started lowering our bags to the ground.

Bam!

A familiar knocking rocked the door of the room. The thick wood wouldn't manage to sustain such blows for long. I had to pick up the pace. The only problem was, the last thing I had to deliver to the ground below was Jacob. There was no way I would rush the lowering of my child down three stories. But I had no choice.

Carefully, I tied the end of the sheet to the car seat handle. I double, triple checked the knot. Once I felt it safe, I slowly lifted the car seat out the window and began to lower. Hand over shaking hand, the seat descended to the ground below.

Bam!

A menacing moan followed the crushing blow of the meaty sounding fist. The single moan became a chorus of moans, the single pound multiplied until a monstrous popcorn cooked on the other side of the wall.

I continued lowering. Echo stood, arms stretched to heaven, waiting for the precious cargo.

Bam!

The door was about to give up the ghost. I loosened my grip and let the sheet slide. The burn of my fingers and palms came on quickly.

Bam!

Bam!

Crack!

The wood of the door splintered. Even with the continued burn, I let the sheets slide through.

The door split in two. The sounds of Moaners filled the room.

"Got him!"

Echo's voice wafted up from below.

It was my turn. With my backpack secured, I swung my left leg over and started out. One of the Moaners managed to get his rotten fingers on my pack and yanked me back into the room. I collapsed on the floor. There were four of them, all glaring down at me with drooling mouths and sour-milk eyes. The fuckers never changed. The same sound, the same look. It seemed *zombie* would never go out of fashion.

"You fucking bastards!"

All four of the undead grabbed at me and lowered their gnashing mouths my way. This wasn't the movies, they weren't about to take turns. My legs were free, so I swung around and kicked up hard. The heel of my shoe connected with a jaw. The disgusting crunch made me want to laugh and puke at the same time. I had no idea why doing damage to a zombie made me want to laugh. There *was* some karmic joy in the act.

I kicked up again, this time a swing and a

miss. Fortunately, the momentum of my kick brought me back down hard enough to remind me I had a gun in my back pocket. It was like landing on your keys, only worse. Thankfully, the gun didn't go off.

My hand shot behind me and pulled the pistol from its hiding place. During the quick arch around my shoulders, I managed to disengage the safety. As soon as the gun was between me and the undead quartet, the trigger was pulled. The spatter of blood and brain clearly indicated the first shot hit the home of homes.

One zombie down, three to go.

The noise took the remaining zombies by surprise. I knew it wasn't possible, but I swear I saw the look of fear flash through their eyes.

I had the upper hand.

The next zombie to come down on me found the barrel of the gun lodged all the way to his soft palette. When the trigger was pulled, the back side of his skull was aired out for his friends to behold. The twice-dead zombie dropped its full weight onto me. The beast was almost unmovable. The body also made a great shield. The hole in the head of the zombie was positioned perfectly so I could see the sites of my gun.

As the third and fourth zombie attempted to get to me through their buddy, I scoped them out, pulled the trigger, and wasted yet another zombrain. Three down, one to go. I couldn't miss.

The fourth zombie grabbed the pile of death on top of me and yanked it out of his way. Face off time. I stood and backed away from the monster. There was no telling how many bullets remained in the gun. To be honest, I didn't have time to find out. Instead of diving deep into the land of fighting, I pocketed my weapon, dove for the window, grabbed the sheet rope, and lowered myself out of the room. I know it would have been more responsible to take out the last zombie – but I had to get down to the ground and make sure my baby was okay. And there was no way I was about to be a hero, only to wind up orphaning Jacob. He was my soul purpose, I wasn't about to let him down.

The zombie reached out with his hands and grabbed. He got lucky and tangled his fingers up in my hair. I wasn't going anywhere without inflicting some serious pain on myself.

"Come on Bethany! We have to go, now!" Echo called up in desperation.

Oh how I wished I could. But with zombie fingers tangled up in one's hair, it's not terribly easy to get away. All I could do was hope for the best. The best, of course, didn't include me forcing my way down and losing a large hunk of hair in the process.

I still had my gun. The only challenge would be to continue to hold onto the rope with one hand and aim the pistol with the other. Fear was a powerful motivator. I twisted the rope around my right wrist and, once the rope felt secure enough, released my left hand so it could reach around into my pocket and grab the weapon. As soon as my arm reached around me, my body started spinning. The tangled hair started growing tighter with each spin. The flesh on my skull grew angry with strain. I wanted to kick physics in the junk at the moment. There was no time for high wire acts.

My fingers felt the cold metal of the pistol and grabbed. As soon as I had my hand wrapped around the handle of the weapon, I swung it around and forced the barrel into the right eye of the zombie. I could feel the squish and pop of the eyeball and, when I did, I sent the barrel on home. The gun dug in about an inch until it hit bone. The brain of the zombie made for the perfect silencer. When the trigger was pulled, the sound was like an overripe watermelon crashing and splashing to the ground and nothing more.

There was no time to cheer, no time to enjoy the victory. Any moment the hotel would be overrun by Moaners. The second the scent of live flesh traveled around area, the place would be crawling with the walking dead.

I hit the ground running – literally. My feet barely gave my body time to recover from the transition to solid ground before I was sprinting, full steam, to the car. Echo already had Jacob buckled in and both passengers were impatient to get the fuck out of this undead dodge.

As the Audi tires barked their frustration at my punching the gas pedal to the floor, I saw a mass of Moaners converging on the parking lot. How we managed to get away so close to critical mass, I'll never know.

"Oh my God! That was ... oh my God!"

Echo's voice rattled with fear. I had no way of knowing what the girl had experienced before we met, but now I'm beginning to think she hadn't fully felt the icy grip of the Mengele Virus at its wicked best.

"Yeah, a horde of zombies. We're safe now Echo."

I reached over and placed my hand on Echo's thigh. The girl needed comforting and I was the obvious lucky winner.

I glanced down at my arm and noticed 'SPA' scrawled in black ink. The twisted nightmare came flooding back in a wash of brown muck. There was something for me to remember – some warning as if comfort was nothing more than a facade for horror. That thought, of course, led to me second guessing everything. Was this trip a mistake or a trap? There was always the possibility that the ZDC was waiting for us in Seattle.

CHAPTER 13

November 21, 2016 4:22 PM
Miles City, Montana

It may as well have been called the 'Miles City Massacre'. The Zombie Response Team was outnumbered nearly ten to one. No one could have predicted such a small town would be so badly overrun by the living dead. When the single truck pulled into the city limits, it was immediately clear they weren't prepared to take on the sheer number of Moaners and Screamers.

The ZRT were militant about their duties. So even though Miles City presented itself as little more than a suicide mission, the deployment would do everything they could to fulfill their task.

Clear the path for Nitshimi and son.

Jonas, the leader of ZRT Unit MC01, had his mobile in hand and Morgan Barnhart's number dialed.

"Talk to me." The imp-ish Texas twang of the ZRT leader rang out on speakerphone.

"This is Jonas, leader of MC01. We have a situation."

A situation. No matter what was going down, *A situation* was always code for *We are fucked*.

"SITREP Jonas."

"I have my entire team here – that's eleven guys. It looks like we're about to face well over one hundred undead. We're locked and loaded, but I can't say I like these odds. Your call?"

Morgan didn't even hesitate to offer an answer. "My call is, you fight. There's no other answer at this point than your taking down every goddamn Moaner and Screamer possible. I can't make this clear enough – that woman absolutely has to make it to Seattle. Do you hear me?"

It wasn't customary to hear the leader of the ZRT barking out such orders. The MC01 unit was most likely on a one way ride out of the Mengele nightmare. Jonas knew Barnhart couldn't pull them out. This mission had to be seen through until the end. If Bethany was lost along the way, the slim chance the world had would be lost with her.

"Give them everything you've got." Was the final call from the ZRT brass. Jonas had every intention of following through with that order – and then some.

"Lock and load ladies. I want full fire as soon as boots hit the ground. Open up and drop the dead." Jonas barked the command to psych his crew up. They were nervous. Jonas liked that a bit of fear was spreading through the group's nervous system. Fear made soldiers sharp. At least that's what Jonas hoped.

The transport vehicle came to a stop at what looked like a high school parking lot. The gate of the vehicle was dropped and the crew's boots hit pavement as soon as they were able to leap out of the truck bed.

The first sight the crew beheld nearly sent

them all packing back into their mother's wombs. Nearly one hundred zombies stood in a row, waiting, as if they were prepared for the fight that lay ahead. It was always one thing to take on a clueless, brainless monster. But at this very moment, it seemed, the zombies had been waiting. But for what? They couldn't have known The ZRT was coming. As the undead Red Rover line stood, it swayed back and forth as one. The Hell-spawned chorus of moans was as disturbing as was the sight of the chorus line of death.

This was going to get ugly, fast.

The first wave of the ZRT unit met the horde head on. From the beginning of the tousle it was clear who would win this slaughter. If the ZRT was going to succeed, the tides of war would have to drastically shift.

The mechanical rattle of machine gun fire filled the area. Jonas knew the noise would most likely draw the attention of even more zombies. Judging from the amount of undead in the immediate vicinity versus the overall population, there was little to no chance the ZRT would win this first assault wave. The bullets punctured the flesh of the living dead. Bits and pieces of meat and bone flew through the air. Not one piece of ammunition managed to penetrate a Moaner's skull. Aim was off. The zombies, on the other hand, did manage to get their cold, dead fingers wrapped around members of the MC01 first wave. With inhuman strength, the skulls were popped like uncooked eggs. Brains squished and slopped to the ground.

And not one zombie bothered to stop and snack.

"What's going on?" Jonas' second in command tossed the question back to an aghast leader.

"I have no fucking idea. But they don't seem to be concerned about brains at the moment.

"This isn't right. There's something going on." Jonas looked out over the carnage, the undead still marched forward. Nearly half of his men were lost. The undead to living ratio was now about sixteen to one. Jonas had to make a decision and make it fast.

They had no large caliber weapons.

They had no grenades.

What they did have was gasoline and fire.

Jonas jumped back up into the truck and started handing out gas cans to the remaining soldiers.

"Take a can and spread out. When they get close enough, we pour and light those fuckers up!"

The men grabbed the cans with a new-found faith in both their leader and their ability to crawl out of Hell alive. Each member of the MC01 squad had seen the effects of fire on the undead – it was disgusting to watch (and smell), but as effective as any other weapon.

"Wait for it." Jonas called out steadily.

Zombies marched slowly forward, the moan of war growing louder.

"Wait for it."

Undead arms reached out in the archetypal zombie pose. Any moment a George A. Romero block party and Michael Jackson flash mob would break out.

Instead, the leader of the MC01 squad called out the order to pour. Gasoline splashed onto the ground, an almost invisible barrier between the living and the dead. When the last dregs of the liquid dripped and dropped to the pavement, Jonas ran to the line of fluid hate, lit a flare, and dropped it in perfect time for the flammable liquid to go up and the zombie race to cross the deadly finish line.

Every member of the walking dead brigade went up in flames. The ragged clothing ignited quickly. After the cloth was devoured by the fire, it was time for the flesh to begin a simmering, pop and crackle barbecue sonata. The smell of burning undead flesh was an affront to the senses.

Some meat was simply not meant for cooking. And even the desperate hunger of the soldiers wouldn't give quarter to the thought of pulling off a hunk of once-human flank and going to town.

The human race had yet to reach a state of cannibalism.

A scant few Moaners survived the flaming wall. Thankfully, the numbers were low enough that a few fired bullets quickly took them down.

Cheers rang out as the echo of the last bullet sang its song of destruction over the parking lot. Jonas grabbed his cell and called headquarters.

"We did it Morgan. All is clear."

Jonas was given the go head to bug out of

the area immediately. He knew Bethany was a highly intelligent woman. The second she saw the smoldering bodies, she'd know something was amiss. Unfortunately, there was no time for cleanup. MC01 was informed Bethany was near. Time to disappear.

The remaining men gathered the weapons and ammo of their fallen comrades, hopped into the back of the truck, and hit the road. Jonas couldn't concern himself with what Bethany discovered. His only orders were to clear the area.

Mission accomplished.

CHAPTER 14

November 21, 2016 6:05 PM
Miles City, Montana

I'd never heard of Miles City, Montana. The *Welcome To* sign proudly informed us it was home to just over eight thousand people. A quick run of the numbers meant there could easily be six thousand, four hundred zombies. That number, of course, assumed the national average of eighty percent amplification of human beings. I could look at the glass half full and say that left fourteen hundred living humans.

In lieu of us making better time across the country, I broke the bad news there'd be no hotel. We'd camp out at the soonest possible safe location, load up on supplies, get as much rest as possible, and head out as soon as the sun peeked its bright head out of the horizon.

I hated the plan as much as everyone. But there were too many miles still between us and Seattle. Besides, the Audi was quickly beginning to feel a bit claustrophobic for my taste.

We pulled into the typical Pump 'N Munch and ran through the usual routine: Gas, food, whore bath, quick check of the perimeter, and back into the car for rest. The only concern to raise its hand was the smell. The air was acrid with the stench of burned flesh. A massive part of me wanted to investigate – but I knew better.

The less we ventured out, the better our chance of survival. Besides, that burning flesh could just as easily be a clan of cannibals waiting for some sweet meat like us to put on their spit.

Pass.

I sent both Echo and Gabe into the building for a supply run. We were nearly out of both food and water. The pickings were slim this late into the game; but I had my fingers crossed for something, anything of substance. If my shoppers came out with nothing but chips and soda, I might well drop to my knees and weep. No food and I may decide to seek out the cannibals and belly up to their bar. We had yet to break into the kibble. I wanted to hold off on that dive into desperation as long as possible.

The station had no electricity, so the pumps wouldn't do their job. The surrounding cars all had been siphoned, so I had to get creative. I found a garden hose, lowered it into the underground tank, sealed off the open end, dragged the hose back to the top, placed the end into a bucket, and released the seal. It took a while, but I managed to get about five gallons before my arms just couldn't heave and ho any longer. I'd finish the job in the morning. For now, I had a few other tasks I wanted to complete – namely, put some food in my gut.

Echo and Gabe had already returned empty handed, save for three gallon jugs filled with fresh water. That meant the menu tonight was fit for a feline. Desperation came sooner than I'd hoped. Echo pulled the bag of dry kibble from the trunk of the car. We sat and stared at one another, waiting for the first brave soul to scoop out a handful and crunch away.

Gabe broke first. His hand came out of the bag filled with the dried bits. Without hesitation, he tossed his hand to his mouth as if he were popping a palm full of Capn' Crunch. The look on his face told us everything we needed to know.

"It's better than starving," I said, as I scooped out my own first taste of cat chow.

It wasn't as bad as I'd assumed. Yes, it was as dry as a mouthful of sand, and had a vaguely fishy taste, but it would fill our stomachs and get us through, until we could locate some real food.

The cold water washed it all down. What I wouldn't do for a mint to get rid of the faux salmon and tuna aftertaste.

We complained a bit, had a couple of much needed laughs, and then each retreated to our own little worlds. I fed Jacob and then turned my attention to my long-neglected friend – my laptop. I had to check email and take care of a little Zombie Radio business. Thankfully, I still had a few working mobile air cards, so I had the ability to get on line. The connection speeds were nowhere near what I was accustomed to, but having a slow connection was better than having no connection.

My inbox was nearly at capacity. Should I have been surprised at how many emails contained pleas for assistance? It seemed every survivor on the planet wished to make themselves known to me. I would give anything to be able to reach out and save each and every one. But that's not the situation. I was lucky to be able to take care of myself and my three travelers at the moment.

What did take me by surprise was one particular email. The email was cleverly sent through a re-mailer – so there was no way to track it. The sender address was completely overshadowed by the contents of the email. It read:

Bethany Nitshimi,

We are impressed. You've managed to elude us for quite some time. But that time is coming to an end. The Zero Day Collective has planted operatives around the globe – each with a single directive, kill you and take your baby. You cannot hide forever. No matter how intelligent you think you are, you will make a mistake and that mistake will cost you your child and your life. Once you are out of the picture, and Jacob in our custody, The Great Cleansing will begin anew.

We have a very special surprise in store for you Bethany – one that will still your beating heart and blacken your soul. Are you prepared for your past to meet your present and put an end to the possibility of a future?

Good luck Bethany.

The Zero Day Collective

I was too damned tired to deconstruct the email. It made perfect sense to take it on faith that something insane was awaiting me, some inescapable trap or new iteration of Zombie

Erectus. There was but one thing I could do at the moment – respond. But to simply respond to an email did nothing more than poke the bear. What I needed was to rally more troops. To do that, I needed Zombie Radio.

Carefully and quietly, I sneaked out of the car with my laptop. I had it on the solar charger most of the day, so the battery had plenty of juice. My plan? Record another Zombie Radio podcast, outside in the great wide open. The dark of the stars and the silence of the night made for a perfect backdrop for recording a war cry to the Zombie Radio Faithful.

Short and sweet was my best friend at the moment. I fired up the recording software, added a single track, and clicked the Record button.

You're listening to WZMB, Zombie Radio, your personal soundtrack to the end of the world. This is Bethany Nitshimi broadcasting to you from the great outdoors. Mother Nature is my backdrop and the sound of little more than the wind is my soundtrack. Ladies and gentlemen of the zombieverse, today I received a missive from the Zero Day Collective. It was actually more of a threat than anything. I thought I should pass on to you the plans this group of mad bastards has in store for this island Earth. First and foremost, they have a plan in motion they call The Great Cleansing. Remember what the Nazis tried to accomplish with their death camps? Multiply that exponentially and you have the situation at hand. The Zero Day Collective are Hell bent on creating a planet populated with clones. Those clones will be defined by the leaders of the 'accepted race of man'.

We cannot allow this to happen. The ZDC claims to have operatives all over the world. I need every member of the Zombie Radio Nation to locate these operatives and take them out. I cannot tell you how to distinguish the Zero Day Collective killers from civilian men and women, but I know they're out there and are willing to die for their cause. I need my followers to take up the mantle of Hero and help me and my cohorts make it safely to our destination. I realize that destination has not been made public – but know this, across the country I travel to create a safe haven for the race of man.

I also want to let every one of you know how much I appreciate your help, support, and encouragement. This war cannot be won without the Zombie Radio Faithful. Even if you do not pick up a weapon, your voice and your soul are heard and felt.

This is Bethany Nitshimi saying Godspeed and good luck.

Silence would be my music for the moment.

With the recording complete, and converted to a stream-able format, I uploaded the file and set up the link on the Zombie Radio site. Next in line was a simple email to Jamal.

J-Tiz,

What the fuck is Miles City, Montana? Where we are is WTF. We're close. Next stop, Helena, Montana. I assume the Zombie

Response Team is with you? If so, give Morgan Barnhart my love and tell her thanks for the escort of Ninja assassins. I'd love to know how she's tracking us. Dare I turn this into a game?

Love in binary,

B to the ethany.

That was it. My brain desperately wanted more stimulation, but the laptop battery had to be saved. The solar charger worked very slowly, and didn't work when the sun was tucked away under the horizon. Fancy that.

There was, however, something else my brain could gnaw on – Dr. Michael's notes. She traveled with them everywhere. Fortunately, the horde attack that took her down, hadn't the intelligence enough to search and seize her binder of notes. I, on the other hand, did.

Within the covers of that binder, existed wonders, some of which would take me weeks to decode. As I unwrapped the binder, nervous energy danced just under the surface of my skin. What magical notations would be revealed? A flood of hope that some hidden means of wiping clean this virus, for good, washed through my system.

When the cover opened, an envelope dropped out and drifted to the ground between my feet. On the sealed envelope was my name and nothing more. My fingers nervously tore at the paper to get to the mystery inside. A single piece of paper, perfectly folded and creased, written in the same hand as was the name on the envelope.

Dear Bethany,

By now you know of my sacrifice. What you do not know of, is the truth. You, of all people, should be given the courtesy of knowing exactly what has happened and what could very well be. I hate to seem the coward, in giving you this information posthumously, but there was no other way. Bethany, there is no known cure for the Mengele Virus. That was all a ruse to get you and your friends on my side so you would help me to escape the hands of the Zero Day Collective. That does not mean there is no hope. Out of the lie I perpetuated with you, is born a very real and undeniable truth – a truth you are probably already aware of.

The salvation of mankind rests in you and your baby. Bethany, you will eventually find out that Jacob is immune to the virus. That immunity most likely was spread to you as you carried your baby to term. But that resistance to the virus comes with a price. The Zero Day Collective will do everything they can to get to Jacob. You cannot let them take your baby. You must find safe haven and locate someone to help you create a true cure for the Mengele Virus from the blood of your baby.

It sounds cold, but the needs of the many...

I'm very sorry I lied to you and your friends. Had I not, I feel you wouldn't be traveling this long road alone.

Be safe Bethany.

Danielle.

The darkness of the evening engulfed me. I felt small, frightened, and alone. Tears dropped from my cheeks and splattered the note, making translucent circles on the delicate paper. There was no cure. Nothing. For the last year my ego allowed me to jokingly say the fate of man rested squarely on my shoulders. Now that there is an absolute truth to that, the weight pressed down forcing me to my knees.

I cried in silence, letting the drops of despair tap out a sorrowful rhythm on the pavement below me. The sound was barely audible, but loud enough to remind me how much I hurt. Spasms racked my muscles, as it all crashed through the barriers of my mental and emotional walls. There were no strong arms to wrap around me for comfort, no hushing voice to say *It'll all be okay*. At this very moment in time, the universe had no intention of making anything easy. My heart ached, my brain wanted nothing more than to shut down.

Lies. It was all lies. *No cure.* The image of the words flashed into my mind's eye again.

Before I could pull myself together and stand, frail arms snaked around my shoulders.

"Bethany?" Echo's voice was a whisper of concern. "You okay?"

I forced the lump down my throat.

"I'm fine Echo, thank you."

I lied. Just piling on the deception. But there was no reason to worry the girl. Let her think the same thing as everyone else – a cure is out there, waiting to be had.

Echo started to help me up, but before I

made it to my feet, an all too familiar sound bounced off the space around us.

"Oh God no. Not more of them."

"Echo, get in the car. Now."

A Screamer was out there, getting close. It could smell us, could probably smell Jacob. What the bastard wouldn't smell now was fear, not from me. After reading the letter from Danielle, fear had left the building of my heart.

I was immune.

Once Echo was back inside the relative safety of the car, I popped open the trunk, pulled out my collapsible pike, and had it ready to rock.

Let the fuckers come. Let them bring everything they had to this wrecking machine called Bethany.

The sound continued growing nearer. It was like a long, drawn out reverse Doppler Effect, straight out of the bowels of Hell. Wherever the beast was coming from, he would arrive any moment. When he did, Hell's playground would break out in a dual to the undead finish.

Screeching echoed all around me. There was no way to immediately discern where the point of origin was. Based on the fading of the echo, it was safe to assume the sound either emanated from the North or the East. With that assumption, I ran away from the car to meet the monster in an open field. The pike felt solid in my hands, my arms felt fearless on my shoulders.

Was I kidding myself? Would this new-found reckless abandon find me nothing more than pulp flowing down the esophagus of the undead horde? Fuck.

A cloud of dust appeared on the horizon, due North. He was coming. Fast. The scream grew louder, fiercer. The sound cracked and popped the air around me. Shortly after I discovered the dust cloud, the figure appeared – its arms flailed wildly at its sides, its legs pumped violently on the ground. Any minute, any second.

The beast screeched to a halt, standing nose to nose with me. He sniffed deeply and roared out an angry disapproval. Rotten breath burned my nostrils, made my stomach want to turn inside out. Other than his standard issue, Hell-spawned rage, what caught my attention first was his eyes. The eyes weren't glazed over with a layer or twelve of wood glue. This fucker had the whitest whites and the bluest blues I'd ever seen. Those ice-blue orbs glared deep into me, searched for something it knew was there. Could it possibly know what flowed through my veins was immune to its special flavor of hate?

He roared again and yanked out fistfuls of his own hair as his voice reached a fever pitch. The hot air fuming from his mouth smelled of vomit, piss, and rot. At that very moment my brain finally caught up to my fear and reminded my hand it was holding the one thing I had on me that could stop the zombie from making a meal out of my skin and sinew. Before I could run the pike through the monster's skull, it screeched again and wrapped thick, muscular arms around me and squeezed. The vice-grip around my mid-section forced the wind from my lungs and continued the clamp-down.

I kicked out.

I rammed my forehead into the beasts' face.

I screamed.

I cried.

Nothing worked. The zombie continued screaming and squeezing. Sparks started flashing and flickering in my peripheral vision, heralding imminent blackout. After that, who knew what the Screamer would do to me.

And then, something happened. The beast let me go, as if it had simply been switched off. When the monstrous arms released me, I dropped to the ground gasping for precious breath. From the Screamer, loud snorts of air released in clouds of steam – which struck me as odd. Up until this point, I believed zombies had no use for their respiratory system. Like their hearts, much of their major organs were just waiting to sluice out their anus in a wash of gelatinous ooze. But this thing standing above me was breathing – hard. It looked down and released another monstrous roar as it pulled out the remaining clumps of hair. The thing stared at me and tilted its head to one side and then the other. What happened next sent the ice-cold waves of shock through my system. The zombie pointed at my gut and tilted its head again. It knew what was once in me, knew I had given birth to something familiar.

The monster was cognizant.

This was a total game changer.

Slowly my hand felt around on the ground,

until my fingers made contact with the metal of my pike. All I had to do was get to my knees and, with a forceful upward swing, run the deadly end of the metal shaft through the lower jaw and into the brain stem. The angle was simple geometry – child's play.

Another roar, only this time the thing's fingers dug deep into the flesh of the skull and pulled away chunks of meat. Ice blue eyes glared down at me. Flaring nostrils billowed winter's mist my way.

My fingers hit cold steel. Carefully, I wrapped my hand around the pike and looked down to make sure I knew which end meant business. If I timed it perfectly, I could jam this bitch home without the zombie knowing what it was that severed his spinal cord from his abnormal brain.

Abby something.

Why my brain flew back to the Mel Brooks film, I'll never know. Maybe it was having a rather large, monster standing over me. Had this beast broke out into strains of "Putting on the Ritz" I'd probably run my own skull through with the pike.

The zombie screamed and his eyes briefly closed.

The metal of the weapon sang a deadly song as the end scraped the ground. With a single, upward thrust, the tip met the underside of the undead jaw and punctured the flesh. As soon as I felt the meat sack give way, I stood and slammed the pole upward as hard as I could.

When the pike breached the top of the skull, the crunch made me want to hurl. I slammed the flat end of the pike on the ground and the zombie did its best maxillofacial pole dance until its jaw hit dirt. My hand wrapped around the blood-slick metal and yanked up.

My heart thumped and thudded. Air continued in raspy gasps. I was alive. Another of the undead horde met its demise at my hands.

The tattered shirt, torn from the dead zombie's back, made for a sufficient cleaning cloth for the pike. There was no reason to scare the piss out of Echo and Gabe.

"Jacob!"

I couldn't believe I'd left my baby's side. Promise broken. There were certain die-hard rules to live by in the apocalypse. The Prime Directive-level rule was to not let the savior of the human race out of your sight!

My lungs were already burning. After my sprint back to the car, I assumed those same lungs would revolt and either give up all together, or leave my body for a less harmful environment.

Jacob, Echo, and Gabe were all tucked safely away in the car.

Small miracles.

Echo saw me, flung open the door, leaped out, and wrapped her skinny arms around my chest. Thankfully, I didn't have some strange reflex and run her through.

"Oh my God! I thought you were going to die! Bethany, you can't leave us like that. Holy —"

Echo's words were overtaken by sobs. I returned the embrace and promised her I wasn't going anywhere.

When Echo pulled back from me, tears were still draining from her eyes. "You're the only family I have now. I've lived on the street long enough my own family no longer exists. If I lose you, I lose everything."

I wasn't about to tell Echo the reason I wouldn't be going anywhere was my immunity to the virus. That information had to remain locked safely away in my mind. Instead I just reassured her as best I could (without giving away the grand plan) and helped her back into the car.

I picked up the notes and the laptop and climbed into the driver's side seat. When the door gently closed shut, the silence inside the car was a magical delusion. For the briefest of moments, everything was okay.

The laptop sat at my side, calling me to reach out and share the news.

I refrained.

CHAPTER 15

November 21, 2016 7:05 PM
Zero Day Collective Mobile Headquarters

"Commander Faddig, we have confirmation of Bethany's location. They are currently in Miles City, Montana. What are your orders?"

The officer pulled off his headset to make sure he could clearly hear his commander's demands. None came. Instead, Commander Faddig stared out into some unknown region of space. There was some thought or plan germinating deep inside the brilliant mind of the Commander.

The Zero Day Collective was still rebuilding. The process was taking far longer than expected. The collection of enough undead for the drop ships had become a challenge, thanks to the lack of living men and women ready to handle the dirty work. Fortunately, time was on their side. It would take Bethany at least two more days to reach her destination. By then, they'd either have enough undead soldiers or Faddig would have to step into action himself.

"How is the collection going?" Faddig's voice was low and menacing.

"Still behind sir."

Failure had already set the Zero Day Collective back far too much. It was no longer an option.

"I want you to dispatch every man, woman,

and child we have available to the collection teams. God damn it those drop ships better be filled with the undead before Nitshimi reaches her destination. And just where in the Hell is she going? That woman doesn't do 'random'. She's filled with purpose, it's what drives her. I refuse to believe she is heading across the country for a change of scenery."

Faddig menacingly crossed to the soldier, grabbed him by the arm, and yanked him to his feet.

"If you can't find out where she is going and what she is doing, I'll have you replaced."

The young soldier saluted with his free arm. Sweat quickly formed on the soldier's brow. The insinuation was clear – in Zero Day speak, *replaced* was a very permanent situation. Being replaced ended in a simple, tragic foregone conclusion – death. But death, within the Zero Day Collective meant one thing – ZOMBIFICATION. If you were no good alive to the ZDC, you'd certainly be of some use dead. And with the current count of zombies, a lot of internal death had occurred.

"Are there particular collection teams you want to focus on sir? And is there someone in particular you would like heading up the new collection effort?" The soldier quickly focused Faddig's attention to a task other than immediate execution.

The commander went silent. His mind stepped back to an earlier moment with Subject 001. A thinking zombie. Faddig picked up the phone and called the bio-tech lab.

"Faddig here. Could you have Subject 001

ready for a deployment in one hour? Good. Have him prepped in Deploy Six. I'll meet you there to introduce the rest of the crew and give you Subject 001's mission instructions."

As soon as the phone went silent, Faddig turned to the soldier. "Give me three of your best and have them report to Deploy Six in one hour."

Without another command, Faddig marched out of the room, his crisp, pressed suit rustling with each step. The sound of his polished shoes hitting the concrete floor was a comforting rhythm. Though not truly a soldier, Faddig was a man used to power, used to those around him bowing down to suck at his teat and polish his shoes with their thick, pink tongues. His power was a seductive mistress that had him rolling over in bed to bare his ass.

In the apocalypse, no one can hear you scream – especially not in the bedroom with your face buried in your pillow.

When Faddig arrived at Deploy Six, he was early. Not that it mattered, the commander was always early. His punctuality gave him time to ponder his next step. From this point on, even the tiniest of moves was crucial. If the Zero Day Collective didn't retrieve that baby, all was lost. The future of mankind would be left to chance and chaos – which led to freedom of speech, thought, and liberty. That would not do.

Before any of the collection crews arrived, the lab tech appeared with Subject 001.

"Why do I have the feeling you've something planned that far exceeds our current capabilities?"

"Because you know me all too well, my friend." Faddig almost laughed, which made the tech very nervous.

Faddig never laughed.

"I'm sending out Subject 001 to head up the collection of the undead. I want someone singular in focus, someone who won't waver and who won't fuck up."

The tech sucked in a deep breath to argue with the commander, but was met with Faddig's palm to his cheek.

"I hope you were not about to question my demands. I will have you amplified if that's the case."

The tech simply stood at attention and saluted.

"That's what I thought. I want you to instruct Subject 001 he is to lead the crews in the collection of as many of the undead as possible. Bring them all back here to be prepared for drop ship deployment. The second we learn Bethany Nitshimi's location, we'll be sending in one hell of a welcoming party. Is that clear?"

"Why don't you command the subject yourself?"

Just as the tech replied to Faddig, Subject 001 stepped forward.

"I await your command." Subject 001 spoke with a strange, rasping echo in its voice. The sentient zombie stared at Faddig, some odd understanding graced the monsters eyes.

Faddig smiled. The Zero Day Collective just reclaimed the upper hand.

CHAPTER 16

November 22, 2016 9:05 PM
Spokane, Washington

I drove. And drove ... and drove. And for the first time since the Mengele Virus hit, experienced almost an entire twenty-four hour period where nothing of consequence happened. No zombie attacks, no communication from the Zero Day Collective, no mental or emotional break downs. Not even the slightest bout of teen-angst drama was unleashed. This was also the first time in a long while I went an entire day without getting my geek on. I felt completely disconnected from the real world – or at least that virtual real world I called '~/' (aka 'home'). That was time I'd make up soon. During the long period of silence I managed to enjoy, thanks to Echo and Gabe napping as I drove, it dawned on me that we were little more than sitting ducks.

So the second we pulled over into the usual truck stop du jour, I had the laptop in hand and fabricated a bit of a lie for the sole purpose of getting the Zero Day Collective off our track. How did I know they were following me? I didn't, but it was a safe assumption to make. The ZDC had been following me since the zero day – or so it had appeared. With each move I made, they seemed to be one step ahead. It was time to belay that.

The plan was simple. All I had to do was log

into my server, back-date some files, re-post some blog entries, and unleash a flurry of search bots on my own site. Once those bots picked up the content, the Zero Day Collective would have no trouble finding out we were on route toward San Antonio, Texas. Why San Antonio? The Zombie Response Team. It was a risk, but one I felt had to be taken. If my assumption was correct, Jamal was in cahoots with the ZRT and would get word to them the ZDC was heading toward their front door.

All I had left to do was contact Jamal. But this communique would be sent gift wrapped in a very special encryption matrix we called *The Sports Bra*. It was nearly impossible to get to the delicious contents out of *The Sports Bra*, unless you knew the trick. Only Jamal and I knew the trick. The message was simple:

J-Tiz,

Inform ZRT the ZDC is heading to San Antonio. Use of deadly force encouraged.

B-Zip

The encrypted message left my machine and had me feeling a bit more confident we'd make it to our destination. I closed the laptop as Echo and Gabe returned to the car.

"Score!" Echo cried out in joy as she held up plastic shopping bags filled with actual food. "No kibble for us tonight!"

I laughed and nearly wept. We had been snacking on kitty kibble for so long I swear I had developed a purr.

"I could kiss you both! Holy shit, is that

actual soda I see in that bag?"

The shiny can teased me from within the plastic sack. When I saw that, I did cry. That's right, I broke down at the sight of soda. It had been so long since the bubbly delight crossed my taste buds. Hope had left the building of my heart at the thought of ever tasting one of my only vices again. But when Echo pulled out a gleaming can of Diet Mountain Dew, I nearly peed my pants with joy.

Once a geek, always a geek.

"B, the place has showers. The water's not hot, but it's running." Gabe's eyes nearly rolled into the back of his head.

That was all I needed to hear. Although it hadn't been long since my last shower, the apocalypse was quite good at making one grow pungent quickly. I was stewing in my own funk. The cold water wouldn't ease my achy, tight muscles, but I could luxuriate in a bit of cleanliness for a moment.

"Echo, would you do me a huge favor and change Jacob for me? I'll feed him when I get back from the shower."

I thought world-war teen was going to break out, but Echo just smiled and agreed. She had developed quite a bond with my baby. That was a blessing I wouldn't ever have counted on, but it certainly helped me do the things I needed to keep us safe. There were brief moments of horrible guilt that I was not spending enough time with Jacob – but this was the apocalypse and the rules of society were flushed down the toilet. So the care and feeding of baby Jacob would be shared, guilt free, with my sister in arms, Echo.

Who still had no last name.

Curious. Everyone had a story, and a last name. Note. To. Self.

Before I settled into the driver's seat for yet another evening of cramping, cold sleep, I held my baby in my arms and gently rocked him. His big eyes stared up at me – they were his daddy's eyes, so soft, so caring, so strong. Every time I thought of baby Jacob, my heart was torn to bits with guilt. This baby was brought into such a broken world. No one should have been born under these circumstances. How could this baby have a future, when the very word itself had become a foreign concept to the human race. *Future*? Did we even deserve such a luxury? After our Grande Mal fuck up, does the human race deserve a second chance?

My mind's answer to the question was very different than that of my heart. But because of the baby boy in my arms, I had to pull the answer from my emotional core, otherwise what's the point of Jacob continuing on?

Jacob coo'd and pointed up at me with the tiniest finger. I kissed his forehead and sucked in the fresh smell of baby.

Baby huffing.

"I love you my dearest baby boy."

For some reason, the haunting melody to the Leonard Cohen song *Everybody Knows* popped into my head. I sang the ironic twists and turns to my baby as I slowly rocked his tiny body in my arms. His smile never once faded as he drifted off to sleep. Back into his bassinet he went, without so much as a peep.

Getting a baby to go to sleep is better than any drug. It will calm you, soothe you, and put you into a place of peace you thought you never owned.

***

Nightmares had become just another part of the landscape of the new world order. If you weren't having nightmares, you probably weren't alive.

This time around, within my nightmare, we arrived in Seattle and drove the car directly up to the entrance of the underground city. Seattle's streets were completely bereft of life and/or death. As the car came to a stop, the doors slowly and silently opened. I stepped a foot out into a low-lying fog so thick my leg disappeared up to my knee. Jacob was handed to me by unknown arms. The baby slept soundly. Seattle's streets were a void of silence.

In front of me was a set of gilded double doors that stood over sixteen feet high. The handle on the doors was carved from human bone. As I reached out to open the door, it effortlessly swung open on silent hinges. Beyond the door was darkness and a warm, inviting sensation, impossible to resist. My feet carried me forward without my brain fully understanding what was happening.

As soon as the doors shut behind me, a massive, wild, completely silent party broke out in front of me. Strobe lights flashed a blitzkrieg display of blinding light. The floor was filled with countless lunatic, undead dancers. In the dancers wildly flailing hands, were flickering green glow sticks.

Undead rave.

Something pulled me forward. I stepped down onto the dance floor, only to find it covered entirely in snakes. There was no way to step in any direction without crushing one of the slithering reptiles under foot. Before I realized it, snakes were overtaking me, slithering up my legs. The shiny creatures had the lower half of my body completely encased. I couldn't move.

Another wave of serpents made their way to the upper half of my body. This time they worked in conjunction with one another and squeezed tightly around my torso until I couldn't breathe. Somehow, a collection of snakes managed to pull Jacob from my arms. I was helpless to do anything as I watched the snakes slither off into the raving crowd with my baby. My mouth opened to cry out, but one of the snakes made its way in between my teeth and down my throat. The ability to breathe was completely revoked from my system.

Stars danced in front of my now-tunneling vision.

As I started losing consciousness, the sound of Jacob crying echoed through the mysterious building. The dancers seemed to writhe and pump to the rising and falling sound of my baby boy's cries.

"Jacob!" I tried to scream. I felt the snake slither its way further down my throat. When the tip of the tail disappeared between my lips, I panicked. I was encased in a skin of serpent with one of the beasts writhing within my gut. I felt synapses in my mind snapping and misfiring. My muscles locked up. Death was drawing ever nearer.

Just before the Grim Reaper had its way with me, I jerked awake to darkness and silence. The cold breath hanging in front of my face was illuminated by the full moon that shined down through the windshield of the car. A quick look to the back of the Audi confirmed Jacob was fine. No snakes had taken up residence inside the car.

There was something about the nightmare that begged to warn me. From deep within the core of my conscience, I could feel the metaphor of that snake winding its way around the entrails stuffed within my abdomen. It had to be the ZDC. But what was warning me? Was there something now twisted around the double helix of my DNA, encoded to send me some sort of Bat Signal when the ZDC was near?

It was three in the morning. Soon we'd be heading off – the last leg of this long journey. Hopefully, at the end of the road, a new life awaited us all. But for now, sleep beckoned me from the beyond.

CHAPTER 17

November 23, 2016 9:23 AM
Seattle, Washington Underground City

Morgan Barnhart was almost always up before everyone else. It had become routine – wake at six AM, stretch, yoga, breakfast, gather intel. All of this, of course, was precluded by an enormous cup of coffee. Although the massive dose of caffeine seemed counter-productive to the yoga, there was no way her eyes would remain open throughout the day without the hit from the dark bean. And being in Seattle, why not take advantage of some seriously good coffee?

Or so she would have, had the apocalypse not leveled humanity.

"The Great Equalizer, that Mengele Virus." Morgan whispered to everyone and no one. Of course, no one else was awake to hear her micro-cosmic waxing of the philosophical. Or so she thought.

"You're right. Fucking virus pretty much leveled the playing field." Jamal awoke as soon as he smelled the coffee brewing. "Sorry. My nose can smell a pot brewing in the next state. It's hell in the morning – like living in a roastery. Mind if I have a cup with you?"

Morgan smiled and nodded her approval. There was something about Jamal she liked, trusted.

"So, Jamal, what's the real plan with your

underground city? Is this going to be your own personal playground or what?"

The young man stared off in the distance, unsure how to answer the question.

"Honestly, I'm just holding the fort down for when Bethany arrives. What we do will be her call."

Morgan stood quickly, almost knocking her mug onto the floor. She caught the heavy ceramic cup before gravity got its heartless fingers on the handle.

"Are you fucking kidding me? We're just waiting around? Isn't that a bit, I don't know, insane?"

Jamal laughed. The sound carried with it an undertone of tragic irony.

"You obviously haven't the slightest clue who Bethany is, do you?"

The young woman stood, staring at Jamal. The sideways tilt of her head and the purse of her lips answered the question well before a single word was uttered.

"Of course I know who Bethany is. The entire goddamn world knows who Bethany is."

Jamal's laugh echoed into silence.

"You might know of her, but you don't truly know Bethany Nitshimi until you've actually experienced her. She is the single most brilliant mind you will ever know. Any plan I could piece together would only pale in comparison to her ideas. So why bother trying when I know the perfect plan is only a days car trip away?"

Jamal had received the latest text from Bethany letting him know they were driving, straight-shot, from Spokane to Seattle. They would arrive before nightfall and whatever great plan Bethany had would be set in motion.

"There is something we can do though. Where's your nearest full-scale team?"

Morgan walked over to the Battle Table. Covering the entirety of the table was a tactical map of the United States.

"Portland, Oregon. Why?"

Jamal joined Morgan at the map. "I want you to bring them here. I have a bad feeling the Zero Day Collective is going to throw the kitchen sink at us to get to Bethany and her baby. I want to be prepared. Will you call them to us?"

Morgan and Jamal stared at one another for a long moment. There was no flirting going on, just pure strategy and work. Finally Morgan broke the silence.

"Yes. I can have them here before Bethany arrives."

Jamal gave Morgan a pat on the forearm.

"Great. Make it so."

With his best Picard maneuver tossed off for fun, Jamal grabbed his mug and made to suck down the bitter coffee. As soon as the hot liquid touched his lips, Morgan could tell Jamal normally drank his coffee with sugar and cream. Unfortunately, the apocalypse stole those luxuries away from mankind. Post-Mengela Virus, coffee was to be had au natural.

"I'll send word now. They'll be here in a few hours."

Jamal smiled at Morgan. "Thank you. And

as soon as Bethany arrives we'll all meet and sort out the plan of attack. I can tell you this for certain – our single most important job is to protect Bethany's baby."

Again, Morgan made with the *tilty-puzzle* face.

"You don't know about the baby do you?"

Morgan shook her head.

"You haven't read the book have you?"

Once again, Morgan shook her head.

Jamal gestured Morgan over to a computer terminal. "Sit down and read. You may as well consider these the first and second testaments of the new world order. The book, I Zombie I, was written by Jacob Plummer. The blog is Bethany's. Between the two of them, you'll understand the full story. The single most important bit of information you will take out of that is Jacob impregnated Bethany after he was infected. The resulting baby has become the target of The Zero Day Collective. For some reason, they will stop at nothing to get that baby back into their labs. Once Bethany arrives, it will be our duty to make sure that never happens. If we fail that, we fail the human race. Should the ZDC get their hands on Baby Jacob, their Great Cleansing will succeed and we'll all be nothing more than worm food for the undead."

Jamal's words settled uncomfortably under Morgan's skin. She knew of the Zero Day Collective. She even knew they had some diabolical plan that included the end of the majority of the lives on the planet. What the endgame of that plan was, she had no idea.

But 'Great Cleansing' was quite clear in its intent.

With a newer, more powerful motivation under her wings, Morgan turned to read the book and the blog of Jacob Plummer and Bethany Nitshimi.

Her eyes would be forever opened to a deeper, darker truth.

Before Morgan set about to plow into the words displayed before her, she pulled out a smart phone and sent a message to the commander of the Portland, Oregon division of the Zombie Response Team. The message was simple:

Pull out of Portland. Head to Seattle immediately.

Once the message was off and received, Morgan knew the troupes would arrive, packing powerful heat and an even more powerful attitude.

Just as Morgan turned to Jamal to inform him the message was sent, a klaxon ripped through the air.

"What the hell is that?"

Jamal ran to a computer terminal, sat, and started typing commands. "I set up a perimeter alarm with software that would monitor movement. If the camera caught human sized objects it would begin monitoring. If the movement had the typical characteristics of a zombie, the alarm would sound. I plan on integrating it with a fully automatic weapons system, so that if zombies are detected, they will be shot remotely. It's a brilliant piece of soft—"

"So we have zombies is what you're saying?"

Morgan's face offered an odd smirk, as if there were a level of thrill building at the thought of zombies marching toward the gate of the castle.

Jamal continued on at the computer, scanning through the different camera views, until he came upon the site of the action.

"Shit. There's hundreds of them. Fuck! What are we – "

Morgan pulled a radio from her belt. "I got this. Josh, this is Morgan. We have a large-scale breech at..."

Jamal picked up Morgans cue. "Near the intersection of Columbia and First."

Morgan relayed the information to Josh and followed up with the order to take out the undead threat.

***

The intersection of Columbia and First was close. The first response team was assembled and directly underneath the location of the zombie army within minutes. Each team member was armed with weapons of silent destruction. The goal was to not bring any unnecessary attention to the location – especially attention of the undead kind. So swords, bats, pikes, and bows were the order of the day.

"Ready to wipe clean the streets of the undead?"

"Ready!" The soldiers barked.

"I count to three, this door opens, you unleash bitter Hell upon these sons a bitches!"

A nervous energy spread through the Zombie Response Team members. They gripped their bats, knocked their arrows, some whispered prayers to one God or another.

"One."

The energy rose.

"Two."

Swift, shallow breathing overtook the men.

"Three."

Josh flung the door open, the hall was bathed in the near-blinding, white light of the sun. Through the brilliant rays of light, the wavering, shadowy forms of the undead could be seen. The Josh-led Zombie Response Team spilled out of the Underground City and immediately spread out. The team was outnumbered by at least ten to one, odds the men were used to. But the ZRT were trained assassins of the undead, odds meant nothing.

Without order or thought, the men with the bows scrambled to higher ground, taking perch on roofs and fire escapes. Arrows flew through the air, embedding themselves into the rotted flesh of the undead.

Josh ran from the door, metal pike in hand, heading full steam towards a solo Moaner. The point of his pike struck home and impaled the Moaner in the neck. The tip of the pike pierced the Moaners spine and the beast dropped to its knees. With a swift kick, the Moaner slid backwards off the metal pole. Sticky, brown blood slopped and splashed. The leader of the ZRT team took no time to celebrate his kill and set off to strike another blow for human kind.

It was impossible to tell how many of the undead had been sent to their final grave, but the street was still thick with melee.

"Buckshot! Watch out!"

A call from one of the bowman echoed off the walls of the nearby buildings. Buckshot was one of the senior members of the ZRT. In typical fashion, Buckshot was taking on two Moaners at once, and was unaware of a third party wanting to join in on the dance. Buckshot cracked his bat down hard upon one of the first two zombies, sending its brain matter flying in all directions. The gore splattered Buckshot's face shield, obstructing his view. The second zombie's arms flailed out in the air-space between itself and Buckshot. The bat swung hard and connected with the zombie's right elbow. The sound of the bone crushing would have sent chills down through the spine of even the hardest of asses. Fortunately, everyone else was far too busy crushing skulls and piercing brains to notice.

The now, one-armed zombie lunged forward, taking Buckshot by surprise. The weight of the undead bastard forced the fighter backwards, into the powerful arms of the zombie sneaking up from behind. The monster's rot-filled mouth opened up and clamped down on Buckshot's neck.

As the zombie enjoyed his meal, every bowman in the area took aim and fired. Five arrows hit their mark – the top of the zombies head. Buckshot was the last meal the Moaner would have.

There was no time to mourn the loss of their comrade in Armageddon. The bowman turned their attention back to the battlefield and let loose their scorns and arrows.

The battle raged on, with little more than the sounds of moans and the slicing and dicing of undead meat to punctuate the scene. When finally the last of the zombies were felled, the tally of men was taken. The Zombie Response Team had lost three good men.

Josh collected the weapons and armor from the downed men. It was a task he hated, but with the scarcity of tools nothing could go to waste.

When the remaining men stepped back through the door, they each whispered the names of their fallen friends – a ritual that came about after a particularly bloody battle in San Antonio. They called it the Undead Alamo.

CHAPTER 18

November 23, 2016 12:17 PM
Zero Day Collective, Zombie Collection Unit
Unknown Location

Subject 001 flew the drop-ship deftly around the landscape of the city. The heat signature on the radar drew an undeniable picture – there was massive movement of an undead nature. When the zombie pilot flipped on the external shotgun mic, the chorus of moans and screams bounced off of the metal walls of the ship.

"We have confirmation." Subject 001's ghost-like voice filled the soldiers in on the SITREP. "Setting down near the mass of undead civilians."

The over-sized drop ship came to a gentle rest on a four-lane thoroughfare that cut straight through the heart of the city. The sound of the landing deck motor roared to life. As soon as fresh air and light entered the cargo bay, the captive men and women within began screaming for help.

It was the SOP for a collection: Secure numerous living humans within a cargo ship, open the gates to the vessel near a crowd of zombies, and let the living draw the dead into the trap. The plan never failed.

The sounds of the humans wafted out of the ship and caught on the tail wind to be swiftly carried to the ears of the beasts. Once the sound of the living found its way into the ear canals of the dead, the zombies instantly turned their attention toward the drop ship. But that wasn't enough. The Zero Day Collective had to be sure to consume every available undead resource in the area. That is why Subject 001 was sent on the mission.

With the drop ship secured, Subject 001 unlatched his harness and made his way out of the cockpit and to the main exit. When the door hissed open, the undead pilot lowered the ramp to the ground.

Subject 001 glided down the ramp like the Ghost of Hamlet's Father; effortless, as if he were floating just above the metal below his feet. When he hit the pavement below, Subject 001 pointed his feet in the direction of the zombie horde. Within the recesses of his mind lay a programming few knew of. When the sound of the moaning crowd crossed the threshold of his ears, the programming kicked in and Subject 001 knew exactly what he had to do. He had a strange role to play in this circus of the damned. The Moment Subject 001 was within ear shot of the undead mass, he opened his mouth and released a sound so bizarre, no one would ever be able to explain. The noise was half music, half horror. A string quartet, tuned to the key of Hell, with undertones so atonal any semblance of melody would only serve to threaten the listeners sanity.

The sound spewing from Subject 001's mouth caught the attention of every zombie in the area. They turned and began to march toward the nightmare waltz.

Back inside the staging area, the soldiers all watched a live video feed of Subject 001 in action. No one within could explain what they witnessed. But when they saw the horde coming their way, denial took a back seat to duty.

"Here they come." One of the foot soldiers spoke nervously.

The junior soldier in the group revealed his fear when he reached up to re-adjust his helmet with a shaking hand.

"Pull it together soldier. It's about to get massively fucked up in here. When those Moaners reach this ship, you're going to witness, firsthand, how picnics happen in Hell."

The rest of the soldiers laughed at the expense of the young man.

"Why you so scared, bitch? There's a wall of three inch thick steel between us and them. There's no way they can get to us."

There was no reply, just the frightened look of a child who'd just seen his first horror movie and was about to have his bedroom light turned off.

"Don't tell me you've never seen this shit before? Come on! It's the fucking apocalypse. Zombies are as common as crabs in a whore house. You can't be afraid of a slow-ass, piece of shit Moaner."

Tears streaked down the young man's cheeks.

"You've gotta be kidding me! Seriously? What the fuck are they doing shipping out newbies on a collection? You have to have a stomach for this shit. The sounds alone will keep you from eating for weeks. Goddamn it!"

The team leader unleashed his fury on the wall behind him. The beat down he gave the steel served as little more than a percussive underscore to the crescendo of moans in the cargo bay of the ship.

"Listen carefully kid. You're about to get one hell of a show. If this doesn't put hair on your chest, nothing will."

The screams of the living shook the walls of the ship. As the sounds of the Moaners reached a peak, the human voices seemed to fold inside out. Heads bounced off the steel walls, bones were cracked, flesh was ripped and chewed. When the young solider looked through the tiny window that overlooked the cargo bay, he sucked in a gasp of terror. The bay was filled, asses to elbows, with zombies.

"Shit." The boy whispered.

"What do you see?"

The young soldier was mesmerized as he stared out into the hold. When his superior clocked him in the helmet and repeated the question, he finally remembered the mission.

"It's full of 'em. The humans are all dead."

"Lock and load baby!" The commander whooped and smacked the large red panic button that raised the drop ship's cargo door. The Moaners were busy cleaning up after the brain matter buffet and didn't realize they were being canned and carried off.

The closing of the cargo door came to a loud, metallic end and the drop ship lifted off.

The zombie pilot pointed the ship back towards the Zero Day Collective. They would return, unload their cargo, load up a fresh buffet, and head out to lather, rinse, and repeat.

CHAPTER 19

November 23, 2016 9:25 PM
Seattle, Washington

I never thought I'd be so happy to see a city skyline. When the Space Needle came into view, I nearly cried. I had to be honest with myself; I wasn't quite sure if we'd make it alive, or with our sanity intact. But here we were – complete. Jacob was cooing in the back seat, Echo and Gabe were gabbing about some odd pop culture meme, and I was desperately watching street signs.

"Echo, I need your help. We have to find Fourth Avenue and Yessler Way."

Echo and Gabe went silent as Echo focused her attention out the passenger-side window. I needed to call Jamal and let him know we had arrived, but I was too unfamiliar with the city to make the call.

"Over there! Fourth Avenue! Right turn." Echo squealed.

I turned the wheel to make the turn and slammed my foot down hard on the gas. The car took the turn with a squeal just as Echo screamed.

"Look out!"

The city street was filled with the walking dead. Moaners, Screamers, and a few evolutionary left turns no one would have predicted. The burning of rubber filled the air as the car came to a jerking halt. The undead flash mob turned to the car in a synchronized, dance-like movement. As soon as I slammed the car in reverse and punched the gas, the Screamers among the crowd took off after us. The sound was a chorus of demons and devils amplified and filtered through Purgatory's own recording studio.

"Bethany! Get us out of here!"

"I'm trying Echo! Be my eyes for me. No, the other way!"

Echo had turned to watch out the rear window. I needed her to follow the trajectory and movement of the Screamers giving chase. One wrong move on my part and we were nothing more than canned snack food.

"Shit! Bethany, one of them is about to—"

Echo didn't have to finish the sentence. The sound of the zombie's feet slamming down on the roof of the Audi was punctuation enough. I punched the gas again, jerked the wheel, put the car in neutral, tapped the brakes, and let the car start spinning. As soon as the front end was at ninety degrees I put the car in third and waited for the completion of the one-eighty. Once the geometry lesson was complete, I mashed the gas and the car took off.

The slamming of fist to roof informed me the zombie stunt man was holding fast. Dents began forming in the ceiling of the cockpit.

"Fuck!"

"Bethany, can he break through that?"

I really didn't want to answer Gabe's question. Screamers had proved that nothing could keep them from reaching fresh brains. And given the fact that Jacob was within this moving metal box, there was extra incentive.

Before my mind could rationalize a plan, Echo made a quick demand.

"Stop the car!"

"What? Why?"

"Just trust me, Bethany. Stop the car."

There wasn't time to argue. Rock 'em, sock 'em zombie was about to break through the roof of the car and we were about to become the main course for one pissed off undead son of a bitch. As my foot graced the rubber of the break, Echo grabbed the pike from my bag, opened the door, and leaped out. She landed on her feet with the grace of a panther and immediately leaped onto a dumpster. I couldn't believe my eyes. All of a sudden the girl was some sort of kick ass super hero without the costume. She had the pike extended and was spinning it around as if she had been possessed by the spirit of Thor himself.

The monster roared and leaped down from the car. It spread it's arms and flexed muscles I never knew the human body contained. The Screamer's neck was Batman's cowl, without the S & M rubber look.

I couldn't let Echo try to take on this thing alone, superhero action figure or not. My hand shot out for my bag and returned with my gun. Using a gun in this situation would not end well; but I couldn't let that fucking monster crack open Echo's skull.

Not on my watch.

"Stay in the car Gabe. Let nothing touch Jacob."

As soon as my feet hit cement, my arms

shot up to take aim. There was no shot to have. The beast was in mid-air, leaping toward Echo. She whirled the pike around just in time for the business end to meet the eyeball of the beast as it landed on the dumpster.

The Screamer went silent. Echo kicked up hard and the zombie slid off the pike and came to a hard crash landing on the ground below. One tiny, volcanic splash of brown zombie oil from the eye socket was all the confirmation I needed the thing was dead undead.

How in the hell?

I couldn't even finish the question before the sound of pissed off Screamers (as if there were any other kind) let us know the gang was on its way.

"Get back in the car!" Echo called out as she jumped from the dumpster and landed beside the Audi.

I managed to convince my brain to remind my feet how to run and made it safely into the driver's seat. The Audi took off with a screech to shame the screaming army just yards away. The turbo kicked in and the car sped off toward Yessler Way.

"How did you," I started.

"You don't survive on the streets for long without picking up some skills. I did a lot of training with these dudes that called themselves the Homeless Street Ninjas. I know, it sounds crazy; but they were legit. It was a thing. Without their help I would have been raped, beaten, and who knows what else."

I couldn't believe it. I had a fucking street hero with me and had been doing all the fighting alone.

"Why didn't you bother to let me in on this? I could have used the help."

"You asked me to protect Jacob. I did. This time, I had to protect you. I'm sorry. Why don't we argue about this once we've found your friend?"

It's hard when your logic is bested by a teen. I felt like handing in my Mensa membership.

"There's Yessler!" Gabe shouted from the back seat.

My little tiff with Echo almost caused me to miss the turn. Thankfully, the all-wheel drive spun on a dime. All we had to do now was find Fourth Avenue and we were as home free as one could enjoy at the moment.

As I drove slowly down Yessler, my guilt grabbed my gut and yanked it downward. Sometimes I wanted to punch my conscience in the face. Other times, I was glad I owned up to my humanity.

"Echo, I'm sorry for busting your chops. I get it. We all have secret lives, pasts we'd either like to forget about or already have. But our situation kinda warrants the revealing of truths that could help forward our cause. So, in the spirit of survival, if you have a super power, share it."

We all laughed. It was the only honest reaction that could follow such a demand. The laughter reignited our purpose and our hope. Sure this nightmare sucked the barrel full of monkeys out of the party, but hope still existed. It had to; else there was no reason to continue on.

"Shit!" Gabe exclaimed.

I slammed the brakes down hard.

"I can't believe it." Echo chimed in.

"We made it."

I couldn't help but laugh out loud again. The world was bedlam, rubble strewn about the land, but we made it across the country to help rebuild it all; one piece, one moment, at a time.

I slipped my phone out of my pocket and dialed Jamal's number. As soon as he answered, I had but one simple thing to say.

"We're here."

Of course Jamal knew we were here. He'd be tracking us the whole time. How could he not? It was just a matter of pushing a tiny tracking app onto my phone. I knew he'd do it. Did I complain? Not once. Knowing the second best hacker in the world had the back of the best hacker on the planet was fine in my book.

A heavy door swung open. Two enormous men in Kevlar hustled out and stood on either side of the entry. The guards held serious firepower in their hands and had Hell Fire grenades strapped to their bandoleers. Someone certainly knew what they were doing.

"B-Zip! Fuck! Hot as evah!" Jamal's voice carried out the door, preceding his lithe body by just a fraction of a second.

When his long arms appeared from the darkness, they were spread in a gesture of embrace. Our arms wrapped around one another, his nearly squeezing the breath from my lungs.

"Jesus, it's good to see you Bethany."

"I never thought I'd see this day Jamal."

It had to be clear to everyone around us, there was a history. It was undeniable; the length and strength of the hug, the deep inhalation of breath, the relaxation of every muscle while at the same time an inexplicable tension rose from our cores. It all spoke of 'story yet to be revealed.'

"Let's get you and your friends inside."

Jamal pulled away and turned toward the door. He gestured for me to head in first. I denied his request and insisted Echo and Gabe lead the way. As Echo passed, she handed Jacob's bassinet over to me.

"Holy shit. Is this him? Is this *the one*?"

Jamal stared, wide-eyed, down at the still sleeping Jacob.

"Don't go all Matrix on me Jamal. He's not Neo and this is not the Nebuchadnezzar." I smiled at Jamal and gave his shoulder a nudge.

"But you still make one hell of a Trinity. I'll never get the vision of you in that body suit out of my mind."

I winked at Jamal and entered the building. A few short seconds later, the heavy steel door slammed shut behind us. With the sunlight barred from entry, the darkness was almost overwhelming. Within a few seconds, my eyes adjusted and the environment was nothing more than a behind the scenes look at a haunted house.

"You're going to shit yourself when you see command central. I've set up an entire data center down here. We've got one hell of a Beowulf Cluster – twenty-five nodes, baby! Slammin'. The temperature is perfect – no need for a cooling system."

Jamal was getting a serious nerd-on. It was one of his charms.

"J-Tiz, I love you and your geeky ways, but what we really need is sleep. You can show me nerd-central tomorrow. And by the way, this is Echo and Gabe. Gabe, Echo this is Jamal Tisdale. We go way back, so he's safe."

"Yeah, B and I pre-date the Pentium—"

I stopped my boy before he got revved up. Thankfully, it didn't take much. If anything, Jamal was understanding of my needs. He always was. Why I broke it off with the man I'll never know.

Maybe the Universe was trying to tell me something. If so, the Universe would have to wait until tomorrow before I'd listen.

CHAPTER 20

November 24, 2016 11:34 AM
Underground City Seattle, Washington

I believe, for the first time in my post-Mengele life, I slept a full twelve hours. The glorious feeling in my head was inversely proportionate to the feeling in my back and legs. I didn't want to stand. I just wanted to remain horizontal. In corpus delicious. But Jacob had other plans. Waking to his cries made me instantly realize how bad of a mother I had been over the last few days. I had become so focused on getting us safely to Seattle, I forgot to be a mother.

"Good morning my special man. How's the savior of mankind feeling today?"

Thankfully, Jacob wasn't aware enough to develop the ego associated with being mankind's one chance for salvation. The cries issuing from his mouth certainly spoke highly of the standard-issue infantile ego. He was the center of a very tiny universe that would hopefully grow and flourish.

The bottle of formula quickly silenced Jacob's cries, just in time for Jamal to knock on my door.

"I think we're going to have to develop some sort of child care down here in Undertown."

"Undertown? Seriously? You couldn't come up with a better name? Sounds like something a frat boy would call the package within his tighty whities. Come on, you've got to find a better name than that."

I was mostly teasing Jamal. The man was brilliant – in so many ways. But creativity was not his forte. The man could code in nearly every language known to nerd-kind, could recite Pi (and, on a side note, eat pie) like no one I'd ever known, and his knowledge of security systems far exceeded the sum total knowledge of the NSA. But put a crayon in his hand, and his IQ seemed to plummet back down to mere mortal level.

"It's my city, I'll name it what I want. Maybe I'll just call it Jamaltown."

Our laughter caused Jacob to spit out his bottle and kick his legs in a frenzy of giggles.

"There's a meeting about to take place. I'd like you to attend. What do you say?"

The look on the dear man's face clearly indicated this meeting was of some importance – that and it would probably break his heart if I turned him down.

"I'll get Echo and Gabe to watch Jacob. You're right, we need child care. Oh, and health insurance and a 401k."

***

The meeting room was nothing special, just a large round table with a single laptop. Seated around the laptop were the very friendly faces of complete strangers. They each looked upon me as if I held the keys to the kingdom of heaven and was about to hand said keys over to one lucky person.

First to introduce herself was Morgan Barnhart. She was a wisp of a girl with an adorable face that spoke volumes to a nerd like me. She could make you swoon before you realized she had you under some strange spell that rendered you powerless to resist her charms. Her cohort in crime, Joshua Garcia, was a big man with a ham-sized fist that could crush your skull as he yelled out the lyrics to Avenged Sevenfold songs in a throaty, bear-roar of a voice. He was Chewbacca to Morgan's Leah.

Yeah, I said it.

We all sat. Jamal stood. There was some irony to the motion I wanted to track down. My brain wasn't functioning properly at the moment.

"I wanted to bring Bethany in on this meeting mostly because she'll be involved in about every meeting we'll have. I've made no bones about the fact that she will be the facilitator, and the designer, of all operations from this moment on. If anyone has any objections to that, I suggest you pack up and haul ass. Anyone?"

No one packed up, or hauled ass.

"That's what I thought. Okay, Morgan, I'd like you to start the meeting off by explaining to Bethany the situation?"

Morgan didn't bother to stand. She didn't need to. Her elf-like voice had no problem commanding attention.

"The Zombie Response Team's mission statement is to protect and sever. We've mostly accomplished this by banding together to create the biggest enterprise of individuals ready to fight against the undead, as well as help to educate others. We have formed self contained pockets in all the major cities across the United States. The goal of each pocket is to begin rebuilding those cities and fortifying their defenses against the undead. So far the plan has worked – but not to the extent we'd like. We need a way to help survivors find us."

Jamal stood back up and interrupted Morgan.

"This is where we think you could help Bethany. You picked up Zombie Radio where the original DJ left off. We have to assume some of his listeners stayed tuned in. If we can harness the power of that medium to guide people to the locations of the ZRT pockets, we think the cities would more easily rebuild."

The whole of the idea spun around the meat of my mind for a moment. By the time the synaptic dance was concluded, I had one major concern.

"If we broadcast the locations of the ZRT teams, we run the risk of the Zero Day Collective locating and neutralizing them. It can't work that way. It won't work that way. To do this right, we'd have to go the opposite route and have the Response Teams go to the survivors."

Morgan and Joshua started to protest. I silenced them with a raised hand.

"Hear me out first. We announce to listeners to raise a flag to indicate their location. The ZRT teams could then search them out and take them back to their respective cities. That way you eliminate the possibility of the Zero Day Collective locating and destroying each and every Response Team headquarters. It'll take more time, but the end result will be far greater. I can make the announcement on Zombie Radio; inform everyone to raise a large white flag to let the teams know their whereabouts."

Everyone at the table took a moment to ponder the idea. There was only one objection, and a strong one at that. Morgan stood and addressed everyone at the table.

"This plan would jeopardize every survivor. You have a bunch of white flags raised and the Zero Day Collective could drop bombs or even drop ships full of the undead."

Her concern sunk in – deep. She was right. Either way we risk the ZRT teams or the survivors. We were going about this all wrong. I closed my eyes to let all possible outcomes retract to a single point. From that single point, I could follow the path of each solution to see which route offered the most plausible success. It was little more than probability and statistics.

"I use Zombie Radio as a ruse. Morgan, you and Josh contact all ZRT leaders and let them know they are to start searching out survivors and returning them to the safe zones. Not a word of this leaks out through any channel. I will pick up the broadcast on Zombie Radio that the ZRT headquarters have all been overrun with the undead. The teams will then start searching the cities to locate survivors. No flags, no welcome parties. Your men and women will have a harder time locating civilians, but eventually word of mouth will spread and the survivors will be more likely to show themselves. A simple lie, to draw the heat away from your teams."

I stared around the table. All eyes were upon me and all mouths were shut. It seemed my plan had legs. Morgan and Josh eventually agreed it was the best route and would contact their leaders to set everything in motion. As for my part, I just had to conjure up some serious acting chops to make the demise of the ZRT believable. On the off-chance the Zero Day Collective was listening in, I wanted to make sure they believed this like white trash on wrestling.

"B..." Jamal was still seated at the table. He had a very familiar look in his eyes. The man wanted something only I could give him. "I need your help."

Jamal and I had a pact; not one of those 'If we're both alone when we're forty" pacts. This was serious, and often led to deep, chocolaty trouble. In a nutshell, we never refused. If one of us needed a favor, that favor was always granted. That was actually how I wound up falling in love with the man so many years ago.

Favors.

God damn it.

Jamal looked around the room, clearly nervous or paranoid. The door was standing open. He stood, crossed to the door, looked out, and then slowly sealed the outside world away from out little sanctuary. When Jamal sat back down, he took my hand in his.

"You're the only human being on this planet I trust. I brought all of these people into this place because I was certain of their loyalty. But..." His lip quivered. Jamal allowed doubt to creep into his mind. Jamal rarely allowed doubt an audience of his faculties. "I'm not sure any more. I've heard rumblings and seen suspicious things. B., I need you to check everyone out. Make sure no one under this roof has ties with the ZDC. I'd do it, but I'm not nearly as tied into this web as you are. You know things I don't, so you could more quickly spot the red flags. I don't want to lie to the world. If we are to offer salvation from this insanity, we do so honestly and without even the slightest threat that the Zero Day Collective is going to find us and pull the carpet out from under our feet."

I placed my free hand on Jamal's cheek. The sincerity of the man broke my heart. He hadn't changed a bit. Underneath the boy-genius exterior was the heart of the truest, most sincere man I'd ever known. Jamal was the incarnation of truth. Amplify him and his inner zombie would moan the truth. There would be no lie zombie lie from the mouth of that monster.

"Of course. Set me up a work station and I'll get to it."

Jamal smiled a wicked smile only I could decrypt. He had something for me, something big and juicy.

"I have a surprise for you."

Jamal led me to another room. As soon as he opened the door, I knew immediately what the man had done.

"Your very own broadcast studio. Soundproof and zombie proof. Once you're in here, you can hop up on soapboxes as high as you like and no one will interrupt. You also have a fully networked and firewalled computer that has a point to point connection with my cluster – should you need the extra iron. Oh, and there's a Linux box in there serving as a full-blown media server with over a terabyte of music on it. The Princess, nay, Queen of the airwaves may entertain her subjects to her heart's content."

The wicked-evil grin that chased around Jamal's chin and cheeks made me want to kiss him and kiss him hard. I refrained. Why? I had no idea.

We both walked into the studio. I shut the door behind me so the frankness of my next question wouldn't escape into the wild.

"Why do you suspect foul play? What's going on?"

Jamal stopped in his tracks and continued looking away from me for a moment. When he finally spoke, his eyes remained elsewhere.

"You won't believe me B."

A strange pause danced around the room. The silence of the soundproofing was disconcerting enough to make my skin slink around the meat on my bones.

"It's the apocalypse, douchebyte, I'll believe anything."

Again Jamal made with the pause.

"I have no proof. All I have is gut instinct and my gut is telling me there's a ghost in the machine."

Jamal knew I loved it when he dropped the Gilbert Rile description of Descarte's Mind Body Dualism. Jamal was brilliant, even when he contradicted his Vulcan-like passion for truth and fact.

I closed the gap between the two of us. "What would someone have to gain by being dishonest here and now? It's not like there's profit to be made. And the only true power to be had is in survival."

When Jamal turned to me, the look on his face was a mixture of content and ill at ease. I wasn't sure which projected emotion to latch onto.

"I know it's crazy Bethany, but there's something not right. The reason why I want you to look into this is because you're crazy brilliant and you'll approach it with an objective mind. Do what you can to assuage this Pon Far raging within me."

"Ooooh, I always did love it when you spoke Vulcan to me. Okay, you've got yourself a deal – on one condition."

"Name your price Nitshimi."

I could have so milked this for all it was worth. I decided, however, to play nice.

"If I come up with nothing, you have to trust me."

We hugged on it – and nearly kissed to seal the deal. The awkward moment led to an even more awkward departure of Jamal. I wanted to spend some time getting to know my new Bitch Cave. But before I got too comfy, I had to retrieve my babies – Jacob and my laptop.

CHAPTER 21

November 24, 2016 6:34 PM
Zombie Response Team Headquarters: San
Antonio, Texas

San Antonio was the first to begin the fortification process. The idea to wall in the city was Morgan's. The goal was to encircle the metropolitan area and exterminate any infected humans. Once the undead were cleared from within the city wall, those inside would be safe.

In theory.

The wall took nearly a year to build. It wasn't pretty, but the barrier to entry offered more protection than staggered guards and barbed wire. The only problem with the wall was that it prevented survivors from gaining access to safety – unless they were brought in. That's where Morgan's plan came into place.

"Sir, we have received word from commander Barnhart. We are to begin sweep and rescue missions, starting in concentric twenty-five mile radius circles. As we locate uninfected survivors we are to bring them into the city."

The Sergeant handed Commander Koenig the print out with Morgan's communication. Koenig was thrilled to finally have orders that included a little action. To this point, most of what he did was plan the guard rotations and make sure the soldiers were getting sleep, food, and exercise. Every now and again a fight would break out or a small horde of zombies would attack the wall in vain. That was the extent of the excitement within *New San A*. So these new orders were a gift from God. Something to do.

Koenig stood and pulled down his jacket to smooth the wrinkles. "Sergeant Walker, put together a group of men, arm them, and pack them off in two transports. I want them locked and loaded in thirty."

Walker spared no time in saluting and slipping out of the office. He had a list of men he created for just this purpose. The group was versatile and merciless. He called the men together and gave them their assignments. Koenig was part of the detail. No way was he going to miss out on the chance for a little action. Besides, the wall made him claustrophobic most days. He could use the escape, the distraction from monotony.

***

The twin transports sped through the gate just before it was lowered and locked. New San A took no chance. The cloud of dust kicked up by the transports veiled the city wall from the rear view mirrors. Thanks to the apocalypse, Texas winters were almost as hot as summers – minus the moisture.

Planning a perfectly concentric route was nearly impossible, but the team navigation specialist did his best. He knew the empty transport had room for twenty-five to thirty people. They would drive until the transport was filled, turn back, deliver the survivors, and return to the last point of contact.

Along the way, they would take out any hostiles necessary. Said hostiles appeared far sooner than they thought possible.

"Samuel to Koenig. Undead activity spotted directly ahead. Your orders?"

"Koenig to Samuel – engage undead immediately."

Lieutenant Samuel brought the transport to a stop one hundred yards from the cluster of zombies busy with a small group of survivors. As soon as he stepped out of the transport, the screams punched him in the gut. Zombie Response Team had a name for that – PARF (Post Apocalyptic Reaction Fatigue). The screams of dying humans filled the landscape. Just before the sound becomes innocuous, it begins to hurt like a stomach cramp. When it happened, all you could think of was puking out the pain and the sorrow.

"Lock and load people!"

Instantly the soldiers poured out of the lead transport, guns ready to unleash their fury. Like a choreographed ballet, the men spread out over the landscape and silently moved toward the target area. Once the soldiers were within range of their target, they would wait for the order and rain down second death on the undead.

The moans and screams grew louder as the men drew closer. Trigger fingers were itchy to take down the bastard children of mankind.

As a unit, the team reached the kill zone and dropped to the ground in order to get into position.

But when scopes went to eyes, the scene immediately folded inside out, became a newer, uglier nightmare. What was going on went beyond description.

"Sir, Lieutenant Samuel here. I—" Samuel was unsure how best to describe the horror he witnessed. "These Moaners ... they're just ... Jesus Christ!"

"What is it Lieutenant? SITREP now!" Command Koenig demanded.

"Sir, the zombies are tearing the limbs off of the survivors and strapping the torsos to their backs." The lieutenant knew his description did the horror before him no justice.

"I don't understand Samuel. Explain."

The lieutenant swallowed hard. "It's like they're wearing the armless and legless torsos as backpacks."

Static filled the radio before the Commander replied. "To what end?"

"It's not clear sir. Maybe they're carrying them for food. I don't know. It looks like we've lost all survivors. What are your orders?"

A pause. The moment didn't lend itself to pauses. Hesitation led only to desperation in this type of situation. What they needed was immediate and clear action.

"Do not engage enemy. Return to transport immediately."

The Lieutenant couldn't believe his ears. He thought it imperative to take out as many of the walking dead as possible. A single Moaner or Screamer was capable of spawning thousands more of its kind. That alone was reason enough to want to take out each and every member of the undead community.

But orders were orders. And who was a lowly Lieutenant to question the orders of a venerated and decorated Commander.

"Retreat! Now!" Samuel barked the order into his radio. Without question the men silently fell back from the site of horrors.

As they ran back, Samuel could see the look of disbelief on the faces of the men close by. This was bound to happen. What some of the men failed to see was the importance of returning alive – and with survivors. Blasting away at a small pack of Moaners might save a few lives, but it would, in the end, cause a ripple effect the small army wouldn't be able to handle.

Everyone knew sound attracted the undead.

Unfortunately, enough sound had already been made. Before the men could reach the transport, the screech of Screamers ripped through reality. The sound bounced off of every wall in the area. It was impossible to discern the source of the location.

The small group of men huddled together, shoulder to shoulder, facing out in a small, tight circle. And as if the men were all connected to some collective consciousness, they all began slowly moving the circle clockwise. The lock-step, side-march was a hypnotic dance of death waiting to be performed for the perfect audience.

A cloud of dusty mayhem rose in the distance. Like a small pack of Tasmanian devils, the whirling chaos grew closer, louder, and ever more deadly. Once the group of men spotted the source of the noise, the spinning circle broke and formed a line facing the oncoming hell spawn.

One of the soldiers pulled a pair of long range binoculars out and immediately had the enemy in focus.

"There are two of ... fuck me sideways. This is not good."

"What is it Brinkman?" The commander ordered.

"These aren't ordinary Screamers sir. Sir, they're wearing some kind of armor. What the fuck? Sir, these things look like they're covered in bone."

As the group of soldiers tried to gain some semblance of coherence within the words the soldier spoke, the Screamers came into view.

Brinkman was dead on – the zombies skin had naturally evolved into a bone-like plating.

A screech ripped everyone out of their lost mental anguish and back into reality.

"Fuck this noise." One of the soldiers hoisted his gun to this shoulder, held his breath to aim, and pulled the trigger.

From the chest of the oncoming zombie came a puff of dust. The marksman hit his target, but the bullet bounced off the exoskeleton

"Fall back. Fall back!" The commander shouted

Every member of the unit stood to run – minus the marksman. He chambered another bullet, aimed, held his breath, and pulled back the trigger. Another tiny puff of dust wafted in the wind. The action only served to piss of the zombie even more.

Another round. Another breath. Another shot. This time the shot hit home and nailed one of the oncoming Screamers in the left eye. The first of the armor plated zombies went down. The second continued onward. The rest of the men were already tucked safely inside the transport.

"Brinkman! To the transport. Now!" The commander insisted.

The marksman had better plans. When he was trained by Morgan and Joshua, he was never given the option to retreat. From Brinkman's perspective, you served until you died. He wanted an honorable death and this would bring just that to him.

The sound of the second monster reached a deafening, fever pitch. For a brief moment, everything went into slow motion. Brinkman could finally see the movement of the Screamer in perfect, three dimensional, stereophonic color. The arms and legs were a frenzy of motion. The description of bone armor was dead on. Covering the entirety of the thing's body were plates the color of dirty ivory. The thing moved like a manic marionette, arms and legs flailing in a nightmarish, chaotic dance. The roar of the solo monster was different than any other zombie he'd ever heard – some bastardization of metallic scratches with an overtone of Godzilla.

Brinkman sucked in a deep breath and held it tight within his lungs. His right cheek rested comfortably on the worn spot of his guns' wooden stock. Since the zombie never stopped moving, the shooter had to find the pattern within the movement. Once the pattern was discerned, he could anticipate the movement and place the shot accordingly.

The thing was growing dangerously close. The monstrous sound vibrated loose metal and threatened to shatter weaker glass.

"Brinkman! You have your orders. Get into the transport."

The order was summarily ignored. He had to get the shot. The shot was life, was salvation.

Jerk right, hang forward, snap back, droop left.

Jerk right, hang forward, snap back, droop left.

The pattern revealed itself. Brinkman would get his shot.

Just as the foul creature was about to droop left, it leaped into the expanse of space between where it was and where Brinkman knelt. The bullet shot out of the gun and cut through the empty air, coming to rest six inches into a wooden poll holding up a hand-made sign proclaiming "Jesus is Lord". The bone-armored zombie came down on the shooter and swung a forearm out at his head. Brinkman's skull erupted like a rotten watermelon, the pulpy juice sluicing the ground around the killer and killed.

An unnatural, undead roar of triumph shook the ground. The commander of the ZRT team shouted the orders to move out just before the zombie gave chase. The army-issue

Hummer had just enough horses to haul it, and its cargo, safely away from the monster. The beast finally gave up pursuit of the transport and released a screech of frustration.

The game had changed. The bogeymen had evolved into something far more dangerous. Mother Nature seemed to somehow change sides and give the ghost in the human machine the advantage.

The Hummer sped off. The team still had a mission to complete, humans to search for and rescue. Koenig sat in the back with his men. For the first mile not a word was spoken. Men exchanged glances, but nothing more. Eventually the silence was broken.

"What do we do if we run into something like that again?" The speaker went by the name 'Brimstone'. He fancied himself a comic book artist. His nom de plume came from one of his favorite characters he was developing before the apocalypse robbed him of his chance at fame and fortune.

"We don't miss."

Koenig's answer drew a few chuckles from the men.

"Seriously – don't miss. You've trained for this. Everyone in this transport can shoot the shit out of a swallow at one hundred yards. You guys don't miss. Ever. I suggest you remember that simple fact."

CHAPTER 22

November 24, 2016 7:20 PM
Underground City: Seattle, WA

Jacob cried until his face was blood red. It broke my heart to see him struggling to breathe from whatever it was that made him weep. That was one of the hardest aspects of new motherhood – not knowing what to do to comfort my baby. I wanted to fold him up into my arms and protect him from the hate and sorrow that seeped into every crack and crevice of the landscape. But I wasn't going to be *that* mom, the one that suffocated her child to the point of stunting his emotional and mental growth. I wanted Jacob to have a healthy understanding of what was going on around him. I assumed it would be the only way my child, or any child, stood a chance at survival. Truth. Because of that, my baby would hear my cry for help over the air, would watch me weep for loss, and would get to see me celebrate the destruction of what was once a human being.

But at the moment, my baby was with me in a make-shift recording studio, where he would experience his mother call out to the crowds and ensure them that this revolution would not, in fact, be televised.

Good evening Zombie Radio Nation. It's me, your host, Bethany Nitshimi. I am here with the progeny of one Jacob Plummer to inform you that you are, in fact, still alive. If the words I am speaking are making sense to you, you my dear friend are still very much human. And this is Zombie Radio 2.0. That's right my gentle nation, your replacement DJ is here to help you rock in the latest evolution of mankind and avoid having the man's hand down our pants grabbing our junk without consent.

That sounded disgusting. Just when did I start using words like 'junk'? Especially in the presence of my baby. What's going to happen with him? Will his first word be some trashy explicative he heard issued from my very mouth? Has my child been pre-doomed like the rest of humanity? To that I say 'nay nay'. But how can I be so confident when the living are outnumbered by the dead and damned ten to one?

I can, because I'm still here. The odds did everything in its power to bend me over and have its mighty way with me, but I refused to give in. I fought and I won. My very existence proves that we can and will survive. The Zero Day Collective has lost and soon their experiment will turn its rotten maw back on the creator and bite the hand that did feed it.

Did I say The Zero Day Collective lost? What does that mean exactly? Are they dead and gone? No. Unfortunately some of those bastard mad-men lived to fight another day. They might be outside your door, hoping to drag you into the filth and rot of their experimentation. But we have one thing on our side that the bogeyman failed to consider – we are intelligent. I know that might seem a bit contrapuntal to the average state of man, prior to the release of the Mengele Virus. But I like to think of the great amplification as a reboot – a culling of an average herd. I know, I know, that sounds horrible. But seriously – the truth of the matter is that only two types of people will have survived The Zero Day Cleansing: The intelligent and the resilient. Ignorance and stupidity will have no place in the new world order. I guess that's not entirely true. Just look out your windows. The undead, shambling horde represents the new caste of ignorance. Slack-jawed followers loping around with just enough lower-motor function to seek out sustenance. They're out there – waiting to dine on the gray matter of the elite thinkers. Don't fall prey to the wandering souls.

So, what can you do? Simple. You can wait. There is a group out there, The Zombie Response Team, looking for you. They are our new heroes. Right now there are teams searching the barren wastelands of the country in search of survivors. When you see them, let them know you are alive and they will bring you to safe zones where you can breathe in the air of freedom from the undead tyranny. But do not try to find them, their headquarters have been destroyed. I cannot tell you where they are for fear the Zero Day Collective might hunt them down and decimate our last, best hope. Be patient – they will find you.

And know this – as the ZRT searches, I will be hard at work developing the cure for this sick-fuck disease. Have faith, Bethany is on your side and I will do everything I can to bring the living back to prominence and Providence. That's right bitches! Let's get biblical!

On second thought, let's not. I've already had my share of run ins with zealotry. But thinking biblical makes me think of Genesis and that is a perfectly good segue into a song. Here's Genesis and "Land of Confusion."

The trusty sound of Phil Colin's voice guided me into some sort of happy trance. I did it. My first 'real' broadcast complete with song. I wasn't a DJ, that's for sure. I didn't have the sexy voice or the constant stream of pop-culture references, but I did have plenty to offer.

This is good. I could easily turn this into something to help save the world.

"What do you think Jake? Is Superman right here, standing in front of you making goo goo faces into a bassinet filled with the real savior of humanity?"

My little boy stared up at me, a gigantic, toothless grin beaming up into my eyes. He had no idea what was going on around him. All that mattered to Jacob was that his belly was full, his diaper was empty, and there were plenty of things to gawk at. Oh, would that life were so simple for everyone involved.

I queued up a solid hour worth of music. There was no way I was about to ball and chain myself down to a desk and a mic. There was a cure to find, humans to save, and a collective of mass murderers to track down and destroy.

"Momma's a busy woman Jacob." Jacob cooed up at me, his eyes twinkling in the light from above.

A soft knock came from the other side of the door. When I opened the soundproof entryway, Morgan was standing, framed in the doorway. As soon as she saw me, she started clapping.

"Brava Bethany Nitshimi! I knew there was a reason why you're my hero."

Morgan's arms reached out and wrapped around my neck. It had been a long time since a hug was a part of my life. My body melted into the embrace. It felt so good, even coming from a stranger. I didn't want the connection to break.

"I was listening. What you said was perfect. In so many ways, the world needs you. If there's anything I can do to help, just let me know." Morgan pulled away, her cheeks as red as mine felt.

As soon as I heard the proclamation, my brain went into over drive. What did I need help with? The answer popped out of my mouth before it seemed my mind knew what was going on.

"I need help locating a chemist and a biologist. The cure didn't work. In fact, Dr. Michaels was lying all along. But I'm convinced one can be synthesized. Problem is, I can't do it. So if you can find members of those professions among your survivors, we might have a chance at beating this back."

Morgan's face immediately registered deep thought – a good sign. I already liked the girl, even before the soul-restoring hug.

"I'll see what I can do. I'm fairly certain we have at least one of those among us. He might not be here in the underground city, but he's within our reach. I'll poke around and see what I can find out."

Morgan left, a bit lighter on her toes than when she arrived. As she vanished, the first song faded only to be replaced by another; this time, the screeching guitars of "Welcome to the Jungle" filled every corner of my broadcast room. The sound of Slash's familiar wailing brought to light an idea.

The Obliterator.

I knew my next stop. Jamal had wanted to somehow join his Zombie Recognition Software with the right weaponry to defend the underground city. That solution required laser sighting and some incredibly complex software. I had a much more elegant – but just as effective – solution.

***

"...but my goal is to lessen the undead population. Your idea would only scare them away. How does that help the greater good?"

Jamal had a point. But the immediate need was the safety of the people within the confines of these underground tunnels and rooms.

"Look, I know this idea doesn't feed your mass destruction needs, but it does fulfill what should be our Prime Directive – survival. With your recognition software already in place, I can have the Obliterator up and running in less than a day. At least it will keep us from succumbing to an attack."

Jamal started deeply into my eyes. I could

see wheels of genius turning a Turing Test, grinding and pulping the possibilities.

"Fine. But I don't want you screwing with my original code. I'll give you the API and you can write the software to communicate with whatever hardware you create."

Before we could continue on with the conversation, a near-deafening alarm sounded.

"Oh fuck!"

"What? What's 'Oh fuck!' mean Jamal? Is it what I think it means?"

"Yes. We're under attack. Get rid of the baby and meet me in the command room."

As I ran with the bassinet in hand, I couldn't believe I was responding to 'Get rid of the baby'. I couldn't just *get rid* of Jacob. What I could do was hand him over to Echo until this attack was under control.

When I threw open the door to mine and Echo's temporary room, I was greeted by Echo and Gabe lying on the bed, hands in a mad frenzy of seek and destroy.

"Don't you knock?" Echo shouted and she pulled the covers to her chin.

"I don't have time. You need to watch Jacob. This place is under attack. Gabe, you're a good shot, right? We could probably use you."

The young man looked up at me as if I'd just sprouted undead breasts that sprayed rotten milk over the room.

"Fine. Whatever. I don't have time to convince you. Just please watch Jacob for me Echo."

After I was assured my precious child would

be safe, I took off, full-tilt, towards the command room. The alarm was still roaring its angry tune. I wanted to cover my ears, but needed my arms to move people out of the way.

People. Strange how I had yet to really notice the actual people here in the Underground City. I must have been so deeply lost in my own little world, my eyes were blind to the world around me. Too bad there wasn't time to offer up hugs and handshakes to every survivor.

When I finally reached the command center, Jamal was busy discussing the strategy with Morgan and Josh. When Jamal caught sight of me, he immediately seemed to relax.

"Bethany, I need you to listen to something."

Jamal went to a small console and moved a slider to the half-way point. The sound that greeted my ears was a mixture of the familiar and unfamiliar. But no matter how much of the sound I knew, the sound I didn't know carried with it a level of disturbing I had never experienced.

"What is that?"

The sound was a random rattling mixed in with a strange, discordant noise of the undead.

"When I show you the video that goes along with this sound, you'll wish like hell you could erase it from your mind." Jamal warned.

Morgan stepped over to a television monitor. "My men in San Antonio reported similar iterations of the zombie species." Morgan flipped on a flat screen monitor. Jamal was right. I immediately wanted to poke out my mind's eye for ever glimpsing what I saw.

Bone covered zombies. The undead with an exoskeleton. Every inch of the beasts was covered. Hundreds of the hulking monsters were heading directly toward the underground city.

"How did this happen? The armoring?" Morgan's voice was a fearful whisper.

"This isn't mother nature's own evolution. My guess is the Zero Day Collective had a hand in this change. I saw worse mutations when I was being held captive by the bastards. You can't imagine what the ZDC is capable of."

But I certainly could. I'd witnessed, far too often, what contemptible acts human beings were capable of. This new modification of the undead? Child's play.

It was Josh's turn to raise the hand of concern. "How do they know we're here?"

Jamal stood and, in his reply, offered a bit more information about what he'd accomplished so far. "I'm fairly certain it's the mass of people collected here in the city. The zombies must be smelling or hearing us."

The word *mass* certainly piqued my interest. "Just how many people are down here Jamal?"

Jamal looked at me with a tilted, quizzical head. "I figured you would have already made the rounds or hacked a few accounts by now to have every piece of information you needed. Are you hacker slacking B?" The gentle smiled returned to Jamal's face. "There's just over five hundred survivors down here. You need to get out of your shell and look around. It's a real block party down in this bitch! And now baby – you's the DJ!"

Five hundred. I thought my days of living among that many were over.

"I hate to break up whatever it is you two have going on there, but we have a large amount of bone-covered zombies heading our way. If we don't stop them before they reach us, this block party might be called on account of death." Morgan brought Jamal and I back to reality.

Immediately, everyone at the table went silent. Eyes cast shadows of doubt and fear across the table at one another.

"What kind of weaponry are we looking at?" Josh was the first to speak.

"Oh we're loaded for Armageddon. I planned this city to include a fully stocked bar and armory."

"Jamal, we can't pop out of the streets with guns a blazin'. We make that much noise and there'll be more than bone-armored zombies to deal with. We'll wind up with the entire undead population of the state of Washington on our hands."

We had two clear choices in this situation – lead or scare the bastards away.

"There is one noise we can make that will solve our problem."

Everyone at the table looked at me as if I were crazy. Before I could voice the answer to the unasked question, a dirty grin spread across Jamal's face.

"B, you are brilliant beyond my wildest, sexual fantasy. What all do you need to piece together an Obliterator?"

I wrote down the list of hardware for Jamal to hunt down. He promised he'd have it all prepped and ready for me to work on within minutes. I should have been surprised by his one eighty on the Obliterator – but the armored zombies served as major game changer. While Jamal went hunting, I remained in command central to explain to the remaining soldiers of the new world freedom just what an Obliterator was.

"Jacob Plummer discovered the primary reason the undead were cracking open the skulls of the living was because of a high-pitched, oscillating sound. That sound was a side effect of the Mengele Virus and the only way to stop it was to tear out the brain. And, before you ask, yes they thought they were actually helping the living. It's crazy, I know. Together, he and I discovered the exact pitch and oscillation of the noise and were able to reproduce it. When the undead hear the sound it's like fingernails on a chalkboard, post apocalyptic style. The sound either sends 'em running away or cracking their heads on the pavement to silence the noise. What I plan on doing is setting up a device, an Obliterator, to create that deadly music. We'll amplify the sound, place it outside the entryways to the underground city, and drive those bastards as far away as we can. Every zombie within ear shot will shit their pants and run like frightened children."

Morgan and Josh tossed blank looks my way. Their eyes were filled with doubt that a simple sound could repel the undead.

"Trust me, this works."

I wasn't about to sit at the table and argue what I knew to be fact. I had too much work to do and not nearly enough time to get it done. I wanted to be ready for Jamal as soon as he returned with what I needed. After clearing off the command central war table, I began the process of gathering the tools necessary to build the newest iteration of the Obliterator. Fortunately, I had the specs memorized, so there was no need for me to retreat to the nearest computer to bring up the blueprints. I could build these bitches in my sleep.

What I did need was tools. I assumed Jamal wouldn't try to build his very own city without a stockpile of tools. My assumption proved correct. After very little digging, I uncovered a veritable shop-class filled with every tool imaginable. By the time I returned to command central, Jamal was there with everything necessary to build one Hell of an Obliterator.

"Check these out B. Loudspeakers capable of Manowar-level decibels."

I got Jamal's reference. One of the man's secret passions was heavy metal. Manowar was his favorite, probably due to their speaker-ripping blend of chainsaw guitars and D&D references.

He was correct, at least in theory. The loudspeakers he produced were certainly capable of ear-drum splitting levels. We wouldn't need that much power. So long as the drivers could produce the necessary frequencies, the hardware wouldn't need to cause the entire block to tell us to *turn it down*.

"What do you want to do with your life?" Jamal smiled.

"I wanna rock."

My reply had Jamal smiling and nodding his head. It's nice to know, even in the middle of the apocalypse, some things will never change.

"Plus ça change, plus c'est la même chose."

"B, you know I love it when you speak *Rush* to me. Oh wait, that's French. Even hotter."

Once upon a time, we stopped ourselves just before *the* moment. On top of the Henry Vogt school of Comp Sci building. Had it not been for the blaring of a fire alarm calling us down from the roof, our lives probably would have been completely different. Of course, that singular moment in time wouldn't have stopped the Zero Day Collective, but it certainly ensured enough romantic tension to always somehow pull us together.

"So," Jamal broke the moment building between us. "What's up with your fellow travelers? Brother and sister?"

I wasn't sure where J-Tiz was heading with his line of questioning. I didn't want to think, for a second, the man had developed some strange YA fetish and was about to go all Twi-hard on me. I gave Jamal *the look*.

"Wait. No! Fuck no! Come on B, you know me better than that."

One thing so marvelous about having such a tight connection with another soul – the ability to almost read each other's mind. Jamal and I had always been so good at finishing one another's sentences, thoughts, code ... everything. In some ways, we were like a creepy pair of twins from any given clichéd horror film.

"I just mean ... where'd you find them? Small talk, girl! Get with the program."

As I filled him in on Echo and Gabe, two things hit me: One – I never really learned much about Gabe. Two – I entrusted the most precious cargo on the planet to a rogue teen girl and young man I knew nothing about. And the last time I saw them, they were caught up on a hormone tsunami.

"Oh fuck, Jamal. I left Jacob with those two. I'll be – "

Jamal stopped me before I took off. He was pointing toward the exit of the room. When I turned, Echo was standing in the doorway holding Jacob's bassinet.

"He wouldn't stop crying. I figured he wanted his mom."

It was clear Echo had joined Jacob in the tear-fest. I ran to her, took the bassinet, and held Echo's face gently in my hand.

"Echo, what's wrong? Did Gabe—"

"He didn't hurt me. But when Jacob wouldn't stop crying, Gabe got all weird and said he had to leave."

Echo wrapped her arms around me and the flood gates opened. I wasn't sure what was happening. Had her hormones taken over and kicked logic to the curb? It didn't feel that way. I knew well the siren sounds of the hormonal teen and this was not it.

"What's wrong Echo. You can talk to me."

The young girl pulled back and looked up at me. Her eyes were salty fountains flooding the landscape of flesh below.

"It's crazy. But, just hearing Jacob cry for you made me realize what I'd missed out on. I've done my best to convince myself that I'm not afraid – but I am. And until you came along, I had no one. Now I'm afraid of losing you."

The surprisingly strong arms wrapped around me once more. I mistakenly glanced over at Jamal who was Cheshire-grinning from here to Wonderland. I held out the bassinet to Jamal who immediately picked up on the message and grabbed Jacob from me. With both arms now free, I returned a solid embrace to Echo.

"Echo – with what I know, and what I've survived, I don't think you have to worry about losing me. You stick with me and everything will be okay."

God, I hated making promises. It seemed every time I made a promise bad things happened. Especially to young girls. But how could I not? If for any other reason than to honor the memory of Susan. I had to protect this young girl.

"Promise?" Echo's eyes nearly sucked me into a game of hormone twister.

"Promise."

And there it was. The word of doom spoken. I may as well pinky swear and go all rom com sisterhood and swear we'd be double-dating as soon as I ended the apocalypse.

Good God what has become of me? I was a hard-core hacker with a streak of punk as strong as my monthly desire for chocolate. Yet here I am, the second time in a year I've been overly protective of a young girl.

"Echo, I need you to do me a favor. I have to build a device to protect our new little world here. Can you hang out with us? Keep me and Jacob company for a while?"

She had no idea the plan was to keep her here so I could watch out for her. The girl was riding a roller coaster of emotion. There was no way I'd let her out of my sight now.

The twinkle in Echo's eye was all the answer I needed.

"So, what are you building?" Echo grabbed Jacob from Jamal and sat down, cross-legged, on the floor.

I explained, in lay-girls terms, how the Obliterator came about and how it was built. There was no small sadness in knowing the retelling of Jacob's story was getting easier and easier. Maybe seeing Jamal again made that possible. Or maybe the apocalypse simply healed all wounds to the heart faster. Was that a sign love would become a thing of the past? I couldn't imagine the human race surviving without the effect of Cupid's mad-bastard arrow.

Fuck. Listen to me? Up until the last year, my life was ruled by ones and zeros. Love was nothing more than this intangible collection of endorphins and hormones acting as neuromodulators for the brain. Like everything else, love could be broken down by science. But I've let that prime directive slip by me. I lied to my own core system of beliefs and tenets.

The lies keep piling up.

"So what does the Obliterator sound like? Will it hurt if I hear it?"

It was nice to see Echo take such an interest in what I was doing. Everything shared with her from this moment on would go a long way to ensure her survival.

"Nothing more than an annoyance to you and me. But to the undead, it's like Fran Dresher's voice through a megaphone crafted from the larynx of Gilbert Gottfried. You won't believe their reactions. They'll run away crying to their zombie mommies."

Echo laughed. I couldn't remember the last time I heard a young girl laugh from the gut and the heart. It was refreshing. My arms wanted to reach out, pull her to me, and never let her go.

God, I almost *rickrolled* myself. The apocalypse is truly and unmistakably dry-humping me from every angle.

"It's ready for a test. I'll keep the volume low so it doesn't hurt your ears in this small room. Ready?"

Echo put her hands to her ears and nodded.

"One. Two. Three!"

The too-familiar, high-pitched oscillating sound jumped from the loudspeaker and punched me in the gut. The volume was much higher than I expected. Echo looked at me with a furrowed brow and yelled.

"I thought you said it wouldn't hurt. You must have an incredibly high tolerance to pain!"

I eased the volume back down to a less painful level, just loud enough that we could hear it and still talk at normal decibels.

"Is that the sound? That's what causes the undead to crap their diapers?"

"The very sound. I've heard it so many times I can almost produce it myself. This beautiful music will keep those monsters from storming our castle."

Before I could shut the sound off, Jamal was at my side.

"Do you have the numbers for the sound coded into a usable API I could add to my Watcher program?"

"You're still watching Buffy reruns aren't you? You always had a thing for blonds."

"Oh ho! And Bethany drops the B-bomb on me. Girl, you know my needle always points to red. Always has and always will."

Echo's laugh instantly turned Jamal a deep shade of embarrassed. Like catching your parents making out in front of the TV.

"And where's that needle pointing now?"

We all had a good laugh, which was cut short by the entrance of Morgan.

"Guys, I hate to interrupt the pajama party, but the bone-zombies are getting really close."

I turned the sound of the obliterator back up to inform Morgan we were ready. And with that, Jamal set out to send a crew outside to hang the loudspeakers above all the entryway doors. Once the loudspeakers were plugged into the system, all we had to do was fire up the software.

Jamal and I shared a desk with two computers. We had a bit of coding and compiling to do – which would take us all of ten minutes. We were both so accustomed to one another's style, it never took us any amount of time to combine efforts (or code).

"Damn B, your code is almost as sexy as you."

Blush. I could feel it. Within the span of, what, thirty minutes I experienced more firsts than I had in years.

"So does that sound have to play all the time?" Echo reminded us she was there – and also reminded us to use our age-appropriate voices.

Fuck.

"Actually Echo, we've combined Bethany's alarm with my zombie recognition software to create a system that would only turn the noise up if zombies are spotted. That way we don't have to hear that sound playing twenty-four seven. Otherwise, we'd probably all lose our minds."

Jamal flashed his big, toothy smile at Echo. Had the girl been over eighteen she'd be little more than a puddle of moist. Jamal had that way with the girls. Echo thankfully tossed him back an innocent smile. The girl was immune to Jamal's charm. Lucky thing. Without so much as a flinch, Echo grabbed Jacob's bassinet and informed me she was going to head back to her room for a little quiet time with her favorite little human.

What in the Hell would I do without my babysitter?

The sound of a voice cracked out of a radio. The last of the loudspeakers was mounted and hot. Jamal grabbed the radio and called back.

"We'll run a test. I want everyone to report in as soon as you hear the sound." Jamal turned to me. "B, would you do the honors?"

I ran the command for the test program, *obliterator --testmode*. Shortly after I hit the Enter key to execute the command, the reports poured in. One hundred percent success rate. Now that we knew all speakers were in working order, I issued the command to start the software in Watcher mode. Now all we could do was sit back and wait for the undead to arrive. If everything worked as planned, the zombie horde would be instantly turned away, bearing insufferable pain.

CHAPTER 23

November 25, 2016 6:21 AM
Unknown location, Zero Day Collective: Zombie
Collection Unit

The drop-ship returned with its third load of undead cargo. This time, the awaiting officer in charge had different orders.

"Prep the ship for drop-off. We're dumping an undead payload in San Antonio, Texas."

The pilot of the ship titled his head, unsure of what was going on. "I was told – "

"Do I look like I give a damn what you were told? Pilot, you are to pack the belly of that ship with zombies and fly it to the coordinates transmitted to your flight deck. Are you incapable of doing your duty? If you are, I can have you dismissed and relieved immediately? I don't think I need to tell you what happens to soldiers who have been relieved of duty from the Zero Day Collective."

The soldier stood at rigid attention. "No sir! You do not sir!"

The barked response echoed off the metal walls of the hanger.

"I want you in the air as soon as possible."

The commander turned and marched off. No more information was offered. None was necessary. The pilot did not need to know anything about the mission other than what his cargo was and where it was going.

Everyone knew the process for getting the

zombies onto the drop ship. Without something to entice the undead into the belly of the metal beast, the monsters would either stand and sway, or tear one another limb from limb. The only route to success was with living flesh.

While the pilot was out gathering up the last payload, another soldier was tasked with collecting a few desperate civilians to serve as the proverbial dangling carrot. The civilians were told only that they would be fed – just not that they would be fed *to* something.

The civilians were brought out in chains, and forced up into the drop ship. Their desperate screams and pleadings rattled the belly of the machine. The cries of anguish over-powered the sounds of the shackles being locked to the back wall of the drop ship.

The ground soldier stepped out of the ship and stowed himself away, surrounded by the thick steel walls of the control room. The Moaners and Screamers would never breach the walls of control; it simply wasn't possible.

"Release the hounds!" The pilot laughed as he slammed his open palm onto the giant red button to release over one hundred Moaners and Screamers onto innocent victims. When the call of the undead echoed off the inside of the drop ship, the pleas from the humans rose once again. Cries for help were immediately overpowered by the ripping of flesh and breaking of bone.

Death.

"Hit it Roscoe!" The pilot called out to the foot soldier, who then took his turn to slam his open palm onto another switch; one that closed the doors to the drop ship, sealing the beasts within.

"Locked and loaded."

As the door to the drop ship roared to life, the undead continued on with their reverse Darwinian buffet. When the heavy metal door sealed out light and sound, the pilot kicked the engines up to speed and the ship began its journey down the short runway.

"This is Air Romero calling base. I'm in flight and bound for San Antonio, will report back when the package has been delivered."

The pilot cut off communication and took a quick glance at the intended coordinates. He knew the area and knew landing was going to be as much of a *fuck off and die* as was taking off. With a three hour flight ahead of him, the best he could do was relax and enjoy the peace. At the moment nothing could touch him – it was just him and the bluest sky he'd ever seen.

And a plane full of zombies.

CHAPTER 24

November 25, 2016 10:45 AM
Zombie Response Team: San Antonio Unit

"Samuel to Koenig. We're coming in hot with a transport full of survivors. We're going to need a medical team at entryway three. Have a full surgical unit prepped; we have a couple of fairly serious wounds."

The Lieutenant didn't bother to wait for a response. He knew the pat answer that would follow – bring them in and head back out. That seemed to be their entire MO now – survivor sweeps. It was becoming quite clear they were to cover the entire seventy square miles of the metropolitan city, until all survivors had been moved into New San A. Thank God the transport had an MP3 jack – otherwise, navigating at speeds of twenty-five miles per hour would quickly grow suicidal-tiresome.

The transport pulled up to the dock and began the unloading process.

That was when Hell decided to stop by for a visit.

It all began with a deep rumbling sound, almost like a distant thundering herd of cattle running. When the all-too familiar lowing and moaning sound tickled the tympanic membranes of the ZRT soldiers, everyone knew what was coming. An undead swarm was about to wreck the party.

A silent alarm sounded. In place of the

usual klaxon was a pulsing red light, informing anyone in the know the undead were closing in. It was action stations and go time for all packing and able to use.

"Koenig to Samuel. SITREP."

Lieutenant Samuel did his best to gather all the necessary intel to give his commander a full report. Unfortunately, all he knew was that a mass of the undead were closing in. That, of course, was good enough to order every man he had to *Arm for Harm*.

When the orders were given, to the untrained eye, it would seem chaos had infected the headquarters. Those in the know, however, would be witnessing a danger ballet so beautiful in its execution, it would steal the breath of even the hardest hearted of drill instructors. The scrambling sounds of chaos lasted all of ten minutes. Once the dust had settled, every soldier had a gun trained on the swirling cloud of dust just within eyesight.

The whirling Hell-dervish drew ever closer. The sound was filled with dissonant undertones, disturbing beyond any imagination. All soldiers knew the drill; no firing until given orders. Wasting ammunition was a new cardinal sin in the religion of realism. All soldiers held their shot and their breath.

The size of the dust cloud being kicked up meant a horde. A horde meant many bullets would fly. Many bullets could easily translate to many a missed shot. No one needed a Vin diagram for that eventuality.

"What kind do you think we'll be up against

sir?"

Lieutenant Samuel looked down at Corporal Beaner, the youngest of all his men. The young man's weapon was shaking.

Samuel lifted his binoculars toward the sandy cloud. The news to report wasn't good and wouldn't ease the young Corporal's mind one bit.

"Judging from the height and density of the cloud, I'm guessing we're going up against Moaners and Screamers."

"But no Boners?"

The nickname for the bone-armored zombies was tragic, but no one seemed to think the undead would mind. The name also tempered the fear instilled by the new flavor of fear mongers.

"I can't say. Let's just concentrate on getting your first shot off. Remember, steady breath makes steady aim."

Samuel patted Beaner on the shoulder. The act seemed to bolster the kid's confidence enough to keep him from wetting himself with fear.

The binoculars eased back up to Samuel's eyes, only to see the oncoming swarm of monsters well enough to know he and his men were swimming deep in the waters of trouble. There were no Moaners in the horde – this was nothing but Screamers and Boners. The situation jumped instantly to Defcon 1. The pistol was cocked. Nuclear war was imminent. All just metaphor for *Oh shit!*

The Lieutenant brought his radio to his lips. Everything seemed to slow down around him.

This was a moment he never wanted to see happen – a fight to the end. Only one side would come out victorious. Samuel had to do everything in his power to make sure the spoils of this war was not brain-pan soup.

"All soldiers prepare to open fire on my mark."

Judgment day came in all shapes and sizes.

"Soldiers ready."

Every soldier and civilian knew death longed to crack open their skulls and dine on the sweet meat within

"Soldiers aim."

The apocalypse was hungry.

"Fire!"

The heavy metal popcorn brought New San A to life. The collective trigger finger of the ZRT danced across the metal of the gun. Bullet after bullet sailed through the spans between barrel and beast.

"They're not going down sir!" Beaner cried out.

"Keep firing soldier. You don't stop until either you or those bastards are dead. You hear me?"

"Yes sir!"

Beaner continued rattling his death-dealer at the oncoming monsters. Still, the dust cloud marched toward the city. Eventually flailing arms could be seen, just above the nearly six foot high wall of flying dirt and flesh. The way the arms moved clearly indicated Screamers. Scattered within the pale, rotten fleshy arm meat was the tragic site of hardened bone.

Samuel trained soldiers and soldiers never

left their post. Even when the beast of beasts was revealed among the bringers of pain and suffering, not one man budged. All weapons continued to heat up the air. Slowly but surely, the number of zombies dwindled – at least the Screamers. As for the Boners, the bullets bounced and popped off their exoskeletons, only serving to piss them off even more.

The scratchy, metallic screeching of the Boners cracked through the air, raising the arm hair and fear level of the soldiers. Lieutenant Samuel's radio lit up with voices.

"Sir, they aren't going down!"

"Sir, what are we going to do?"

"Sir, should we retreat?"

They may as well have been lobbing Nerf bullets at the zombies. With little thought on the matter, Samuel opted to go with a few rounds of the heavy artillery. It was standard operating procedure to avoid using anything louder than a machine gun. Samuel switched his radio to simultaneously broadcast to all listening channels; he wanted to be sure no soldier missed his message.

"Break out the heavy metal. I want anything larger than M82s to open fire."

The rattling of machine gun fire evolved into a deeper, deadlier tone. The cloud of dust rose higher. The monsters continued onward.

Suddenly, the death dealers were upon the New San A Zombie Response Team. The sounds of large caliber machine guns were replaced by cries and gasps for help. Those cries went unanswered. One by one the soldiers were robbed of limb, life, and lobe.

With a single crunch of bone-covered forearm, the Boners gained access to the brains of the men.

Zombie crack.

One of the Boners spotted the Lieutenant and rushed toward him; his rotted eyes locked onto his next meal. Before Samuel was peeled open, he managed to contact the ZRT leaders to inform them the city had been breached and destroyed.

The triumphant roaring and slurping echoed into the phone and through the streets and alleys of New San A. The Texas City protectorate had perished and a new Hell-spawn army had arrived to wipe clean the slate of man.

CHAPTER 25

November 25, 2016 12:01 PM
Seattle, Washington Underground City

"We've been compromised. Hundreds of them; all Screamers and Boners. I have no idea where they came from. All of my men are down. I repeat, all of my men are down. There's a new type of undead. They seem to be wearing—"

The horrific screech of the monsters nearly blew the tiny smart phone speaker out of its casing. Morgan sat the phone down in front of her and dropped her head. Tears plipped and plopped onto the glass front of the smart phone.

"They're dead. All of them. How did this happen? How did all of those monsters find their way to my men?"

I didn't want to speak, to confess the answer to the question. The attack had to have been my fault. Hundreds of the undead had to have been the work of the Zero Day Collective and I led them to San Antonio. Me. There were two clear paths for me to follow. I could lie and keep Morgan and Josh oblivious to my connection with the event, or I could confess and ensure truth is the driving force behind every action taken. Lies on top of lies on top of lies. The discord of untruth had already grown so thick, it was impossible to know how long it would be before we'd reclaim any semblance of honesty. I'd much prefer my baby grow up in a world that was founded in honesty. The shit sandwich was already too steamy and too thick. I had to find a much higher road.

"This was all my fault." My voice was undercut with a guilt anyone should be able to pick up on. "I led the ZDC to San Antonio. I planted a false trail that would misdirect them away from us. I assumed there would be enough fire power in San Antonio to fend off an attack."

Josh immediately grabbed Morgan to control her. Blood rose to her cheeks and forehead in a hot rush of rage.

"You were wrong!" Morgan's words shot out of her mouth with a contrail of angry spittle. "Now my men are dead. All of them!"

"She couldn't know what would happen, Morgan." Josh's deep southern voice caressed the air in an attempt to calm the ferocious woman in his grasp.

"What right did you have? You led those bastards straight to them!"

Tears flowed down Morgan's mottled cheeks. Guilt flowed through my veins.

"What the fuck?" Jamal jumped in, hopefully to save my ass. "It's the apocalypse, we're all in danger at every damn second of every day. Bethany did what she did to save herself, her baby, and this underground city. I'm very sorry about your men, but I'm not sorry B didn't lead the ZDC here. I highly recommend you two get over your anger and your guilt respectively."

How Jamal knew what was pounding my conscience didn't surprise me. The man could read me like he could read a line of PHP code. After his outburst, the room went silent. Josh released Morgan from his beefy grasp and everyone took a deep breath.

Morgan sat at the table and glared for a moment. The tears finally dried up and her breathing returned to normal. How long before she pulled out a knife and sliced my throat? Hopefully Morgan would get busy enough to forget what had happened. I could only hope. Eventually she pulled a US map front and center. "Josh, we need to split up Austin and retake San A."

"Why don't we move Austin and Houston both to New San A. The facilities at San A are superior and it's better armed. With the amount of men we'd be moving from those other cities, they could surely take out a horde of zombies."

It was nice to see them at work. We all needed to focus on the task at hand. That task? Securing our safe haven. With the barrage of horrors from all angles, I lost track of what it was I was doing. My sense of direction and focus was lost. But with the realization came a crystal clarity I hadn't had for a while.

"Jamal. Did you have any luck finding a chemist or biologist?"

Before Jamal could answer, Morgan stood and with wide, excited eyes, addressed the question.

"We have a chemist in Portland. We could get him here in three or four hours."

I gave Morgan the go head on the chemist.

She and Josh dismissed themselves from the room, leaving Jamal and I alone.

"Thank you for saving my ass." My head found its way to Jamal's shoulder.

"You owe me one."

"Actually I think I owe you like five. How exactly do you plan on collecting that payment?"

I didn't even have to glance at the man do know his smile nearly ripped the cheeks from his face.

"You are a bad, evil man Jamal T."

"You make me that way Bethany N."

Our eyes locked onto one another, the end result was all too obvious. Just before our lips made contact, a high pitched scream tore the mood asunder. The voice was Echo's.

"Bethany!"

The sound of my name sent shudders of cold shock through my system. When Echo rushed into the room, the look in her eyes threatened to force me to my knees.

"They're gone. Bethany. Jacob and Gabe are gone! I laid down to take a nap. Jacob's bassinet was on the bed next to me. When I woke he was gone. I ran to Gabe's room to see if he had Jacob, only he wasn't there. I've looked everywhere. Bethany, I'm so sorry! What do we do?"

My heart took a nose dive into the well of my gut. How could I have been such a fool to trust a man and a young girl I had only just met.

"Fuck!"

The word ripped out of my throat and

echoed off the walls.

Jamal ran to a desk and grabbed a radio.

"We have a breech in security. A young man in jeans and a black sweatshirt, carrying a bassinet. Stop him at all costs, but do not, I repeat, do not harm the infant. This man must not be allowed to reach the surface."

Jamal clipped the radio onto his back pocket, grabbed a pistol, and reached for the door. Before his hand could turn the door knob, he turned to me. "Bethany, I promise you I will bring Jacob back.

I wasn't about to sit back and wait it out while Jacob was being carried off. When Jamal tried to stop me, I shook my head. The look in my eyes clearly communicated my intention, because Jamal held the door open and nodded me through.

"You want a weapon?"

"You have extras?"

"You don't know the half of it."

Jamal's words were assuring – especially after he handed me a Glock 9MM pistol. He didn't even bother to ask if I could 'Handle a weapon'. He knew better.

My feet met the floor of the hall at a sprint. I had no idea where I was going, but I assumed neither did Gabe. Jamal's shoes violently slapped the floor of the underground city behind me.

The obvious plan would be to run to what was Gabe's room and then branch off from there. Certainly there had to be some method to the man's madness. But then, how could there be method when he clearly had no idea the precious cargo he carried. Unless.

Just as I reached Gabe's room, the radio in Jamal's pocket crackled to life.

"The male has been spotted. He reached the ground level and was picked up by a black sedan. We couldn't get a clean shot. He's gone."

The pronouncement dropped me to my knees, the flood of tears polka-dotting the ground below me, even before I could suck in air and release a wail.

"Get a team together and track that car down. Find them and return that baby, no matter the cost. Is that clear?" Jamal barked.

"Yes sir."

The radio went silent. I did not.

"No! Oh God no! My baby."

I felt an arm around me and assumed it to be Jamal's. He spoke, but his words didn't register. The only sound I could hear was that of my cries and my heart and breath catching in my throat.

"Did you ... oh no!" The guilt-ridden voice of Echo made itself known.

"What are we going to do?"I could hear the words, but no meaning registered.

"Jacob!"

My legs lifted me from the ground and carried me swiftly forward. I had no idea what I was doing – anything but nothing. There was no way I could do nothing – not when my baby was most likely being carried back into the arms of the Zero Day Collective.

I came to an exit and flung the door open. Daylight stung my eyes. Silence deafened my ears. Somehow I expected, like a bad

Hollywood movie, to step outside and see the black sedan just pulling away. For the first time that I could remember, I wanted my life to be produced by Hollywood – to know that, in the end, my baby would find his way back into my arms. Unfortunately the apocalypse wasn't that kind.

"Bethany!"

Before my brain could register the warning, the Screamer was on me, knocking me hard to the ground. The crash landing knocked the wind from my lungs, but not the gun from my hand. The zombie had my head in his cold, fetid grasp before I could muster up the consciousness to take aim. The beast had me pinned to the ground, his heavy body seated on my gut, nearly stopping all breath from entering my lungs.

Crack!

The beast smacked my head onto the hard ground.

Crack!

Stars and sparks danced in my field of vision.

Crack!

My vision started to tunnel.

The monster let loose a raging roar. It had to know how close it was to dining on a brain-feast fit for a zombie king.

The next sound was that of a large-caliber weapon, followed by the wet thunk of a body hitting the ground. The stars in my vision remained, but the weight of the zombie was gone.

"Bethany! Are you okay?"

Everything fizzled.
"She looks like..."

CHAPTER 26

November 25, 2016 6:22 PM
Seattle, Washington Underground City

"Jamal, she's waking up."

The near-whisper of Echo's comforting voice pulled me out of the worst headache-laden sleep of my life.

"Jacob!" Reality sucker punched me in the heart when I realized what had happened. "We have to get out and find him."

"Morgan already has every Zombie Response Team on alert. If they spot him they will do everything they can."

"No. I have to be out there. I'm Jacob's mother. Do you understand how important that baby is to me and to this fucking planet?" My throat hurt. My gut hurt worse.

Jamal came to my side. The look on his face was as readable as it always was – he had a logic bomb to drop on me.

"It's too late for any of us to go up top in a desperate attempt to search for something when we have no idea what we're looking for. Did Gabe remain in the car, or did he get transferred to a helicopter, or did he drop Jacob off at the car and leave on foot? Besides, Bethany, that's not what you do best. You're not a fighter, you're a thinker. The best chance you have of recovering your child is to use your best weapon – your brain. And the last time you went up top, you were almost taken down by one of those armored zombies. Thankfully, a large caliber bullet, fired at close range, managed to make its way through the exoskeleton. Those things are bad ass by the way!"

"Jamal, you know—"

Jamal silenced me with a gentle, warm palm to the cheek.

"B. I'd do anything for you. If I thought I had a chance to go out there and bring Jacob back in I would do it. But we already have hundreds of people on the lookout. So what we need to do is concentrate our efforts in the best way we know how."

He was right. As much as the swelling ache in my heart wanted to contradict every word he uttered, Jamal was dead on. It would be foolish of me to think I could chase down the Zero Day Collective on my own. And who knew what kind of head start they had and which direction they went. If Jacob was to be found, I'd have to launch my own flavor of search and rescue mission.

I swung my legs out of from under the bed sheets. My bare feet hit the cold, stone floor.

"B. what are you doing? I thought I made myself clear."

"I have an idea Jamal," was all I needed to say. My cohort in many a crime immediately caught the hacker-twinkle in my eyes. He didn't smile as he normally would when he spotted said gleam. I respected that restrain. Now was not the time for smiles.

I pulled my Doc Martins on and pointed my feet towards the broadcast studio. My laptop was in there and that computer had everything I needed at the moment.

"You gonna fill me in B-Zip?" Jamal fell into pace at my side.

"Simple. I'm going to cobble together a script that will collect every transmission and every communication that has occurred within the last week and in real time. That script will then search the collected data for anything pertaining to the Zero Day Collective, Jacob, Gabe, me, our location, and anything else I might deem pertinent to the situation. When the script finds something it will alert me and I will then alert whichever Zombie Response Team is in the target area."

We walked a few paces in silence. I could tell Jamal was mulling over my plan. He'd have an opinion any moment. His opinion would probably be filled with Devil's Advocacy. Was I breaking countless laws? Yes. Did I give two shits about breaking those laws? Hell no. All I cared about was locating my baby and I would do any goddamn thing under the sun to make that happen.

"It's perfect." Jamal shocked me with his decidedly positive statement about a plan that had no testing, no theory, and no moral compass. "It's clearly our best chance of locating your son."

Jamal followed me back to the studio.

"I'd ask if you needed any help, but I already know the answer. It's not like I had any insight to offer for the task at hand. You are the script master, if I recall."

Jamal flashed me a bright, hopeful smile.

He really was doing everything he could to make me feel better about losing my child. I wanted to tell him the gesture was, at the moment, pointless and for him to save it for when I had Jacob back in my arms. Instead, I smiled back at him and fired up my favorite text editor on my laptop.

"Actually, there is something you can do for me Jamal."

"Anything."

Jamal's enthusiasm was a blessing.

"It won't be easy."

"Nothing ever is where you're involved." A wink followed the slam, lessening the blow.

"I need back doors into all the major phone carriers. Can you get them for me? Preferably in the form of ports twenty-one, twenty-two, or five hundred thirteen. One of those three is bound to be open just enough so that I can get through to sniff their data stream. I get the back doors pieced in with a little shell magic and we'll have a continuous flow of information that can be sorted through. If the ZDC had any communication with our friend Gabe, we'll know and can act accordingly."

"*Accordingly,* meaning find the fucker and take him down?"

Jamal grinned his most evil of grins. I wish I had it in me to return the look.

"I've really missed working with you Bethany. I've never in my life known someone that could look so lovely hunched over a computer keyboard hacking out code like you. It's the most pure and beautiful art I've ever seen."

For a brief moment I thought about diving headfirst into that pool of reminiscing, but the code held a stronger sway. When I glanced Jamal's way, he immediately saw the story in my eyes.

"I'm sorry B – I don't mean to—"

"It's okay Jamal. Really. I can't tell you how much I appreciate what you're doing. Let's focus on getting this up and running and then we'll talk about the past, present, and future. I promise." My words mingled with the sounds of two keyboards ticking and tacking away. It was like old times. Memories of Jamal and I hacking away into the wee hours in graduate school, racing against the clock to finish a final coding project. Too much Mountain Dew and too little romance. That was all blown out of the water as soon as the code compiled. While the other über nerds were celebrating with video games and Battlestar Galactica marathons, Jamal and I were ripping one another's clothes off.

"Done. I have your back doors and I've already worked them into an API for you. All you have to do is link and compile." Jamal handed me a flash drive served up with the most adorable of smiles.

God, how can my heart feel anything but broken right now? I wanted to cry again. Rage out against every machine I could find until my inner Hulk had smashed all signs of civilization. Nothing was fair at the moment. Everything sucked. And even still – there was Jamal, that man I called mine for a brief period. He could wrap his arms around me and

I'd forget everything. Or so I wished.

"Done. Now, let's hope this bitch works."

I saved the script with the name *save_my_baby.sh*, copied it over to the server, gave it executable permission, and ran it. I had a second terminal window open, running the tail command on the output file of the script. At first the tail was empty, but after a moment, text began flying by. The script was working.

"We did it! It's collecting data from every phone provider in the country. AT&T, Verizon, Sprint ... they're all there. Now I just have to sit back and wait for the regular expressions to work their magic and send me the alerts."

Jamal came to me and gave me that hug he knew I needed. All I could do was breathe in the moment, take in the oh so brief peace his embrace brought.

"By the way, the Zombie Sensing Obliterator, aka ZSO, is now operational. It wasn't working when you went up top because we failed to load the main application. Newbie mistake. I blame it on the apocalypse. That'll never happen again. But this area is pretty much surrounded by the undead just out of ear shot. We're safe, but we're not going anywhere for the time being."

As the embrace lingered, a rather odd thought bubbled to the top of my mind. "How big did you say this underground city is?"

When Jamal pulled away, the look on his face was curiosity making love to trepidation. "It's roughly thirty-five or so square blocks. It's not that huge, but there are plenty of tunnels that intersect and finger out. Why do you ask?"

"Just a hunch, but how do we know Gabe escaped? How do we know it was him getting into that car? Isn't it possible he's just down here somewhere, waiting to be picked up by the ZDC? My baby could still be here."

Before I could continue on, Jamal had me by the shoulders and stared deep into my eyes.

"B. I've had every man and woman I trust scour this place. He's not here. The possibility of—"

I stopped his logical train of thought before it could leave the station of his mind.

"No. I refuse. Knowing what's out there and him having the encumbrance of an infant, it is possible he could still be down here. You could have missed him."

Desperation had crept into my voice. I didn't want to admit it, but it was there. Before I could swan dive into that black abyss, a stranger's voice broke through the building fog.

"I was told you were looking for me."

The voice belonged to a wisp of a man, easily in his sixties, skin like hot cocoa, wearing an adorable old-man cardigan, baggy pants, an odd sort of drivers cap, and a very misplaced twinkle in his eyes.

"Oh my God! I completely forgot. Bethany, this is Dr. Theo Amos Williams. He's the chemist from Portland.

The impish man came to me, arms extended, with the biggest, brightest smile I'd seen in over a year.

"Dear God in heaven, I am so honored to be in your presence Miss Nitshimi. What you have done has been nothing short of miraculous."

And he hugged me. Out of nowhere, the smiling chemist wrapped his arms around me and embraced me in that way only older people can pull off. It was charming, touching – but a bit misplaced.

"I'm sorry Dr. Williams, but the only thing I've managed to do is lose what might possibly be the human race's only salvation."

Theo looked at me with the cocked head of a curious spaniel. "I don't follow."

"Jacob was taken from me."

I brought the doctor up to speed on the entire situation. When I finished my tale, he wasn't nearly as convinced as I that all was lost.

"The miracle that coursed through that baby's blood was made one with your own. Although no blood would have passed through the placenta, if that baby was born with the infection, you would have shared that infection. If the baby was born immune, more than likely, that immunity was passed on to you. Bethany, you are as your child. If there is a cure to be had, we can get it from within you." Theo proclaimed with finality.

The idea that I shared Jacob's miracle hadn't been part of the equation. It was too easy to assume there was something genuinely unique about him, or there was something just shy of fictional to his very existence. I fully understood the biology; mother and fetus do not share blood, but there are certain gases and trace elements that migrate back and forth. It wouldn't be entirely out of the realm of the possible that whatever it was that gave

Jacob his immunity could have transferred into my system.

There was something gnawing away at me. Something angry that wanted to hurt someone.

"If you think, for a second, I have or will give up on finding my son, you are sorely mistaken. Anyone that gets in my way of finding him will witness a wrath unlike any they have experienced."

Jamal came to me with his big eyes and bigger smile. "B. no one is going to try to stop you from finding Jacob. Dr. Williams only wants to work with you to find a cure as quickly as possible. If that means we use you as the prime catalyst for the work, then so be it. Whatever the cost, right?"

My dearest cohort in crime just had to pull our old motto out of his ass and drop it on the floor in front of me. Jamal knew I couldn't resist the old tried and true. It was a phrase we came up with back in school, in the middle of the night while trying to complete one of the single most crucial assignments we'd been given to date. Over and over we tried to get the code to compile, but to no avail. It wasn't until we decided we'd do whatever it took to succeed with the work and wound up bringing in a third party to get an outside perspective. It worked. Of the ninety-seven students in the class, we were the only two to get the code to work. We both graduated at the top of our classes. For all intent and purpose, we were Gods among men.

Jamal was right to drop that bomb on me. This had to succeed. The cure for the Mengele

Virus was beyond me, beyond Jacob, beyond everyone.

Just as I was about to toss down another barrage of verbiage to ensure everyone involved knew the primary objective was the return of Jacob, my phone went off. It wasn't a call – it was an email. The script was throwing out hits on the search strings.

"Shit Jamal." Was all I got out of my mouth before I took off running toward the studio. From my laptop I could access the dump file and search it for anything that might give us a clue as to what the Hell had happened.

I could hear the slap of Jamal's Chuck Taylor's on the cement floor behind me. He was too gangly and awkward to be quick. Typical nerd. I, on the other hand, had the speed of survival on my side. The third-party sounds of Dr. Williams could not be heard. Good boy for staying behind. I'd have to make a note-to-self memo and chat with the man later – if we all survived this horror-fest.

As soon as I reached the studio, I threw myself down behind the desk, logged into the laptop and accessed the file. The file was huge. I had expected a few hits here and there. What I got was nearly ten megs of data on a flat-text file. Thousands of lines to search would take any normal human hours to go through. I, on the other hand, had the power of regular expressions and bash scripting on my side. After a brief moment of cobbling, I had a script ready to sift through the information and leave behind only the bits and pieces that would aid in our search. The resultant file was short enough for both Jamal and I to sift through together.

"Here's a communication from someone named Faddig to a Koenig, ordering him to send enough undead soldiers to San Antonio to..." Jamal's voice trailed off into some black abyss of fear.

"What is it Jamal?"

Silence. The only other time Jamal was ever rendered silent was when he heard Firefly was being canceled. That was almost ten years ago.

"B., The Zero Day Collective only sent enough of the undead to Texas to make you think they were off track."

Another rousing round of silence.

"What?"

"They knew all along where you were and where you were going. They ... fuck. Fuck!"

"Please Jamal, what is it?"

Jamal turned and stared hard at me. The look in his eyes was clear – I wasn't going to like what he had to say.

"Gabe. He was in constant contact with them. He was a fucking plant! And he led them —"

Before Jamal could finish his sentence, the roaring and banging began. It was a sound all too familiar to me. It was a symphony of chaos that forced its way into my psyche in Munich. That horrific noise once again appeared to claim its prize.

"Why is the Obliterator not going off? I thought you said you started the program. Jamal, you said—"

"I know. I did. I started it. I swear!"

The poor man was in hysterics. And why shouldn't he be. His Fortress of Solitude had been found and the hand of evil was banging at the door.

Clang, clang, clang went the zombie.

"Bethany, what do we do? What if they get in? How will we defend ourselves?"

I had forgotten the average nerd's experience with combat ended at the gaming console. Most nerds would be lost in real mortal combat. Add the undead to the mixture and the nerd herd were nothing more than pant-shitting, thumb-sucking, babies. Fortunately, they had me on their side. Since the apocalypse hit, I sort of became the anti-nerd hero.

"We need weapons. Well, you need a weapon. I need to get into a bag in my room and grab my pike. What do you have down here that can serve as your own personal wrecking ball?"

"Are you kidding? We have an armory down here. I managed to stockpile every sort of weapon of undead destruction you can imagine."

Jamal took off with me close behind. The pounding grew ever more relentless. The monsters knew we were here and they wanted to say 'hello'. My guide took a sharp right turn and then an almost immediate left. Jamal was showing a grace and athleticism I'd never seen from him before.

When we finally reached the armory, Jamal stood in the center of the room, arms wide open, spinning in circles to bask in the glory of what seemed like an infinite collection of security blankets.

"Grab yourself a silent but deadly and we'll go kick some zombie ass."

Jamal gestured to the stockpile of various and sundry deadly weapons, most of which fell into the too-loud category for zombie combat.

"We need stealth on our side. Grab something sharp and pointy and let's go. I need to get back to my room."

And that's exactly what we did. Jamal opted for a Klingon-like sword that had clearly been sharpened by a master. The song it sang as it sliced through the air was vicious. As soon as we made it back to my room, the first thing I laid eyes on was the blanket I had used to wrap up Jacob. Memory slammed me in the chest. Had it not been for the pressing matter of life and death at hand, I probably would have succumbed to the weight of sorrow. Instead, my fingers jabbed into my bag and pulled out the collapsed pike that had served me so well. In seconds I had the lethal pole extended to its fullest and ready to do my best Faster Zombie Cat, Kill, Kill!

"Please tell me your plan doesn't involve tracking these things down and getting up close and personal." Jamal's tremulous voice reminded me he wasn't a superhero.

"That's my plan exactly. Now, you're either with me—"

"Don't say it B. Don't even say it."

I didn't say it. In fact, all I did was take off into the halls, leading with my zombie skewer. As we slowly and quietly made our way through the halls, it dawned on me just how creepy this underground city was. Hollywood couldn't have chosen a better location for a haunt-fest. Dust kicked up with every step, there were cobwebs hanging from every location a human hadn't already passed through, doors creaked with a pained effort. This had to be some sort of sick twisted joke fate decided to play on me.

The screaming and odd roaring of the undead made it very clear this was not a joke.

"Holy shit Bethany, I think—"

Another roar confirmed what Jamal was about to cry out. The undead had come to play. The sounds of reckless abandon filled the halls. That sound was soon followed by the shrill cries of human lives being extinguished. I hadn't managed to get around to visiting the entire underground city to introduce myself to its inhabitants. Looks like I'd never get that chance. Few humans could stand up to Screamers and survive.

Another scream set the molecules around my head on fire. Accompanying the familiar screech of Screamers was that same odd roaring I heard a second ago. That sound actually made the hell-born noise from the Screamer seem like music from a merry go round.

"I don't want to recognize that other sound Jamal." I had to voice my fear before it tore out my insides. "Can't we just pretend evolution didn't take the zombies on its Red Rover team?"

"Sorry B, those are Boners."

"And not the good kind right?" I tried to make light. I didn't work. Not with the crusty call of the undead demon lords spilling out all around us.

For a split second we thought about taking off. But the sound-proofing Jamal did to the sound booth made the room an ideal hideaway for us. After Jamal closed the door, even the call of the Circus of the Damned was sealed out.

"Jamal, please tell me you have the means to monitor this underground city from inside this room." I knew the answer to the question before I asked. I asked any way. Reassurance was a precious commodity these days.

Jamal huffed, as if I had just dropped the insult of insults at his feet, and sat down in front of one of the keyboards. After tapping a few simple commands, he had a window open that spanned two monitors. Inside the window rested eight smaller windows, each of which revealed the view of a strategically placed camera.

"There are actually thirty-two cameras. You can cycle through them with the Alt-Tab key combination."

Jamal stood and presented the workstation to me. There was something I had to do. In my panic to locate Jacob, I managed to let Echo fall into the cracks. I sat down in front of the pair of monitors and started cycling through the cameras. It didn't take long before I spotted Echo. She was in a room with Morgan, in what looked like a heated conversation. There was no sound with the image, so I could only assume what was happening.

"Jamal, I have to let her know where we are. If she—"

Before I could take in a breath to complete my next thought, Jamal had a microphone in his hand and was broadcasting a message.

"Echo and Morgan, will you please make your way to the recording studio as quickly as possible."

Jamal sat the mic down and looked to me for some sign of approval. "Hopefully the zombies haven't also evolved such that they can understand the English language. If so, well, we're fucked. If not – we celebrate the little things. What's the next move Cap'n?"

Next move? Was he serious? I had no next move. My next move was cowering in the corner until this all went away. Or at least it would have been – had the world not been counting on me to save its ass. So instead of doing what I'd really like to do, I had to come up with some sort of bad ass way to keep the monsters neatly swept under the bed. Unfortunately, the underneath portion of the bed was already jam packed with horror.

On the screen, both Echo and Morgan were clearing out of the room they were occupying. As they moved, I did my best to cycle through the monitors to track them.

"They're coming our way. It worked!"

And then it happened. Just as Echo and Morgan were about to turn the final corner that lead the home stretch of their journey to safety, irony pimp-slapped them across the face and planted a Screamer in their way.

"Oh fuck!" My voice leaped from my mouth and was sucked dry by the soundproofing on the walls.

I reached for the microphone to shout out some random, probably worthless, command to Echo, when the girl went Ninja-style commando. She dropped to a crouch and, when the zombie was near enough, leaped up and scissor kicked the undead monster's head into the crook of her right knee. When Echo went down, so too did the zombie; only when the zombie went down it was to the tune of a broken neck and severed spine. The Screamer lay, motionless, on the ground.

"How in the name of Kick Ass did she – " Jamal questioned anyone or anything that cared to hear.

"Homeless Ninjas." I muttered, knowing Jamal wouldn't understand the reference.

Both Echo and Morgan ran off again. I continued cycling through the monitors until the two of them were right outside our door. I swung the gateway to freedom open and gestured for the two ladies to enter. As soon as they were beyond the threshold, I had the door closed and locked.

"Where's Josh? Have you seen Josh?" Morgan was near hysterics.

I ran back to the monitors and started cycling through the cameras. The only moving bodies to be found belonged to the undead.

"Wait! Who's that?" Echo screamed and pointed over my shoulder at the fourth window in the second monitor.

There was a man walking slowly through

the hallway. He didn't have the gate of a zombie, but wasn't in panic mode like any rational human would be, given the circumstances. None of us, not even Jamal, recognized the man. When a pack of Screamers zoomed past the man, completely ignoring him, everyone in the room gasped.

"Did anyone else see..." Morgan whispered the very thought that was clanging and banging around in my skull.

The strange scene moved outside of the camera range, so I continued cycling through the camera feeds. No Josh. Morgan was visibly shaking. Tears welled in her lower eyelids. I knew that look and I knew the emotions behind that look.

Loss.

It had become my closest bedfellow over the last year. Loss seemed the only constant in my life and always reminded me how fleeting life and humanity were.

"What do we do if they find us?" Echo was crying. Crying was good, it meant the girl did know fear after all. Fear was, at least, some assurance the girl was alive, aware, and human.

She raised a good question. I had assumed the walking dead wouldn't be capable of finding something they couldn't possibly hear. That assumption was based on how much the standard zombie relied upon hearing. The one thing the Mengele Virus taught me was nothing could be counted upon. Now that zombies could sprout bone-hard armor, who's to say they couldn't regain their sense of sight back in full force?

Like a bolt of lightning, an idea hit me.

"Jamal, tell me this underground city has a public address system."

Judging from Jamal's grin, he knew exactly what I was planning and his answer to my question was a solid *yes*. He didn't even bother to grill me on my plan. Instead, Jamal simply walked over to a console, typed in a few commands, turned to me, and grinned.

"Their ears are yours. Take up the mic again and speak your commands. This feed is everywhere, not just the rooms."

He could read my mind. What more could a woman want?

I grabbed my trusty microphone, turned the volume to eleven, cleared my throat, and began speaking. At first I spoke little more than gibberish and non-sequiturs. Eventually, however, for whatever reason, I started reciting the Preamble to the US Constitution.

"We the People of the United States, in Order to form a more perfect Union, establish Justice, insure domestic Tranquility, provide for the common defense, promote the general Welfare, and secure the Blessings of Liberty to ourselves and our Posterity, do ordain and establish this Constitution for the United States of America."

The sound spilled out from everywhere and shook the walls. The glass of the room vibrated and nearly anything that wasn't bolted down rumbled to the floor in a massive collection of chaos. The monitors told a similar story, only instead of pencils, trinkets, and various implements of work, it was the undead that collected together to form a union with chaos and loss.

"Bethany, what's happening?" Echo was by my side, staring at the monitors.

"They follow the sound of my voice, but the sound just leads them to the next room with a loudspeaker."

I couldn't believe it was still so easy to confound the beasts. It was just like Munich and France – a simple sound to lead the monsters away and astray. But unlike Munich, Father Time and Mother Nature had a few tricks up their sleeves to help even the odds. Just as I thought my little plan a resounding hit, the hideous sight of the next phase of zombie evolution appeared on the monitor.

"Oh my God. Bethany, are you seeing what I'm seeing?" Jamal's whisper-thin voice surprised me from behind.

On monitor number three was the single most bizarre sight the apocalypse had yet to offer. The unknown man we'd spotted on the monitors earlier was standing in the center of a room, holding up a hand. Behind the man was a small collection of Boners – stopped and staring directly at the man's upheld hand. The mutant zombies seemed to be waiting for some sign to continue on. The be-suited man looked around, spoke into a phone, lowered his hand, and continued moving forward. As soon as the stranger began moving, the Boners followed suit.

"Is he—"Jamal started.

"Controlling them?" I continued. "It looks

so."

There was no way. The undead couldn't be controlled. Chaos wasn't made into anyone's bitch. Not the undead, not the Zero Day Collective, not even me. Chaos answered to no one.

"I don't like this. I don't like this one bit."

Before I could continue on, a phone chirped. It was Morgan's. With lightning-quick reaction, she answered.

"Josh? Oh my God! Are you okay? Please tell me you're okay. Where are you?" Morgan pulled the phone away from her mouth and looked our way. "He's still here. He said he's hiding in what looks like a laundry facility. We're in Bethany's recording studio. Can you make it here? Why not? Okay, just wait where you are. If you get a chance, try to make a break for us."

Morgan continued filling Josh in on our situation. It was becoming quite clear the two of them had much more than just a working relationship. By the time I realized that, I had a greater appreciation for the need to get Josh to us in one, uninfected piece. Besides, the man was large and we could use all the muscle we could get.

Problem. How in the Hell do we guide someone to us, when we seem to be little more than caged animals.

A raging hell storm of sound jerked me out of my thought. I had experienced a seemingly infinite chorus of Screamers and legions of Moaners; but nothing could compare to the soul-suffering sounds of what was running free in the halls of the underground city. At that moment, I would have given anything to be surrounded only by zombie 1.0. I could look the original in the sour-milk eye and know, with a certain level of authority, that I could survive the ordeal. What was waiting on the other side of sanity this time, I wasn't so sure.

"Oh my God!" Echo's voice pierced through my skin and straight to my nervous system. When I looked up, I realized why her voice threatened to crack the cloud and make it rain glass shards. Standing on the other side of the studio windows were three of the bone-armored zombies. The low rumble of rage shook the glass.

It was clear they knew we were inside the room, but the Boners made no effort to crash our secret party. Not a single rock-hard hand was raised in an effort to break down the barriers separating the *us* from the *them.*

Jamal's sweaty palm grabbed my forearm. "What are they doing Bethany?"

How could I answer that? I knew the world seemed to look to me as the single-most scholar on the zombie race. But I was not the zombie whisperer. I couldn't put my hand to the glass and mind-meld with the undead.

I could, however, pull one last trick out of my hat.

Very slowly I stood and backed over to the main console and sat in front of my laptop. With just a few keystrokes I was logged onto the machine that contained a sampled copy of the Obliterator sound. Using the secure copy command I had the MP3 file on my laptop and queued up for blast off. With every loudspeaker cranked up to levels that would make Motorhead proud, I spun up the file and forced it into playback mode on the broadcast console.

The beautiful hatred of the Obliterator poured out of every speaker in the underground city. As soon as the noise tunneled its way through the ear canals of the Boners, the beasts dropped to their knees to worship the great God pain. With the zombies mid-supplication, we could easily open the door and skip our way to freedom.

We could. But walking through a hallway filled with monsters born of nightmares wasn't exactly the easiest task for those not washed in the waters of heroics. During my time with Jacob Plummer, I pulled off such bravery. Jamal? Echo? Morgan? I wasn't sure if they were made from the same stuff.

"It's working Bethany!" Echo hurrayed.

"What happens next?" Jamal didn't surprise me with his questioning nature. "Does the noise eventually kill them? I mean, more than they already have been killed?"

The awkward sentence had an equally awkward answer – awkward in the fact that it wouldn't ease the situation in the slightest. Before I could voice said answer, a moment more bizarre than any I had witnessed to date occurred. The strange man we'd seen in the video feed walked through the madness in the hall and right up to the door to the broadcast room. It seemed everything just stopped – time, sound, the universe.

And then, he knocked on the door.

Knock, knock, knock.

As if he were nothing more than our next door neighbor coming to ask for a cup of sugar or invite us to a barbecue.

Everyone in the room exchanged looks.

Knock, knock, knock.

Before my brain could wrap itself around the situation and form any sort of conclusion, the door splintered at the handle and was forced open. The stranger stood in the doorway, his right arm extended out towards me.

"Phone for you Bethany Nitshimi." The voice from the stranger wasn't quite right. The words that spilled from the mouth were a chorus of various discordant monotones, but seemed without life. When my eyes finally focused on the face of the man, it became clear that nothing about him was right. He was dead – or, rather, undead. But unlike every member of the undead nation I had encountered, this one seemed to be sentient.

Great. Now evolution had handed us 'thinking zombies.' Within the breath of a moment, the tide shifted away from the humanity. The Zero Day Collective had my baby and the undead could think and speak.

We. Are. Fucked.

"Phone for you Bethany Nitshimi. This is your last warning." The stranger pulled out a gun and shot the laptop that was feeding the broadcast. The sound of the Obliterator was silenced. The Boners in the hall released a terrifying roar and stood. When they walked toward the room, the stranger held up a hand. The zombies froze in place.

"Take the phone or I release them." The monotone drone spoke slowly and pointedly.

I had no choice. Someone was obviously desperate to speak with me. I had a pretty good idea who that someone was. Or at least who that someone was with. I very carefully stood and crossed to the stranger. There was really no way of knowing exactly what I was dealing with, so caution wasn't something to be mocked.

When I grabbed the phone, the first thing I noticed was how cold the stranger's hand was; the second, how he smelled of ozone and fetid meat. With the phone in hand, I cautiously backed away. The collection of armored death soldiers behind the stranger sent a flood of chills through my system. If this monster released his dogs of war, we'd be human tartar in seconds.

Once I'd returned to the opposite side of the room, I put the phone to my ear and spoke one simple phrase based on nothing but assumption.

"What have you done with Jacob?"

I was met with a brief moment of silence. That silence was a clear indicator of calculation. The party on the other end of the line was weighing their options, trying to decide which hand played best in this game.

"The rumors of your brilliance were not exaggerated Miss Nitshimi." The voice had an accent – maybe Pakistani or Iraqi. I didn't remember any members of the Zero Day

Collective baring any resemblance to that portion of Asia. "I wonder, Miss Nitshimi, would Jacob grow up to be more like his mother or his father?"

A boiling rage shook me from my core. "I swear, if you so much as drain a single molecule from a single vein in my child's body you will regret the day you learned my name."

"Such unwavering confidence. I must say, Miss Nitshimi, you have never failed to impress me or the entire collective. When we set in motion the events of the Cleansing—"

"Do not hand me this bull shit about The Great Cleansing! You know damn good and well that was nothing more than a dog and pony show for your financial backers. You had much grander schemes in mind that would earn you financial returns no one dared dream about."

A light, low laugh spilled out of the phone's speaker.

"My, but you have done your research. But then, I would have expected nothing less."

The mockery undercutting the voice made me want to hurl the phone across the room and obliterate anything remotely connected to the Zero Day Collective.

"Why am I talking to you? What in the fuck do you want?"

"Miss Nitshimi, I have what I want. Your son. It's what you truly desire that I am concerned about."

If ever I was confused, now was that time. The ZDC cared about one thing and only one thing – their Endgame. It seemed I had been a part of that game from the beginning – or at least since Jacob and I conceived our son. The idea that this man actually cared about what I wanted was laughable.

"My guess is this – you want your son to remain alive. Am I correct?"

I couldn't answer. Of course I wanted my son alive; but I wanted him alive and in my care. How could I possibly say 'yes' to having my son alive when 'alive' meant being under the crushing grip of the ZDC?

"The question was not rhetorical Miss Nitshimi. Either you want your son alive or you do not. It's a simple question I would imagine any mother would have no qualm or quarrel answering."

"Of course I want my fucking son alive you son of a bitch!" My voice cracked with hatred. I so badly wanted the anger to carry through the phone and strangle the man at the other end.

"Then we can come to a very simple understanding. You do not attempt to rescue your son and he will remain alive. You do make such an attempt and I will be forced to tear your son apart, molecule by molecule, in the name of research. Do you understand Miss Nitshimi?"

A ten ton straw fell from the sky and crushed the camel's back. If there was one thing I knew, it was that the Zero Day Collective had to keep Jacob alive. Dead, my son was no good to them. The ZDC scientists had to know what made the boy special, what it was in his blood that made him immune. Alive he was a self-sustaining factory of

Mengele Cure. Dead he was but a few doses. It was time to call the bluff.

"Listen to me. The first thing I am going to do is wipe my ass with the little army you sent for me. Once I've done that I am going to find you and I am going to kill you in ways your sick, perverted mind could never possibly dream up. When I am done with you, I will make sure nothing of the Zero Day Collective remains. We took you down in Munich, France, and New York. That was just me and a handful of survivors. I now have a small nation of soldiers and followers on my side."

Just as I was about to drop a few more bombs on my new best friend, I heard the crack and ping of bullets and witnessed, one after another, as the Boners dropped to their final death. When Josh's over-stuffed body engulfed the doorway to the broadcast room, he smiled.

"To protect and sever!"

And with a couple of well-placed shots, the creeping stranger fell to the floor – his head to one side of the room and his body to another.

Morgan leaped up and ran to Josh. With her arms wrapped around his thick neck, she planted a kiss on his lips, putting to rest one of the questions I had filed in the back of my mind.

"I think the Underground is clean now. Unfortunately that includes living humans. We're all that's left." Josh spoke over Morgan's head.

I put the phone back to my ear, a sense of strength driving my words. "Did you hear that?

Your undead goon is down, along with his bone-covered body guards."

The line was dead. The ZDC had disconnected the call. Immediately I started paging through the phone's interface to find some record of the call. There was nothing. The phone had no log of either an outgoing or incoming call. A flurry of explicatives spewed from my mouth before I remembered the program I had running. The call contained enough of the search strings to be easily tracked.

With a purposeful fire under my ass, I hopped over to the desk, slid my now-defunct laptop to the side (the laptop that helped me break the Mengele Virus code – it belongs in a museum) and secure shell'd into the server running the script.

"B, I know that look. What kind of no-good are you up to?" Jamal nearly hopped across the room and landed at my side. Although he could be smooth as chocolate milk some times, grace was not his thing. So, when he landed, he nearly knocked me out of my chair.

"The phone call. It had to have been tracked by our script. If it was, we might find the source location of the call. I get that, I get Jacob back."

My fingers danced across the keyboard faster than they had in a long time. In seconds I had the console of the server up and was running the *grep* command on the dump files. It took no time for the search to come up with the location of the source call. Longitude 61.17 and latitude 150.02. Anchorage, Alaska.

"Jamal, what's special about Anchorage, Alaska?"

Jamal stared hard at me, as if he thought this was some sort of trick.

"It's the sixty-fourth largest city in the US as well as the northernmost major US city."

The dream machine was revving up. He'd start spewing facts faster than the human ear could comprehend any moment. Jamal was funny that way.

"Anchorage makes up almost forty percent of Alaska's entire population, has been named the All American City four times, and in 1867 a deal was brokered by William H. Seward to purchase Alaska from the Russians for seven point two million dollars."

Jamal was just winding up for the good stuff. He'd hit upon something useful any second.

"The city's seacoast is mostly treacherous mud flats, the average summer temperature is fifty-five to seventy-eight degrees and the average temperature is five to thirty degrees. The 2010 census estimated the population of Anchorage at over two hundred and ninety thousand people. Anchorage is home to one of the few Centers for Disease Control. Oh shit."

We had a winner. A big, fat, scary winner.

"You don't think?" Jamal's eyes were as big as pies when he stared deep into my soul in search of some hope that his train of thought was way off.

"I don't know. Those fuckers could be up to anything. We can't assume, we can only act."

When I turned to Morgan and Josh, they

immediately saw the seriousness in my eyes. Their Hallmark moment was officially destroyed and they were both all business.

"Tell me you have a Zombie Response Team in Alaska."

Morgan stood up straight and furrowed her brow. "We do. It's a small one, but we do."

"Contact them. Inform them the Zero Day Collective has arrived on their turf and they are to do everything in their power to hold them there."

Everyone stopped and looked at me as if I had just sprouted a pink Fu Manchu.

"We're going to Alaska." The words dribbled out of my mouth. And then it hit me. Like a sucker punch to the heart, I realized what was happening. My baby was really and truly gone. Before I knew it, the gravitational pull of the Earth tripled and I was on my knees weeping and wailing like...

Like a mother who'd just lost her son.

The whole world seemed to collapse in on me. Justice kicked me in the back, truth smacked me across the face, and righteousness took a leave of absence. All of this coalesced together in my gut and forced out the sound of despair.

My baby was gone.

My baby.

CHAPTER 27

November 26, 2016 3:05 AM
Seattle, Washington Underground City

I was swimming in a sea of blood. Floating within the murky, thick liquid were doll parts – like any given horror film of the early twenty first century. It was a Rob Zombie inbred cannibal fest and I was surely to become the main course. But before any toothless, backwoods, prophet could drag me out of the bloody milk, the sound of crying babies bombarded the air around me. The sound was as deafening as it was heartbreaking.

My legs and arms were exhausted. I wanted so badly to give in and let the dark depths below take me under for my final moment. The sounds of the baby refused to let me go. As I spun in circles, my head barely above water, the heads of the ruined dolls started to change. One by one the faces on the doll heads transformed into Jacob's. My baby. The cries mutated to the voice of Jacob and grew to ear-splitting levels. It seemed imminent that my very skull was going to shatter from the noise.

The mouths of the inanimate heads all opened freakishly wide and blood began spraying from the gaping holes. The fountains of blood raised the level of the ocean. Slowly the bloody water made its way over my head until I was completely submerged.

Drowning in the blood of my baby.

The crushing pressure of the bloody water threatened to cave in the bones of my skull.

When I woke from the nightmare I was alone, swimming in an ocean of darkness. There was no comfort, no hope. After a moment of cold sweat and heart palpitation, I managed to somehow calm down enough to not feel as if I were going to rip off my skin and set myself on fire.

"I'll find you Jacob." My voice whispered over and over until my brain was too tired to remain among the conscious.

CHAPTER 28

November 26, 2016 9:17 AM
Seattle, Washington Underground City

"Bethany! You okay babe?" Jamal greeted me with a wide grin and wider open arms. When those arms wrapped around me, every bit of horror briefly eased away.

"Bad news B." Echo ruined the moment.

"I can't take any more bad news. Please tell me this isn't about Jacob? Is he okay?"

When I looked around the room, it was instantly clear the bad news had nothing to do with Jacob.

"We're surrounded by Boners." Morgan spit out the phrase before Josh could poke her in the ribs and start giggling like a school boy.

"What? I'm sorry, it's funny. Boners! We're calling them Boners." All of a sudden, Josh looked like he belonged in some Hollywood bromance film. "Isn't there some strange irony to be found in calling a zombie a Boner?"

Everyone shook their head.

"You guys are no damn fun." Josh was instantly deflated.

For the briefest of moments, the drowning nightmare came back to me. It wasn't the blood or the sight of Jacob's ripping mouth that tugged at my conscience, but the noise.

"I have an idea." Before I realized it, the sentence escaped from between my lips. All eyes were on me. "Ultra Sonic Weapon."

Thankfully, Jamal and I always thought on some parallel wavelength. Like a too-close couple that always finished one another's thoughts, Jamal and I bore into one another's heads and knew the very through process that ebbed and flowed within.

"Bethany, that is brilliant." Jamal grinned.

Everyone else stared on in confusion.

Morgan raised her hand. "Mind filling the rest of us in on the brilliance?"

I let Jamal have the floor.

"An Ultra Sonic Weapon uses sound waves to injure, incapacitate, or kill a target. Bethany created one as the first line of defense against the undead."

"The Obliterator?" Echo chimed in.

"Exactly. Bethany's new idea, I believe, is to take this one step further and use sound to break through the exoskeletons of the zombies surrounding us. We already have the hardware in place. All we have to do is figure out the right decibel, frequency, and oscillation to ruin that dead man's party."

It was Josh's turn to question. "Can you do that? I mean, won't a sound that loud damage everything in the area?"

Josh had a point. But really, who cared? Nothing was safe from ruin now. The entire planet was little more than a massive heap of rubble. Wasteland was the new urban sprawl. Who gave two shits if Seattle fell to dust. I voiced that opinion and no one in the room seemed to object.

"So long as we are within the confines of the underground city, I don't think the sound will have any effect on us. Twenty feet of concrete and Earth has some fairly impressive sound dampening qualities." Jamal cleared up anyone's lingering fear that a sonic blast loud enough to crack through inch-thick bone armor would have any effect on those of us below ground.

"But what about survivors up top?" Echo's question ground us to a halt. "We can't just go blasting noise loud enough to kill without giving them fair warning. Right?"

The likelihood of there being survivors in the area was minuscule, but Echo was right. Since the Mengele Virus hit, I was in the business of saving the lives of the innocent. But this situation was a bowl full of tricky. I had a son to save and the only thing in my way of giving chase was a horde of bone-armored zombies. Instinct was tugging hard at my trigger finger.

"Simple. Before we blast the sound, we broadcast a warning. Duck and cover your ears bitches!" Jamal to the rescue.

Everyone agreed the plan was our only option. That meant one thing – Jamal and I had to get to work fast to geek out the numbers necessary to break through the undead barrier. We sent everyone else off on a search and recover mission. We had no way of knowing if there were other survivors here in the underground. There was also a need to gather provisions – food, water, weapons. *Always prepared!* Was the new motto of the undead nation.

Caught up in the restored silence of the

room, Jamal and I could do what we did best –
think.

"We're looking at anywhere from seven
hundred kilohertz to three point six megahertz"
Jamal looked up from his keyboard. "B., I
think we can do this."

A sigh escaped my lips. It wasn't
intentional. "We don't really have a choice."

My reply brought the room to an
uncomfortable silence. I didn't mean for my
words to seem so harsh, but there it was.

"I'm sorry Jamal. I didn't..."

Jamal smiled back at me. "No need to
apologize Bethany. I understand. We're all on
edge. You especially. But don't worry, we'll find
Jacob and kick the shit out of the Zero Day
Collective. Remember, you did it once before
and that was when they were at full strength."

Hearing Jacob's name again put my heart
in a vise and wrenched out every ounce of
blood and sorrow that remained. I wanted to
cry and die simultaneously. But if I was to
succeed in returning Jacob into my arms, I had
to refrain from falling apart. I was certain the
Zero Day Collective was depending upon me
donning my finest straight jacket fashion and
living my remaining days drooling in a padded
and stained corner of some forgotten lab. To
that notion I would have but one thing to say:

Fuck you!

Flowing thick through my veins was the
stuff of motherhood. And like a Brechtian
Mother Courage, I would have my child back at
any and all costs.

"You know what we need?" Jamal's voice

yanked me out of my inner turmoil.

"Jamal, if you say we need to run tests on one of the dead Boners, I'll kiss you on the face."

When Jamal's eyes lit up like a metal halide light, I instantly pulled him to me and laid the kiss that we'd both been patiently waiting for on his lips. I figured, what the hell. It was only a matter of time before I moved on from my recent tragedy, so why not take my present back to my past and march it all, hand in hand, into the future.

I pulled away. Jamal's eyes remained closed, the glow on his face was palpable. It was the first time, since we were all raped by Mengele, that I'd seen another human truly happy. All from a single kiss.

"I've been waiting for that since school." Jamal smiled. "You can't imagine what that means to me."

Truth be told, I could.

"Seriously, I'd love to sit here and fawn all over you, but maybe we'd be better served dragging a dead zombie in here and shattering the armor plating off his body with a little night music?"

My proclamation deflated Jamal just a bit. But we both knew the human race couldn't wait for a little hormone tête-à-tête. So we both exited the room in search of a Boner.

Had that thought passed through the space between our minds and infiltrated Jamal's inner circle of thought, we'd be incapacitated with laughter.

"Over there!" Jamal pointed to one of the

armor-clad zombies laying face-down in the hallway. Even dead the things were disturbing to behold. They were much larger than standard zombie fare – in both height and musculature.

"These things seem like they came straight out of Hell. How do you think they evolved so quickly?" I knew there was no way to answer the question, but I asked anyway.

"If I had to guess, I'd say it was similar to severe eczema. The skin cells mutated and reproduced at a rate so fast they built up a hard crust. Because of the mutation, the crust continued to build up and harden, until it formed the exoskeleton." Oddly enough, Jamal's explanation was as disturbing as anything I'd seen. It was also, most likely, dead on.

"You grab the head, I'll get the feet." I directed Jamal, hoping to distract him from lecture mode. The last thing I needed at the moment was information on zombie skin care.

We positioned ourselves at the polar ends of the stilled monster and each wrapped hands around the extremities. On a count of three we *heaved*, but didn't *ho.*

"This thing weighs a ton! And no, Jamal, I don't need you to tell me how much of an exaggeration that was."

"But—"

"A ton. Leave it at that. How in the Hell are we going to move this thing?"

Jamal raised a finger, as if to point to the light bulb that had just gone off over his head. He excused himself and stepped away for a moment, leaving me alone with the undead. How many times had I been face to face with this plague? I wanted to put my foot through the lead-like skull of the zombie. This thing that I stared down upon was the evolution of the death of man. There was some poetry in the moment that I didn't want to acknowledge.

Before my brain could send the order to my foot to crush, Jamal returned, wheeling a dolly in front of him. "Ta da!"

"Really? You want us to strap this thing to that and then wheel it to the lab? Seriously? Wouldn't it just be easier to bring the lab here? Besides, how are we going to test an ultra sonic weapon without blowing out our eardrums, our bowels, and possibly our brains?"

That stopped Jamal in his tracks.

"Well shit. I hadn't thought of that. Wait. We have the sound studio. The STC rating of those walls is seventy-five plus. You could fly an airplane through these halls and that broadcasting room would remain absolutely silent. We set up the testing area in the hall outside the room and you and I will be safe and sound within. I just have to repair the door."

And there was Jamal's *pat me on the back* grin. I had to hand it to the man – he was adorable when he was brilliant. And he was always brilliant.

"Shall we strap on a zombie?"

***

After Jamal had replaced the door to the studio, we grabbed the nearest Boner to be used for the experiment. The Boner we picked out was heavy. Really heavy. Clearly, the bulk was in the armor plating. Even when the thing's arm swung down, the shift in mass nearly took both me and Jamal down to the floor. We did eventually get the zombie strapped to the dolly and wheeled to our makeshift hallway laboratory. Jamal was finishing up the experiment as I went off in search of the others. There was no way we could set off this USW with the rest of our gang wandering around the underground city. The second the sonic waves reset the pressure in the air around their bodies, they'd be deaf, blind, and who knew what else.

So, it was best to locate everyone and wrangle them back into the broadcast booth. That is, if everyone would fit. Who knew how many survivors were hanging out with us in the underground. The only fact I had in my back pocket related to those small groups that went off in search of supplies. I had to be okay with the idea that they would be the only ones that would return with me. Of course if anyone else were to get picked up in the march back, I wouldn't complain – so long as they weren't either zombie or ZDC.

The underground city was a ghost town. The cold, hard floor was lined with the dead undead. Moaners, Screamers, and Boners alike covered the cracked floor. At times it was hard to get any semblance of footing. The idea of slipping and falling on top of one of the undead made me want to will myself into superhero status and fly out of this rotten existence.

Supergirl I was not.

CHAPTER 29

November 26, 2016 12:12 PM
Zombie Response Team: Anchorage Alaska
Unit

The snow fell silently. The heavy blanket of beauty made it nearly impossible to see beyond three feet. It was impossible to use hand signals to the team that surrounded the Center for Disease Control. Since radio chatter was nothing more than a death sentence, the team had to stay as close together as possible.

Breaking into the CDC was impossible – or would have been. Thankfully, one of the Anchorage police officers had not bought into the bribe offered up by the strange group that came in and took over. The bribe was little more than a handful of dollars and a bottle of whiskey. The purpose of the whiskey was obvious. But with nothing resembling commerce remaining on the planet, the dollars seemed a hollow, if not romantic, gesture. That same officer happily helped the Zombie Response Team into the CDC.

"Once inside, we go stealth and split into two-man teams." Captain Jeremy Stinson whispered. His rank was honorary – he never served a second in the military. Even without the training, leadership came naturally and his men followed him, rank and file.

A wind raked bitter cold against exposed skin. The Anchorage Zombie Response Team was tough. Alaska winter was tougher. The soldiers knew they had to get inside. The temperature was plummeting and would soon be below zero.

Thanks to the passed out police officer, the entrance to the CDC was not only unlocked, but unguarded.

"Candy from babies." Manuel Menolos prematurely bragged.

Charlie Sloan smacked Menolos on the back of the head. "You mean candy from pinatas?"

"Watch your face, Biscocho."

Stinson glared at the two men, who instantly dropped back to silence. "Ladies, do I have your permission to return to the mission? Or would you rather do each other's nails and maybe have a panty-clad pillow fight? Whatever you need, I'm here for you."

"I want everyone to file into that building in pairs. Cover every square inch until you find the target. As soon as contact is established, radio your position and stand tight. When the location of the target is known, everyone make their way in and prepare to fight. But remember, the target must make it out unharmed. Anyone shoot that baby and they answer to the entire human race. We cannot afford to fuck this one up people. Are you ready?"

Nods went around the group and the first of the men slipped into the cover of the unknown. Stinson was the last to enter. As soon as he crossed the threshold of the entrance, the door hissed shut behind him. The team was washed away in absolute darkness.

"Fuck!"

"What's going on?"

"I can't see shit!"

"Dios mio!"

And then, the sound of horror greeted the Zombie Response Team. At first it was just a single Screamer's voice ripping through the darkened halls. Joining that wretched noise was another, and then another, and another – until it was a Hell-born cacophony of death. The rattling echo of sound was disorienting. Unable to locate the source, it was impossible to know just where (or if) safety could be found.

"Anyone packing night vision?" Stinson demanded. "If you have it, wear it and lead us out of here."

"On it sir." It was Menolos. Always Faithful was his nickname and with good reason.

"Oh fuck!" Manuel screamed out.

"SITREP Menolos!" Stinson barked.

"Shit! They're surrounding us."

Without second thought, Stinson pulled his only rescue flare from his pocket and ignited it. He instantly wished he hadn't. There are certain situations where ignorance might well be bliss. This was one of those situations. The flare revealed the group of soldiers was in fact, surrounded by the undead. Useless, sour eyes stared on through the dark night. The monsters knew exactly where their target was and there was no obvious means of escape.

The thread of an idea began to wind its way through Stinson's brain.

The leader whispered. "Everyone pull out

your weapon and stand in a circle. Back to center and aim directly outward. As soon as you're in the circle, sound off. When I give the order, aim out and fire."

"But sir," the soldiers began to complain.

"I don't want to hear it. This is our only option. On my mark. Ready. And go!"

One by one, the soldiers announced they were in position. Stinson counted until his last man was in place and then he gave the order to fire.

The deafening sound of too many large-caliber weapons in a too small space rang out. The mechanical death rattle was quickly drowned out by the roaring of Screamers. Accompanying the noise was the strobe light flicker from the weapons, bringing yet another level of horror to the sight.

Without the benefit of constant light, aim was not a luxury the soldiers could afford. It was point, shoot, and hope.

Rattle and roar.

"They're not going down!" Menolos cried out.

"Aim higher!" Stinson replied. "For the head!"

Before a single barrel could raise an inch, a wall-shaking roar crashed through the building. The noise was part Jurassic Park, part Wolfman, part Exorcist. One by one the weapons went silent

"What the..."

Again the monstrous roar washed over the room. Unfortunately, for the soldiers, the current wave of undead paid no attention to what was behind door number three and continued marching inward. Before another shot was fired, the sound of cracking skull broke a brief silence.

"They're on us!" Menolos cried out.

CHAPTER 30

November 26, 2016 1:23 PM
Underground City Seattle, Washington

We managed to locate Echo, Morgan, and Josh. Everyone else had either perished or fled. Unfortunately, that meant my chemist was lost as well. I'd have to remember to hit Morgan up for a backup scientist later on. The thought felt cold on my conscience, but we lived in a state of *only the strong survive.* That did, however, make things simple. Not only could we all fit inside the recording studio for the testing, our chances of survival were far greater than had we corralled together an entire battalion of survivors.

After Jamal explained to everyone what we were doing, we sealed the door shut, and stared out the large inch-thick window. None of us really had any idea what would happen with the test. Theoretically we knew what should occur. But then again, both Jamal and I knew what everything should theoretically do. All things could be derived down to the most basic math equation. Problem was, once you boiled it down to the bare minimum, sifting out the meaning from the remains was often a challenge few could meet.

'Few' rarely included the likes of me and Jamal.

Jamal gave me *the look.* That look was special and would only be picked up by me. It meant *If this fails, it's been a pleasure knowing you.* When my eyes caught Jamal's, a deep sadness threatened to pull the carpet from under my feet. My brain and my heart were overcome with the idea that, should this test go tits-up, I wasn't in any way, shape, or form capable of losing yet another love. If fate was going to give us the ol' reach around, it damn well better grab me first.

"Everyone ready for this? I highly recommend letting your jaw hang open, just in case the change in pressure is higher than I've calculated. Wouldn't want anyone going painfully deaf." Jamal grinned and hunched over a keyboard to tap out a few commands. Finally he held up one finger that pointed straight down toward the keyboard. This was it. Go time!

Jamal handed out precautionary ear plugs and insisted we wear them. He received no resistance. Once our ear canals were sufficiently plugged, Jamal tapped out the final command sequence on the keyboard and hit Enter.

We waited. Seconds ticked by and nothing seemed to happen. My entire body was rigid with anticipation. Any moment the exoskeleton of the zombie would shatter and we'd have our latest, greatest defense against the impossible.

Still we waited. Jamal looked over at me, a concerned look creasing his face. He shrugged and reached to pull out his ear plugs.

And then it hit. At first it was a build up of pressure in the air – like reaching the apex of a flight. But the pressure didn't stop at ear popping. The windows in the room bulged inward and my eye balls felt as if they were being crushed.

As soon as the pressure began to normalize, a wall of sound punished us. Our bodies unloaded contents of either bowel or gut. No one was immune. I was lucky enough to be one of the pukers. Jamal wasn't so lucky. Had I not been caught up in wave after wave of nausea, I might have laughed at the sight of him when he realized what had happened.

When the wave passed, and our insides normalize, we felt another pop. This time the feeling was slight and somewhat distant. I immediately ran to the window.

It worked. The Boner's armor had shattered, the pieces laying on the table or dropping to the floor. The beast's vulnerable body lay prone, ready to be speared, axed, shot, chopped, burned, or piked.

I turned to Jamal and smiled. Understandably, he didn't join me in my celebration. He did, however, give me a thumbs up – all the while refusing to get within range of my sense of smell. The room stank of bile and shit. The second the thought crossed my brain, I nearly vomited a second time.

"It worked, Bethany. We have our weapon. It won't take much time to redirect the program to the external speakers. Unfortunately, we won't have any way to broadcast a warning to anyone. That means a lot of people could die."

Before I could pose a response, my cell phone rang. It made no sense – anyone that would call me was in the very room in which I stood. I never made it a point to give out my number to many people, and surely phone SPAM didn't cross the border between pre and post-apocalyptic America.

"Hello?" I answered anyway. From the tiny speaker on the smart phone, the too-familiar sounds of cries for help spilled out. The pleas were followed by another familiar sound – the roaring of Screamers and death. Finally, a voice. The same East Indian voice from before. The same smug, self-righteousness.

"Do you hear that Bethany? That is the sound of lies. Did you really think we were going to make it that easy on you? Just broadcast the location of Jacob for the entire world to know? The Zero Day Collective is no longer that ignorant. In fact, you could say we're as smart, if not smarter than you."

"Where is my baby? He's innocent. Leave him—"

Menacing laughter poured from the phone. "Oh my dear girl – innocence is extinct. Didn't you know that? The second the Mengele Virus was released, mankind kissed any hope of an innocent soul goodbye. Lies are the new dollar and judging by the collection you have been amassing, you my dear woman are the richest human alive. What say we have a little trade – a truth for a truth. Would that make you feel better Bethany? I'll even go first. Do we have a deal?"

The line went silent. For a second I worried the man ended the call for fear of being traced. When I heard him take an impatient breath, I realized he was simply waiting for my answer.

"Deal," was all I said.

"Very good. Truth: So long as you don't do anything foolish, Jacob will not be harmed."

"Is that a threat or a promise?"

Another round of laughter, only this time it was sans the menace.

"Bethany, my dear, as the name of the game implies – that was truth and no more. Now, your turn."

I couldn't do this. I was about ready to break down. Besides, what truth did I have to offer? Of course, I know what the arrogant son of a bitch was digging for. He wanted me to promise I wouldn't come after Jacob. There was no way in Hell that was going to happen. I had fought too hard and come too far to give up on rescuing my baby from becoming some apocalyptic experiment. Regardless of what flowed through Jacob's veins, he was my baby.

"Tick tock, Bethany."

I looked over to Jamal and pointed to my phone, hoping he'd understand I wanted him to try and trace the line. As soon as he sat down at a keyboard, I knew he got the message. The call had already gone on long enough for a trace, but since Jamal was only now jumping on, I'd have to keep the man going for a while.

"How do I know you're being honest?"

Silence.

"You don't."

Silence.

"Wait, you already handed that truth over to me during our last conversation. If you want me to play along, you better own up to something new."

"Well played, Miss Nitshimi." Another pause. "How is this for a truth? Should you not do as I say, your baby will wind up in liquid form. Now, if you don't mind Bethany, I do believe you owe me a truth."

My mind raced around for some nugget to hand off to the man to appease him. As the plug was pulled on the drain of my thoughts, only one idea continued spiraling down.

"I don't trust you."

"Nor should you Miss Nitshimi. After all, it was the Zero Day Collective, the group for which I work, that caused this nightmare to unfold. We ruined your life, we stole the man you were in love with, and now we have your child. How could you possibly trust us? Very good. At least I know you are honest."

Jamal was waving to me. When I looked over he was giving me the thumbs up. We had a location. The game of cat and mouse was done.

"I have another truth for you. So long as you don't do anything foolish, I will allow you to live. I'm done speaking with you. The next time you hear my voice, it will be the last voice you ever hear."

And with the tap of a smart-phone button, I managed to retain my edge. Yes, my baby was out of my hands, but he was alive and, as far as I understood, safe. So long as I did nothing foolish, Jacob would remain alive. Of course, the big variable is *foolish*. Who gets to define the terms? Well, that was a simple question to answer – The Zero Day Collective. I assumed by *foolish* the man meant me not attempting a rescue mission. That being the case, I'd have to figure out a way to covertly remove Jacob from the care and feeding of the ZDC.

"Good news, bad news, and good news. Which do you want first?" Jamal half-smiled. "Never mind, that's a stupid question that doesn't really apply to this situation, based on the relativity of—"

"Jamal, the news," I begged.

"I have the man's location. He's on a plane. I have all pertinent flight information."

There was one thing Jamal overlooked. It was the apocalypse and the old-world rules no longer applied. Planes didn't have to register flight plans or gain permission to land. There were no longer no-fly zones. Chaos had its way with the human race and it's every man, woman, child, and monster for themselves.

When I explained this to Jamal, he had a plan. Jamal always had a plan—it was part of his charm.

"We can have the Zombie Response Teams on the lookout at every major airport. They spot a plane landing, they check the fuselage for the identification number. If any team spots the aircraft in question, they radio it in and we're on them."

Back to the issue at hand. Our underground city was still surrounded by Boners. Even if we did get an ID on the plane, we couldn't go anywhere, at least not until we break through this first line of defense.

"How long will it take to get the sonic weapon ready Jamal?"

Before I could complete my question, Jamal was tapping furiously at a keyboard. When he looked up at me, the sinister grin on his face gave me all the answer I need.

"Fire it up baby!"

Jamal stood. He was in lecture mode – I could always tell.

"I don't know how well protected we will be underground. What I am about to unleash will be Man O War compared to the Celine Dion we just experienced." Jamal immediately knew none of us got the reference. "Decibels. Man O War holds the record for the loudest decibel level for a live concert, whereas ... oh never mind. It's going to be extremely loud and I can't be certain there will be no ill effect down here. I will set the device off with us in this room, which will further shield us from the sound."

Jamal and I tossed knowing glances toward one another. Untested experimentation was all fun and games in graduate school; but the real world, even a post-apocalyptic world, was no place to play mad scientist. Even so – what choice did we have?

Jamal stood behind the computer, his finger held aloft above the Enter key. I could hear my breathing and my heart pounding. The entire scene seemed to drop into an over-used, Hollywood slow-motion moment. Jamal's long, delicate finger moved centimeter by centimeter until the tip managed to compress the key to execution.

We held our breath. Not a heart did beat, or an eye did blink. All was perfectly silent. And then, a massive thump jarred the entire underground city. It was a single hit from a seismic tidal wave that threatened to tilt the Earth on its axis. The thump bounced us from the floor and tripped our feet from under us.

And that was it. No sirens, no screams, and no undead battle cry. This could easily become one of those life-defining moments. What could have possibly been our last chance was nowhere near a sure thing. Did it work or are we still surrounded by armored zombies?

Jamal sat down at the work station and began clicking and typing again.

"Our external cameras will tell us right away if..."

Jamal went silent. Something was wrong.

"What is it?" Echo's voice clearly indicated she understood all was not right in wonderland.

We all stood behind Jamal and stared on the monitor. Immediately I understood Jamal's silence. Although the weapon did exactly what it was supposed to do – shatter the exoskeletons on the Boners – it failed to rid us of the problem entirely. One by one, the zombies were standing back up. Yes they were shedding their bony skin, but they were still alive. All of them. We still had no way of escape.

Jamal stood and turned to address us. "Okay, we have plenty of firepower. If we all arm ourselves we can – ."

I stopped him cold.

"I'm sorry. I can't do that. I was privy to that scenario once before and it didn't end well. That time it was trained soldiers that went up against an undead army and none of them survived. If you think we have any chance, you're sorely mistaken. We need a plan that keeps us all alive – not something pulled out of a military-fantasy movie. We need reality."

"We need a tank," Echo said, almost jokingly.

"We have one. Sort of."

It was Josh's turn to surprise us. The man who spent most of his time in the background, waiting to lock and load, lobbed his gentle voice out into the room causing all heads to turn.

"Morgan and I arrived in our ZRT Truck – it's armored and stocked. If you're looking to plow through a line of zombies, it'll do the trick."

"Why didn't you..." I started to ask before I realized the only thing that mattered was that we had a way out. "Is this truck close?"

"Less than a block away." Morgan chimed in.

"Oh shit." Jamal's voice shattered the good vibe that was building.

"No more bad news Jamal. Please."

"I'm sorry Bethany, but our sonic blast shattered the drivers in the speakers. The Obliterator is off line. All of those zombies out there? The smell of our flesh? They'll be heading our way."

Josh wasted no time, grabbed the door, and nearly ripped it off its hinges. "Then if we're going to bail, we better bail now."

No one argued. We all took off running. Morgan insisted we make a pit stop at the armory in case we have to defend ourselves on our way to the truck. Smart girl. I insisted I stop and grab a backpack with a laptop, an aircard, and a copy of the *save_my_baby.sh* program. We'd need the ability to locate transmissions if we were going to be serious about tracking down the Zero Day Collective. Something I took very, very seriously.

At the armory, everyone but Echo and I grabbed guns. I had my pike in hand and I pulled out a bow and quiver of arrows for Echo. It seemed a bit cliché, but it made sense that a young girl would be less capable of killing a friendly with an arrow than a gun. Of course, I've seen the girl in action – there was probably little (if anything) to worry about.

We were ready to fight. All we had to do was make it to the truck alive.

Before we reached the door I asked Josh to make sure he had the keys. I wasn't about to let plot convenience theatre smack us upside the head with an *Oh shit, I can't find the keys!* moment.

We reached the door. Jamal hesitated, his hand on the handle. None of us were sure what was on the other side of the door. It could be freedom, it could be the end. Either way, we had to pull it open and go through, guns a blazin' or not.

When Jamal threw the door open, the cold afternoon air bit into our exposed skin and the sunlight made pinholes of our eyes.

The undead were not in the immediate vicinity. Lady luck would get a big kiss on the face later.

"This way." Josh whispered.

We took off after Josh. For a big guy, the man could haul ass. Of course it helped to light a fire under your feet when you knew there were hundreds of the undead coming your way. As we sprinted, our lungs were punished by the sharp, cold air and our ears were assaulted by the hate-filled sounds of the on-coming undead horde. Jamal was right – they knew exactly where we were, and they were un-dead set on cracking open our skulls.

"There's the truck!" Josh barked out.

And what a truck it was. Calling it a 'truck' was like calling a Hummer a car. This truck was an iron-clad, steel-belted, warrior machine with a large ZRT logo professionally painted on the doors. I was certain we'd all need step ladders to climb on board and the power of the Gods to get the beast moving.

We were a half-block away from the machine when the first wave of zombies came into view. As soon as they spotted us they each let loose a roar to rattle the timbers of the very city. Josh didn't lose a step as he released a shot to drop the first of the monsters.

Monsters was the only way to describe what we were seeing. Stripped of their armor, these zombies looked naked, their skin a translucent pinkish-brown color. But in their nakedness, there wasn't an ounce of vulnerability. There was only rage.

One of the beasts stopped to flex and roar. The muscles in the zombie's neck stretched as tight as aircraft wire, the facial structure threatened to break and shatter under the vicious strain. As the beast was posing, Echo leaped on top of an upturned car, knocked an arrow, and sent it flying straight into the skull of the zombie. The girl didn't even celebrate, she just hopped off the car and continued on toward the truck. Thanks to the apocalypse, even a tween could act professionally.

Josh was the first to the truck. He ran around opening all doors and finally jumped into the driver's seat. Morgan was next to reach the truck, and next to fire off a few shots. Her first two rounds were off, but her third managed to drop the nearest zombie. Morgan then climbed up on top of the truck and sat down behind a large-caliber gun mounted on a swivel.

"Hurry! Get in!" Morgan screamed out as she swung the monstrous weapon around to take aim at the approaching horde.

"You better cover your ears! This bitch is about to get ugly!" Morgan shouted before she unleashed the loudest barrage of hate I'd heard in a long while. The gun was almost deafening. I dared a glance up to Morgan who looked like she was screaming as she fought to control the weapon. Her screams went unheard. The only sound was war and this time, war *was* the answer.

Echo, Jamal, and I quickly crawled into the back seat of the truck. Josh reached across the passenger seat and pulled the final door closed. He pounded his meaty fist on the roof of the vehicle, fired up the engine, and punched the gas. The continued blasting from up top assured us that Morgan managed to remain on the roof. Had that not convinced us, the dropping of the undead would have. Morgan was a dead-eye shot.

"Oh fuck me sore." Josh's deep bass of a voice growled.

When I looked between the front seats and out the windshield, my heart leaped into my throat and bile threatened to spill between my teeth. Less than fifty yards ahead of us was a mass of naked zombies, flexing and roaring. The sight and sound was unnerving. Josh stopped the truck, opened the door, and stood up on the door frame to speak to Morgan. What he said was a mystery and he certainly wasn't about to take time to share with the rest of the class. Instead, he sat back down, closed the door, revved the engine a couple of times, and crushed the accelerator with his size twelve-ish shoe. As soon as the tires started spinning, the monster-truck gun started firing. One by one the zombies ahead of us dropped. It was a fairly simple calculation to conclude there would be no way Morgan could take out every one of the undead before the truck reached the crowd. That calculation could easily lend itself to the hypothesis that Josh planned on ramming the truck into (and hopefully through) the remaining zombies.

"Can Morgan hold on up there?" I shouted over the din of Hellfire.

Josh laughed. "Morgan's grip is rated at seven Gs. She'll be fine." Josh again gunned the engine to send the beast of a truck lurching forward. The mass of zombies flexed their muscles almost to snapping and took off running toward us.

It all came down to a game of undead chicken. Either one of us would flinch and dive off the path or we'd collide with such force that someone would go down. If I were prone to prayer, I'd have dropped to my knees and let loose a litany to shame the Tibetan Monks.

The sound of the gun changed to a deeper, throatier thump. Seconds after the first shot, I realized why it changed – Morgan was unleashing Hellfire grenades from a launcher. One by one the walking dead went up in flames. By the time the truck reached the crowd of zombies, every piece of meat was pre-charred. The collision scattered the ashes of the burning undead to the four corners. One more rev of the engine sent us through the dead-rover line and into the land of the free.

Or so we thought. Once beyond the first wave, a second wave of the undead made itself known. This time the monsters were the more familiar Moaners and Screamers. At least with that came a certain familiarity. Unfortunately that familiarity did us little good, considering the numbers.

"Holy fuck – there must be thousands of them!"

"And me without an Obliterator!"

Echo was right. And I was certain this rolling fortress didn't carry enough ammunition to take down this undead army.

"What do we do now?" I was surprised Jamal asked such a pedestrian question. Normally this was his time to shine – creating resolutions to situations where the odds seemed impossible. His brain worked in just that way. I had yet to see Jamal not rise up to the occasion of disproportionate odds. Certainly he was about to have an 'ah ha' moment wherein the resolution to our current *oh shit* would be forthcoming.

Nothing came. In fact, we all just stared ahead as the walking dead death machine inched closer and closer.

From the roof, Morgan began pounding. Apparently, Josh knew the precise pound as he scanned the cab of the truck.

"Hold on to your butts," Josh said just before punching the accelerator. The truck lurched forward with a monstrous jerk and was at deadly speeds within a heartbeat.

"What's the plan Josh?"

The man with the white-knuckle grip on the wheel didn't even glance my way as he spoke. "It's all Morgan. Three. Two. One."

The sound of Josh's voice was overtaken by the machine gun rattle from above. The fiery contrails of large-caliber bullets flew out from above as the truck of doom sped forward. The parade of death grew closer and closer.

"This is not happening. Seriously, this is not happening!" Jamal cried out, nearly covering his eyes.

"Fuck yeah this is happening! Those undead sons of bitches won't know what hit them." Josh whooped.

"Yeah, but we will." Echo replied, her point understood very clearly.

Jamal pulled his hands away and started taking in the situation. "Josh, this won't work."

From the mouth of the driver came laughter. Laughter. I had no idea humor could be found in such a situation.

"No seriously Josh, this will only end badly. But I have a plan."

Josh ignored Jamal's pleas. "Sorry guy, time for plans is over. Now's the time for action. Our action is to plow through the rank and file of the monsters in our way of freedom. If you don't like that plan, feel free to hit the ejector button attached to your seat." Josh laughed again. "I'm kidding! There are no ejector buttons."

"Josh, listen to me!" Again, Jamal appealed to the reason we all hoped Josh was capable of. "This is all about geometry. Sort of."

Jamal's statement had all our curiosities piqued.

"If you approach that line perpendicularly, and near the center, if the rank and file is more than one deep, you run the risk of getting engulfed once you run through the first line of defense. If, however, you approach at an angle, toward the outside of the line and away from the center, you'll break through and not have to worry about what's behind door number three."

Before Josh could utter a word, he jerked the wheel to the left, changing the course to a near perfect forty-five degree angle. And with what might have been one of the most wicked grins I had ever seen, Josh gave me a glance.

"No, seriously, hold on to your butts!"

As soon as Josh flipped a switch, something happened and the car jerked forward again, this time doing so with quite a bit of force. The engine wound up and the machine gun above ripped the air asunder with violence.

"This is still not an intelligent plan of action!" Jamal shouted above the voice of war around us as he grabbed his seat belt with all his might.

When the truck collided with the wall of zombies it felt as if a nuclear bomb detonated under us. The initial shock nearly snapped my neck in half and slammed the wind from my lungs. But to my shock, the truck continued moving. Jamal's theory was dead on. The trajectory was nearly perfect and we broke through the death march as if it weren't twenty deep. Jamal's theory, of course, didn't account for the flood of thick, lumpy, brown viscera. When the mass of undead were unsealed the truck was awash in their disgusting oil. The smell was far worse than the site. Zombie stench wormed its way into your system and rarely left. You could blow your nose and hose your sinuses down with every nettie pot in sight – death remained.

The collision didn't stop the zombies. Screamers peeled off the million zombie march and, with a scream to shame Jamie Lee Curtis, tore off in our direction.

From the roof, Machine Gun Morgan again slammed her foot down, indicating to Josh to haul ass. This time the hate-filled tattoo of machine gun fire ripped across the horizon behind us, tagging the undead – and every so often nailing them in the off button between their eyes. But their numbers continued after us. Even with the monster truck redlining, the Screamers weren't falling behind. Both Morgan and the truck's pistons continued firing full bore.

But then, something just short of miraculous happened. The Screamers behind us began thinning out their own heard in a maddening display of pure rage. When a Screamer would go down, another would pounce to tear the fallen to shreds, and then attempt to return to the chase. But before the attacker could gain any speed they were taken down by yet another member of the undead sprint to dinner. One by one the fallen fell. This nightmare would work in our favor. With a quick calculation, based on how quickly the zombie numbers were dwindling, and the relative speed of the truck, I realized all we'd have to do is remain just outside of the zombie's reach for about ten more miles, at which point the Screamers would be little more than rotting chunks of half-eaten flesh.

"Oh, fuck!" Josh glanced into his rear view and shouted. "One of those sons a bitches made it to us. The fucker is climbing up the back of the truck. Morgan can't use the gun at that range. She's not safe!"

As much as I hated it, that was Echo's cue. I gave her the nod and she pulled out her bow. I swallowed a melon-sized lump back down into my esophagus and she opened the door and carefully swung her leg out. My hand reached to her pant leg and grabbed tight. Echo looked down at me and smiled.

"I live for this stuff," was all the girl said

before she pulled herself out of the car and onto the roof.

I wanted to stand up through the window of the back door and watch; or at least give Echo a hand with a bullet through the face of the attacking zombie. That would be a mistake and I knew it. Echo was in full-on Ninja mode. If I surprised her and she fell to her death, it'd be Susan all over again. I couldn't lose another young girl. Susan was a broken promise to a dead lover. I made a vow to Echo and had the same heart-breaking need to protect her that I had with that young girl I pulled from the clutches of the mad man that started this wacky apocalypse. There was no way in hell I could look on to see Echo fall to the ground at sixty-plus miles per hour. She and I had this strange, unspoken bond. After surviving the horrors of the apocalypse together, it was easy to feel a closeness with another human being you might not have felt pre-Mengele.

Good thing the girl was always full of surprises. I couldn't see what was going on, but I could certainly hear. There was no pre-teen scream, no ear-splitting roar of victory from the undead. As soon as the machine gun ceased firing, and the zombie thumped off the back of the truck, an arrow protruding from its forehead, I knew Echo had succeeded. Next thing I knew, her Chuck Taylors descended from the roof and she lowered herself back into the seat with a grin to shame the Grinch.

"I am so bad ass. One shot and that Screamer was toast."

Echo was right, she was bad ass and I'd

make sure she never forgot it.

Morgan fired up the machine gun again and littered the road behind us with blistering shells. Her aim was erratic, which was odd considering Morgan had already proved herself an incredible shot. Even though the woman was sexy (in a nerd-tinted, fairy kinda way) she would still crush a man's nuts while batting her eyes and not breaking a sweat. I quickly realized the issue at hand was the pothole-filled road and not a wounded or otherwise fucked up Morgan.

The bumping, jumping, and ill-fired shots went on for a few miles. Eventually the zombies managed to snack their way to thinner numbers and the road below us grew smooth enough for Morgan to finish off the job. As soon as her shots starting hitting home, the undead army began to dwindle enough to assure us we would survive yet another day.

I watched out the window. Three. Two. One.

The last of the Screamers went down.

We made it.

Our tiny collection of survivors pulled out of what could have been the same nightmare I'd lived through too many times since this apocalypse said 'hello.' Granted we did enjoy the help of an undead civil war. Had it not been for the rage-fueled infighting among the monsters, we never would have made it.

Josh brought the truck to a slow stop. After he slammed the transmission into park he flung the door open, leaped out, and screamed Morgan's name. From up top Morgan squealed and laughed before she jumped down and wrapped her arms around Josh's thick neck.

And then they kissed. It was one of the sweetest visions I'd laid eyes on in a while. Their kiss reminded me that humanity hadn't dried up and died off. Life still existed. Humanity remained. No matter how hard the Zero Day Collective punched us in the gut, we'd rebound and swing our own mighty blow.

But even with this tiny victory, there was still a war to wage. The Zero Day Collective had Jacob and I wouldn't rest until he was wrapped up tight in my embrace. I had a new group of survivors along for the ride; and although they weren't special-ops soldiers or molecular biologists, they were warriors to the core. Together we would march our way across the country until we could reach our fingers deep into the chest of the ZDC and rip out its still-beating heart.

CHAPTER 31

November 27, 2016 9:00 AM
Unknown location

The baby cooed and grinned, even as the twenty-five millimeter needle was pulled from its tiny arm. The tests had all been run. Now it was time to get enough blood samples to begin synthesizing what would eventually become the cure for the Mengele Virus.

Commander Faddig rushed through the double doors of the mobile surgical cube.

"Commander! This is a sterile environment. You can't—"

"Don't fucking tell me what I can and can't do. That baby was resistant to everything you threw at it. A little germ here and there isn't going to do a goddamn thing."

Tension mounted in the room. Doctor Kinkaid's jaw flexed in and out as he glared at the commanding officer.

"Are the results complete?" Faddig demanded.

Kinkaid continued staring.

"I asked you a simple question. Either you can answer it, or I'll have those same tests run on you. I'll pose the question one more time. Are the results complete?"

"Yes. The baby is immune to all strains of the Mengele virus. I have injected him with every known mutation. None have had any adverse effects. The child is exactly as you hoped."

Commander Faddig stood over the acrylic bassinet and smiled. The grin on the commander's face wasn't something reserved for a child, but a subject – a project. And baby Jacob certainly was the project to end all projects.

The savior.

The messiah.

The second coming of mankind

"How much longer before you can begin mass production of the anti-viral?"

Doctor Kinkaid took another moment to glare. "We need to not be working within a mobile laboratory. These are delicate procedures, I need stillness and I need the right equipment. If you can get me a proper lab, I could get production ramped up in a few days time. Working within this environment, it could easily take weeks."

Weeks wouldn't do. Faddig had already wasted so much time the board was breathing down his neck. They needed results. The window for the human race would close quickly. If the cure wasn't offered to the public soon, there would be no public to take advantage of. Imminent death was one of the most profound motivating tools. When faced with death, mankind would comply.

"Fine. You'll have your lab. We're being sent to Calgary, Canada. Once there, we'll locate a suitable lab where you can begin your work. But there is something else you must do."

The commander's voice held an ominous tone. The doctor stood, knowing he was about to be thrown for a significant loop. It had happened countless times, since he took a position within the Zero Day Collective. He'd joined out of fear – he wanted to live, to find the means with which to keep his family alive. But when the ZDC made the initial threats, it was immediately clear he had no choice. Either Jonathan Kinkaid sells his soul or the family he promised to protect, at all costs, would perish at the merciless hand of the makers of chaos.

"I brought you into this task force based on your research in the field of cloning."

"I'm sorry commander, that work was halted over ten years ago when human cloning was banned. It went no further."

"Dr. Kinkaid, please do not presume me ignorant. It was not two years ago you presented a viable human cloning process to the Canadian Institute of Health and Research. They accepted your proposal and granted you funding. It wasn't until the Mengele virus was released that your research halted. We need you to pick up where you left off."

The doctor's legs nearly buckled. He had been at war with his conscience since his first work with the ZDC began. But for the most part he was doing little more than mending the wounded, so the war was an easy win. When he was charged with the research on the baby, that war became quite the challenge.

"I'm sorry commander, but I cannot—"

"Doctor Kinkaid, do not act as if you have any choice. You do what we say and your family remains safe. Go against the Zero Day

Collective and your family will die – or worse. Do you understand?"

The doctor remained silent.

"I asked you a question. I will repeat it if necessary." Faddig bristled.

The doctor stood fast by his silence.

Faddig pulled out his mobile and dialed.

"This is Faddig. The Kinkaid family, kill them."

Tears instantly streamed down the doctor's face as if a spigot had been opened and the sprinkler set to soak.

"No. Please don't. Whatever you need of me..." Kinkaid hesitated.

"Belay the order." Faddig barked and disconnected the call.

"Anything you want. Just don't kill my wife and children."

Faddig had him exactly where he needed him. With some men, the instinct to protect was so strong, they would go to any length or depth.

A chilling silence drifted into the room. Commander Faddig stared deep into the eyes of Doctor Kinkaid.

"I need a human clone."

"Of who?" Doctor Kinkaid swallowed a ball of fear into his gut.

A taught silence blanketed the room. The unsaid words quickly became an elephant, stomping about, ready to crush anyone underfoot.

"Jacob Plummer."

The bomb dropped into the middle of the room and sent ear-splitting shrapnel in three hundred and sixty degrees.

"This boy's father? *That* Jacob Plummer? The man that spent his last months protecting the woman you're doing everything in your power to destroy?"

"Yes."

"Why? Why would you want to bring that man back to life? And even if you did, you'd be dead by the time the clone returned to the age in which he died."

Faddig stared deep into Kinkaid's core. He wasn't used to be told 'no'. "We live in a new world, with new rules doctor. What was once impossible is now not only possible, but made practical by the whirling hell storm that threatens to take down our very civilization. You will be given the best equipment and assistance in the world. You will be paid with protection for you and your family. In return, you will bring Jacob Plummer back to life for me. That is all the 'why' you need to know. Is that clear?"

No response came. The commander slammed a powerful fist onto a thick, wooden table. The echo resounded off the metallic walls of the lab within the transport.

"I asked you a question. Is that clear?"

"Yes sir. Perfectly."

The stare-down lasted only a few seconds, before Faddig smoothed out the front of his jacket and returned his spine to the rail-straight position it was used to.

"We should arrive in Canada soon. I will leave you to your preparations."

Commander Faddig slowly exited the room,

leaving Doctor Kinkaid alone with his misgivings and questions.

"Why bring a harmless journalist back to life?" Kincaid lobbed the rhetoric into the air around him. There was no answer to be had. The question only beget more, deeper questions. The one making the most noise inside the skull of the doctor was whether or not Faddig (along with the whole of the The Collective) had lost his mind.

The soft, cooing sound of baby Jacob brought Kincaid screaming back to the now. He looked down into the bassinet to see Jacob smiling up at him. Was it possible the baby knew something? Could this post-apocalyptic messiah have an insight no other had? Was the little guy boring into the doctor's brain in search of a weakness, a deep-seeded fear?

"Well, Jacob, looks like your daddy might be coming back to the land of the living." Kincaid chuckled almost imperceptibly. "Nothing seems to want to stay dead these days. Even death is a lie."

EPILOGUE

December 24, 2016 11:17 PM
Unknown location

Zombie Radio Nation. It's yet another apocalyptic Christmas here on good ol' planet Go Fuck Yourself. This is Bethany Nitshimi here to bring you bad tidings of hate and not even so much as a crumb of fruit cake in your stockings. We've been Grinched and Scrooged yet again this holiday season. But hey, that's okay! We've grown accustomed to this new way of life – right? It's like the old hacker credo, less is more. If you knew your bash scripting, you'd get that joke. Otherwise, ladies and gents, just smile and nod.

Christmas. Yeah. Christmas. A holiday that was, at one point, filled with joy and merriment, now a barren landscape of loss and suffering. It's been over a year. I think. Hell, I don't actually know how long it has been. It feels like a century has passed since I showered. I know, imagine how rank I smell. Oh listen to me, practically resorting to fart and dick jokes for ratings. Look into my eyes, does it seem like I give a shit?

I let a silence waft into the airwaves. I needed that brief moment to collect myself. I had become prone to random fits of anguish – thanks to the loss of my baby. Since the moment of his capture I have daily sworn to all that I hold holy and dear that I would return that baby to my arms. One way or another, Jacob will be reunited with his mother.

I'm sorry.

Another silence.

It gets lonely in the apocalypse. I never thought I'd spit those words out, but it's true. Even with friends and loved ones by my side, loneliness still manages to creep its bastard way into my gut. It doesn't hurt that the only remaining family I had was ripped from my arms.

Before I could choke out the next words, Jamal was standing at the window of my new broadcast booth holding up a hand-written sign. The sign simply said:

We got a hit!

The short sentence had me sucking wind and wanting to scream joy out into the universe. I didn't. The entirety of the Zombie Radio Nation would go deaf at my exhalation. Instead, I opted to let something different flow from my soul.

When was the last time you felt joy? I'm talking the birth of your first child kind of joy, or your first paycheck from your dream job kind of joy. It's out there – still. Even among the trash, rubble, and chaos there is still joy and pleasure to be had.

God, I just wanted to wrap this up so I could know what the hit was. I knew what Jamal was referring too – my tracking script – but had no idea of the details.

Segue. Segue!

If you are listening to me, that means you are still beating incredible odds. The human race is at critical mass and anyone still living is playing with house money. For over a year we've bested the bastards that did everything they could to terrorize and cripple mankind. And even though they're still out there, attacking and corrupting, we're still standing. That's right babies, momma's still standing and she's gonna fight like a mad bitch from Hell until everyone is safe from those makers of mayhem.

Jamal returned with another hand-written sign stating:

Take off, eh!

You know, it's been a long, long time since I've played you a song. I think it's that time again my lovelies. But what kind of madness can I drop on you?

Jamal's sign finally smacked me upside the head. I tossed a wicked grin his way and he gave me his goofiest thumbs up.

I'm going to take you back to the '80s and this strange little tune that stars two comedians and one high-pitched singing, kick-ass bass playing Canuck. Take off ya hoser!

The silly little Bob and Doug Mackinzie song danced out of the monitors as I ran to the door, flung it open, and wrapped my arms around Jamal.

"Your program worked. We tracked down a call from a mobile to Calgary, Canada. Commander Faddig, searching for a suitable lab in order to continue the ground-breaking work of the Zero Day Collective. Morgan has dispatched the Calgary Zombie Response Team on a recon mission. In the mean time, break out your tuque and your parka, we're heading to the Great White North!"

"Cooo, loo, coo, coo, coo, coo, coo, coooo!" I sang out.

"Beauty, eh?" Jamal replied.

Did stereotypes still exist in this post-apocalyptic world? If not, I'd make sure to start some new ones. The first? Pissed off, bad-ass, no-name-taking mother. And that, my friends, was no lie.

ABOUT THE AUTHOR

Jack Wallen is a seeker of truth and a writer of words. Although he resides in the unlikely city of Louisville, Kentucky, he likes to think of himself more as an interplanetary soul ... or so he tells the reflection in the mirror. He's also the author of:

I Zombie I
My Zombie My
Die Zombie Die
Lie Zombie Lie
Cry Zombie Cry
Fry Zombie Fry
Buy Zombie Buy
Zombie Radio
Zombie Radio 2
Zombie Radio 3: Radio Chaos
T-Minus Zero
The Last Casket
Teenage Wasteland
Kiss & Hell

Punk Ass Punk

Suicide Station

Frankenstein Theory

Hell's Muse
The Nails of Calvary

The Dark Seduction

Screampark

Klockwerk Kabaret
Tick Tock Girl

Shero
Shero II: Zombie A GoGo
Shero III: Death by Cosplay

A Blade Away
Gothica
Endgame
Control

Published by Devil Dog Press

A Tale of Two Reapers
To Kill A Reaper
For Whom The Reap Tolls

If you want to receive an automatic email when Jack's next book is released, sign up at jackwallen.com. Your email address will never be shared and you can unsubscribe at any time.

For any author to succeed, word of mouth is crucial. If you enjoyed *Lie Zombie Lie* please consider leaving a review. Even if it's only a line or two, it would make all the difference and would be very much appreciated.

Contact Jack!

To get more information about Jack, stop by his web site, jackwallen.com and learn more. You can also send Jack an email to jack@jackwallen.com.